I0725143

Lost to Lady Scandal

Book 2 of Lady Knights series

Cara Maxwell

DRAGONBLADE PUBLISHING, INC.

© Copyright 2023 by Cara Maxwell
Text by Cara Maxwell
Cover by Dar Albert

Dragonblade Publishing, Inc. is an imprint of Kathryn Le Veque Novels, Inc.
P.O. Box 23
Moreno Valley, CA 92556
ceo@dragonbladepublishing.com

Produced in the United States of America

First Edition June 2023
Trade Paperback Edition

Reproduction of any kind except where it pertains to short quotes in relation to advertising or promotion is strictly prohibited.

All Rights Reserved.

The characters and events portrayed in this book are fictitious. Any similarity to real persons, living or dead, is purely coincidental and not intended by the author.

ARE YOU SIGNED UP FOR DRAGONBLADE'S BLOG?

You'll get the latest news and information on exclusive giveaways, exclusive excerpts, coming releases, sales, free books, cover reveals and more.

Check out our complete list of authors, too!

No spam, no junk. That's a promise!

Sign Up Here

www.dragonbladepublishing.com

Dearest Reader;

Thank you for your support of a small press. At Dragonblade Publishing, we strive to bring you the highest quality Historical Romance from some of the best authors in the business. Without your support, there is no 'us', so we sincerely hope you adore these stories and find some new favorite authors along the way.

Happy Reading!

CEO, Dragonblade Publishing

**Additional Dragonblade books by
Author Cara Maxwell**

The Lady Knights Series
In Bed with a Blackguard (Book 1)
Lost to Lady Scandal (Book 2)

CHAPTER ONE

London, 1814
Three years ago

MISS JOSEPHINE CASTLE was doomed.

Miss Annabelle Foster had a chance.

But Miss Christiana Harmon would overshadow them all.

No amount of money would make Miss Castle a competent dancer. There might be enough money, however, to buy her a husband. A lesser lord, impoverished and desperate, might be willing to overlook the way she flounced through the room like a pincushion always in fear of the next needle. Dominique flinched as the young woman trod on her partner's foot for the fifth time in as many minutes. A *much* lesser lord, then.

Miss Foster had a chance, but it diminished with each gale of ridiculously loud laughter. The *haute ton* did not like loud women. They liked obedient, soft-spoken, and of impeccable lineage. Miss Foster was the daughter of a new-money shipping merchant with no noble ancestry. She ought to be quiet.

A tinkle of delicate laughter floated across the small ballroom. Ah, yes. Miss Harmon. Dominique found her easily in the small group of dancers, dressed in pale pink and crowned in an ornate diamond circlet. She was not the only one watching. Dominique's mother stood near the wall, sipping tea and examining her pupil's form. On the other side of the dance floor, Mr. Harmon watched his daughter's progress with an inscrutable steely expression.

Beautiful, retiring, and entirely accommodating, Miss Harmon had made a perfect study of the type of wife Londoners desired. She was a graceful dancer to boot. She would find an earl or marquess eager to shore up his finances; a well-placed lord willing to ignore her most damaging trait—she was an American.

As soon as could be managed, these young women—along with the bevy of others under her mother's supervision—would enter London Society and attempt to snag a lord and a title.

Dominique did not give a fig.

Her skin crawled just watching the spectacle.

But she kept the soft smile on her face as Mr. Foster wove his way around the edge of the dance floor, seeking out her mother. Without a thought, she moved to intercept him.

She bobbed a curtsey, even though propriety required no such thing. But these up-and-comers loved the bowing and scraping.

"Miss Foster is progressing quite nicely in her mastery of the quadrille," Dominique said. Another peal of loud laughter screeched across the space. Mr. Foster cringed. Dominique did no such thing.

"Madam Beauchamp is quite pleased with her progress," she said instead.

Mr. Foster's eyes moved over her shoulder to where her mother sipped tea. He was determined to speak with her, then. Dominique shifted subtly to the side. "Of course, please discuss the details with her yourself."

The burly man did not even spare a glance in her direction as he stepped past her to speak with her mother. Still, Dominique's soft smile held.

Most of the time she engaged with mothers or the young women themselves. But Mr. Foster was hoping to secure a lucrative shipping deal with the Crown and hoped marrying his daughter into the nobility would ease the way.

Even as the thought slid through Dominique's mind, Miss Castle's mother approached. Her face was positively morose. Dominique felt a tug of sympathy for the young woman and her family. Of her mother's pupils, Miss Castle was the kindest. But to say she was the least graceful was an understatement of alarming proportions.

And kindness meant nothing to the *haute ton*. Dominique could attest to that fact most personally.

Dominique glanced to her left. Mr. Foster frowned as her mother spoke in rapid, accented English. Mrs. Castle was a half-turn of the dance floor from joining them. Moving with a dancer's ease and confident speed, Dominique sidled over to the punch bowl and filled two goblets. She was back in place and ready when Mrs. Castle arrived.

"Would you care for a refreshment, Mrs. Castle? You look a bit peaked." Dominique did not wait for a response before sliding the drink into the older woman's hand.

Mrs. Castle looked equal parts thankful and defeated. She was not suffering from any illusions with regard to her daughter's prospects.

"Thank you, Miss Beauchamp," she said, though she did not take a sip. Instead, her eyes swung toward the dance floor. A new set was beginning, and Miss Castle, now without a partner, stood on the fringe with a frown that matched her mother's. "I suppose we shall need to schedule another round of dance lessons."

Dominique laid a sympathetic hand on the woman's forearm and squeezed gently. "Perhaps this time we focus on two or three simpler dances. Miss Castle might find it easier to master if she is not managing so many different sets of steps."

The matron's frown remained in place, but she tilted her head as she considered. "What would she do at a ball? There will be more than three sorts of sets—a waltz, cotillion, a reel, to name but a few."

"Miss Castle can conveniently visit the retiring room or seek refreshment during those sets she has not yet mastered,"

Dominique's mother interjected smoothly. She touched Dominique's shoulder gently to alert her to her presence.

A quick glance confirmed Mr. Foster was now weaving his way over to his wife and daughter. Dominique inclined her head at her mother and stepped back, allowing her to step into place in the conversation with Mrs. Castle. It was a dance they had done hundreds of times over the last several years.

When they came to London, her mother had styled herself as a respectable French widow. No one knew them here. They avoided the *ton* and instead sought out the social-climbing merchant class, full of parents eager to auction their daughters off for a foothold amongst the nobility. The nouveau riche did not turn their heads at being instructed by a former ballerina; they would take any advantage they might find—and pay handsomely for it.

"I have closely observed Miss Castle, and I believe…"

The two women's voices faded away as Dominique drifted toward the wall. Her own refreshment in hand, she settled in beside a curtain and tried to disappear. It was difficult; she knew she had inherited her mother's beguiling Gallic beauty. The set of her eyes was just that little bit different, her olive skin a fresh contrast to the milky white of the classic English roses all around her. Dominique had spent nearly a decade fending off interested male parties.

It was yet another reason to avoid formal social gatherings such as these.

Most of her mother's work was done in the grandiose townhomes their clients owned. Private lessons were the standard set by the *ton*, so the social climbers could have no less. They certainly possessed the capital to pay for such things. In private homes, with one or two students, there was no chance they might happen upon anyone who would recognize her or her mother.

But this… this at-home was a bad idea. Although most of the guests were pupils of her mother—they did tend to refer her to their friends and neighbors—Dominique had spotted at least five guests who dripped of the superiority so unique to the English peerage.

One such lady caught her eye across the small ballroom. The woman was tall, with stately grace despite her middle age, and her beauty seemed heightened by the strands of silver at her temples. She watched the afternoon's proceedings with a sharp eye and even sharper posture. A countess, perhaps. Maybe even a marchioness.

Dominique shivered.

She found her mother again, now speaking with Mrs. Harmon. Lovely—that was the last of their clients. Another set or two and they could be on their way. Dominique had certainly seen enough to determine which young women warranted additional instruction; surely her mother had as well.

She swung her gaze out over the crowd again, marking the faces she knew and planning a route around the room. She would offer a glass of punch there, give a word of encouragement here, perhaps confirm a few of next week's appointments. By the time she arrived at the threshold, it would be time to depart.

Dominique nodded to herself in silent confirmation, but as she lowered her chin, her eyes snagged on someone.

Or rather, her eyes *were* snagged.

By the noble lady across the room.

The woman's dark eyes held her own, and slowly, so subtly it would easily be missed by the gentleman who was speaking to her, she tilted her head toward the table of refreshments against the wall.

Dominique blinked twice in rapid succession. She must be imagining things. *What's in this punch?*

But before she could take another exploratory sip, the older woman was curtseying to her companion and floating toward the refreshment table. She was not looking at Dominique. It must have been a mistake, she realized. Relief coursed through her. For a moment, she feared she'd been recognized.

The lady reached the table. She dipped herself a goblet of punch. Then a second. When she lifted her eyes, they went straight to Dominique. The woman lifted the second glass an inch. A beckoning.

Dominique gripped her own, remembering it now and thinking it would save her.

Until she realized it was empty.

Drat.

Her stomach flipped uncomfortably even as her feet carried her around the perimeter of the room. She could not make a scene. Whatever the woman wanted, Dominique would have to manage it as discreetly as possible. Her mother and her livelihood depended upon it.

A small smile played across the dark-haired woman's face as Dominique came to stand beside her.

Dominique kept her back to the swirling dance floor and bevy of guests. Best to keep her face hidden, so any shock or despair was not on full display.

"Good afternoon, Miss Beauchamp," the stately lady said, her voice low enough that Dominique had to edge closer in order to hear her clearly.

"Is it, my lady?" Dominique said.

The lady held out the goblet of punch. Dominique did not take it.

The woman set it on the table in front of them, her smile spreading. "I should think so. Madam Beauchamp has accomplished quite a feat, making this troop of young women respectable dance partners for any gentleman."

"I shall pass along your compliment."

"I would be most obliged."

"I must apologize, your ladyship, but if you are seeking to retain my mother's services, I must report that our schedule is quite full," Dominique said. She kept her eyes on the goblet of punch, on the bubbles rising to the top of the liquid and slowly forming together into a misshapen circle.

"Is that so? I had thought with Miss Fairweather now quietly engaged to her duke, your mother would be seeking a new client."

Dominique's heart stopped. Miss Fairweather had been her mother's pupil for six months. That was not such difficult information to come by, she supposed. But the engagement with the Duke of Chesterfield was secret; it would not be announced in the *London Herald* until next week.

She forced herself to swallow down the lump in her throat. "I am surprised to hear that Miss Fairweather's engagement is now common knowledge among the *ton*."

"It is not."

The was a note of pleased superiority in the woman's voice.

"Dare I ask how you came by the knowledge, then, my lady?" Dominique asked. The woman breathed in sharply, and Dominique steeled herself.

But the lady merely chuckled softly. "You may ask, but this is not the time to tell you. I can only plausibly linger here at the refreshment table a few moments longer."

"I do not understand," Dominique said.

"Of course you do not. But perhaps you would like to." Suddenly, the woman's hand closed around hers.

Dominique snapped her head up to find the taller woman's gaze locked on hers. Just for a moment, those dark eyes bore down as if they could see into her very soul.

Then, a second later, she was slipping away, her attention fixed across the ballroom.

Dominique's heart hammered in her chest, her pulse fluttering wildly. *What just happened?*

She reached for the goblet of untouched punch on the table before her and swigged it back in one very unladylike go. With her back still turned to the rest of the crowd, she lifted her hand and tentatively uncurled her fingers to peer at the note the strange woman had placed there.

DOMINIQUE CHECKED THE address for what must have been the hundredth time since opening the folded card the Duchess of Guilford had left in her hand.

It had been a bit of a scramble to obtain all the information she could about the woman before her mother found her and they departed the party. But what she had found was enough to intrigue her—enough to send her trotting through the streets of London at nearly eleven o'clock in the evening.

The Duchess of Guilford was a wealthy widow and grand dame of the *ton*. That was not so interesting, though worrying enough in its own right. What was fascinating was the duchess's reason for attending the at-home at all. If the story could be relied upon—and Dominique sensed it could, based on the wide-eyed sincerity of the maid who'd recounted it—the duchess was the complete opposite of the archetypal *ton* lady Dominique had constructed over the last two decades of her life.

She already is, you dolt. Respectable *ton* ladies did not secretly slip cards to the help, with nothing more than an address and a time.

The streets were quiet at this time of night. The socialites would be out at their balls and soirees until at least one o'clock in the morning. The working residents of London were already abed; they did not have the luxury of lying in until midmorning.

Bed was precisely where Dominique ought to be—where her mother thought her to be at that very moment. She felt a twinge of guilt that she'd snuck out without telling her mother. She'd never done such a thing in her entire life. There had never been a need. She and her mother shared everything, unconditionally.

Yet something in her gut told her that this particular outing should be kept to herself.

The purpose… Dominique's stomach had been in knots over it all evening.

The most plausible reason for the subterfuge was that the duchess or one of her familiars had learned the secret of Dominique's birth, and therefore her mother's scandalous history, and was seeking to blackmail them.

But why reach out to her and not her mother? What was to be gained by separating them? The secret was a shared burden.

She pulled the hooded cloak forward over her face as a carriage rumbled by, though the interior was darkened. In its wake, she ran across the street and into the small park. Just around the corner was the address printed on the card now tucked into her reticule. She didn't habitually carry the frilly thing, but sneaking around London at night unaccompanied demanded some method of defense. So, Dominique had stuffed her reticule with rocks—in addition to the duchess's calling card.

Rather than follow the well-lit perimeter of the park that would take her directly to her destination, she crept through the grass. As the wet ground squelched under her feet, Dominique regretted her choice in footwear. She'd possessed enough foresight to bring a weapon of sorts, but not enough to choose something sturdier than her dainty silk slippers.

One, two, three... She counted the buildings just visible through the darkened line of trees. *There it is.*

The ground floor was dark, but a single candle glowed in the central window of the upper floor—

"You are early."

Only her dancer's grace kept her on her feet.

Her front foot slid in the mud, which swallowed it all the way to the ankle. She threw her arms up reflexively to counterbalance, as her mother had taught her from the moment she first began to walk.

The duchess's deep, melodic laugh floated across the grass.

It was enough for Dominique to locate her seated on a bench in the shadows, a few yards behind her. Dominique had crept right past her without realizing it.

She straightened, carefully extricating her foot from the mud so she did not make a second downward trip. When her feet touched the gravel path, relief swelled in her stomach. But she did not allow it to show on her face. Even in the dim light, she did not want to give the other woman the satisfaction of knowing how thoroughly she'd off-footed her.

"The kind thing would have been to offer me your hand," Dominique said. She did not straighten herself, but glared at the other woman.

"Perhaps," the duchess said, apparently unbothered by the accusatory tone in Dominique's voice. "But the ability to extricate oneself from difficult circumstances is a useful skill."

"What do you want with me, Your Grace?"

The duchess stood, her face catching a beam of light from the street lamps. She was stunningly beautiful, even at her age. A less secure woman would have been threatened. But appearance mattered little to Dominique. She did not have the luxury for such vanity.

"You ascertained my identity. Very good."

Dominique stared.

"Come along, Miss Beauchamp. Our conversation is best had indoors," the duchess said. She did not wait for a response or to see if Dominique would follow before striding along the path toward the squat row of buildings.

She did pause at the edge of the park, where the darkness was complete. She tarried just long enough to pull a hood over her face. A quick glance toward Dominique—who took the hint and did the same.

Dominique followed her across the street and to a door on the left side of the building.

"Did you note the candle?" the duchess said quietly as she withdrew a key from within the recesses of her cloak.

"Yes," Dominique answered. Confusion and frustration warred for dominance in her mind, but she did not let either of them show as the door popped open and she followed the duchess up a flight of stairs.

At the top was another door, which the duchess unlocked with another key. Only when they were inside and the interior door was again bolted behind them did the duchess explain further.

"One candle means I am nearby, but not in the flat. If the draperies are closed entirely, the flat is occupied. If there is a flowerpot, it means the flat's secrecy has been compromised."

"Secrecy? What need have you for secrecy…" Dominique's voice trailed off as she took in the room—luxurious bed, plump settee, gleaming silver tea service. "Unless this is where you entertain your paramours."

The duchess perched on the edge of the armchair that matched the settee and smiled devilishly. "I am a widow. I have the privilege of entertaining my paramours in my home without the judgmental eye of society being turned upon me. A kindness not enjoyed by you or your mother, I would wager."

Dominique blinked. Again.

The duchess motioned for the settee.

Moving soundlessly, Dominique sank into the seat. "You know about my mother and me… our… situation."

"That you are the illegitimate daughter of Lord Wartham and your mother is a former ballerina from the Paris Opera Ballet? Yes, dear."

Apparently unperturbed by the shock and dismay that Dominique could feel oozing out of her pores, the duchess handed her a glass of wine—it had been waiting on the table between them, already poured.

"How did you find out so quickly?" Dominique whispered. It had only been a matter of hours since their encounter at the party. Only a handful of people in London knew of her true parentage.

"I am quite capable, but such expediency is beyond even my capabilities," the duchess said before tipping back her glass of claret. "When Mrs. Foster mentioned your mother, I looked into your connections."

"Because Mrs. Foster suspected something untoward?" Dominique was already calculating the implications. They were done in London—once the secret was out, there would be no more pupils. They could go to Paris—

"Oh no, my dear. You and your mother have hidden your origins quite well. Lottie Foster doesn't suspect a thing," the duchess said. She sat upright, her back straight and proper, but she was at ease.

How could someone be so completely at ease while they destroyed another's life?

"What is your price?" Dominique's heart twisted as she spoke the words. She had some savings, but she doubted it would be enough to satisfy a woman who was already wealthier than Croesus.

The duchess shifted, the amusement sliding from her face as she leaned forward and peered at Dominique. "You assume the worst."

"Life has demanded that I do so," Dominique ground out.

"Good. Those instincts shall serve you well. In our chosen profession, your instincts are often what keep you alive."

Dominique rocked back violently, nearly tumbling over the low back of the settee. She managed to grab the edge and maintain her balance. Twice tonight that dancer's grace had saved her. What was it about the duchess that was so unsettling?

"I do not understand," she said as she hoisted herself upright once more.

"I am not threatening you, Miss Beauchamp. I am recruiting you." The duchess reached across the table, picked up Dominique's untouched glass of wine, and offered it to her once again.

As Dominique's fingers curled around it, they were not shaking. But it was a very near thing. "Recruit me for what?"

"I assume you are familiar with the legend of King Arthur's Knights of the Round Table?" the duchess asked.

This was getting stranger and stranger.

Dominique took a sip of the claret. "I am."

"Good." The duchess nodded. "What you might not realize is that much like the England of legend, our present-day nation faces continuous threats to our stability and safety."

Dominique cocked her head to the side, frowning. "The war is over."

"The soldiers have returned," the duchess agreed. "However, for a country as powerful and envied as ours, the battles will always continue. But the battles now will be fought in back alleys and ballrooms, rather than battlefields."

In the depths of Dominique's being, a tiny flame burst to life.

The duchess continued: "I have been ordered by Her Majesty the Queen to assemble a special order of knights—the Lady Knights. Each uniquely situated to serve and protect the Crown's interests."

Her words were kindling to the blaze growing within Dominique.

"These women… what sort of work would they be asked to undertake?" she asked slowly.

"Whatever is required," the duchess said, her eyes meeting Dominique's directly. "There will be danger; it is inevitable. I have no wish to lie to you. But I take my charge seriously. I will do everything to protect the lady knights in my care."

"You will be the one leading the Lady Knights?" Dominique asked. It was a critical query that might well determine her answer.

"Yes."

Dominique took another sip of her wine to give herself a moment to think. The duchess waited for her to lower her glass before catching her gaze again and saying, plain as could be:

"I would like you to join us."

If she could not see her own hands in front of her, Dominique would have thought her entire body had burst into flame.

It all sounded thrilling. A sharp contrast to the hours and days spent appeasing the melancholic natures of mothers hoping to auction their pretty daughters off to the highest-ranked bidder. But doubt nagged at her.

"Why *me?*"

The duchess smiled. "Aside from your instincts, which we already discussed, you are a chameleon." The woman's smile only deepened at Dominique's raised eyebrows. "I watched you transform into at least five different women today at the Foster party. You were deferential one moment, consoling the next. Your manners are impeccable; those young women under your mother's tutelage would do well to also watch you."

"You need a young woman who can mold herself to any situation," Dominique said slowly. Understanding was taking shape in her mind.

"Precisely," the duchess agreed.

Another thought occurred to Dominique. "As someone raised on the fringes of society, I am not likely to be recognized… but I already have the refined manners and deportment of a lady."

The Duchess of Guilford dipped her elegant chin in confirmation.

She may have been the first person who saw the situation of Dominique's birth and upbringing as an asset rather than a complication. From that alone, Dominique had her answer.

"Yes."

"Yes?"

"I shall join you as a lady knight," Dominique said. She set her wine down on the table and scooted forward, poised and ready. "When do we begin?"

The duchess looked her over from head to toe, drained her own wine glass, and drew the slender kit she'd earlier used to open the door from her pocket. "Right now."

CHAPTER TWO

1817
Present Day

"LORD, HAVE MERCY!" David ground his teeth as they jolted over yet another pothole.

The first thing he would do upon returning to Winleigh was set up a petition with the parish council to have the road between Winleigh and Andover repaired. How could they ever hope to grow to anything more than a tiny backwater village if the road was nigh impassable?

They could not, he answered for himself. Nor did the parish council of Winleigh have any interest in becoming anything other than a tiny backwater village.

It did not matter, David reminded himself.

He would not be a resident of Winleigh for much longer. Over the past year, he'd spent no more than a handful of days in the town. This last visit had been a matter of hours, and he'd only spoken to one acquaintance for the duration—just long enough to throw his belongings into a trunk and clamber back into his cousin's coach.

Soon, very soon, he would have to make the move to Derbyshire and take up residence with his cousin, Geoffrey.

He'd been delaying for months. Perhaps the condition of this infernal way was the Lord's attempt at pushing him to finally make the move.

And leave them behind?

His elder brother, Thomas. His father.

They were lost to him now. God rest their souls.

What of Dominique?

David sighed heavily. She was not dead, but she was just as gone.

Perhaps once he was settled in Derbyshire, he would renew his search—

"Hell and damnation!" He flew off the seat and sprawled violently on the floor of the carriage, smacking his elbow against the wood-paneled door with a hideous thwack.

If he was in such a condition, he trembled to know what state his luggage would be in when he finally arrived in London. He'd packed everything carefully, but the fact remained that the trunk strapped to the roof of the carriage above his head was receiving just as violent a ride as he was.

If something was damaged, he would replace it. He was not a pauper.

He was about to become an earl.

David shivered.

It still did not quite make sense. Nothing about the past year did.

First, his cousin's wife had quietly slipped away with the cool autumn winds. David's heart ached for Geoffrey's loss. Theirs had not been a love match, but they'd been well suited, and the affection between them was apparent to even a casual observer. But Lily had always been frail. When she died without providing Geoffrey an heir, the family was saddened but not surprised.

There had always seemed a likely chance the earldom would pass to the Grisham branch of the family tree. Lily's passing and Geoffrey's insistence that he would not wed again were enough to assure it.

But even so, David was the second son. His father and elder

brother were hearty and hale.

Until the fire at the foundry.

David's heart clenched.

Back up on the bench seat, he raked his fingernails over the thick velvet padding and tried to work through the pain. It rose in him with the ferocity of a lion. He didn't fight it. He focused on the fibers against his fingertips, the resistance as they caught under his short-trimmed nails. He let the wave of sadness come.

It didn't prick tears to his eyes, not this time.

But David was not fool enough to think that meant the worst was past.

When his heart finally stopped racing, he relaxed his hands and reached for the shade on the window.

The road had evened out sometime in the past ten minutes, while he'd been gripped by the devastation that haunted him. He was no longer in Hampshire. He did not recognize the paths and squat country buildings. His stomach eased a bit more.

It was time to leave Winleigh behind.

This trip to London was the first step in rebuilding his life.

It would also be an opportunity to complete the last round of commissions. He did not know how much longer he would be able to keep at his etchings. How much work did it really take to run an earldom?

Geoffrey would teach him. That was the entire purpose of this trip to London in the middle of the Season.

That sent another shiver through him, though this was one of distaste.

David had successfully avoided the London social Season for nearly three decades. It was only his faithfulness to his family and his cousin that had him *en route* to London now. He knew how to bow and scrape, of course. He knew he ought to address a duke as "Your Grace" and an earl as "my lord."

But in all the years his mother had drilled proper decorum into him, neither of them had ever thought he would have much use for it.

Finally, a thought that did not set him shivering.

His mother was already safely ensconced at Geoffrey's estate in Derbyshire. She'd left almost immediately; the parish priest had barely said the last line of the funeral service before she pulled on her widow's cloak and fled.

David did not blame her, but he missed her terribly.

He seemed doomed to miss those he loved.

Christ, when did I become so damn dark and morose?

His mind ticked off the list back to him—Dominique, Thomas, Father, Mother...

Mother is safe in Derbyshire.

Dominique is...

Gone.

As he always did when she danced through his mind—more often than he would like to admit—David sent up a silent prayer for her safety and wellness. Wherever she might be, he prayed she was happy and healthy. Even if she was no longer his.

BEING A LADY knight was much like dancing. She executed a series of choreographed movements, planned in advance. Such as bumping into Jacquetta in the hall and knocking her reticule loose, so the other woman would have a pretense for dashing off into an occupied wing of the house.

Other times, she had to adapt quickly—as one might when a partner stepped on their toes or another pair took a misstep. Dominique had to abandon her fact-finding excursion to York, disguising herself as a man and riding through the night in order to get back to London in time for this meeting.

She swept through the doors, having watched Jacquetta and Red enter. She was developing a headache from the pins in her hair, but there was no time to think of that even if her fingers itched to pull them out. The duchess would arrive soon.

"Chafing a bit tonight, are we?" Jacquetta was already seated, golden blonde hair flashing along with her grin.

Dominique's eyes were daggers when she turned them on her friend. "I have worn many costumes. But of all the maids I've portrayed, the duchess has the most annoyingly exacting uniform protocols. This cap is attached with no less than fifteen pins," she huffed as she dropped into the chair beside Jacquetta.

"Drink?" Red held out a flask, which could belong to no one other than Jacquetta.

It might ease Dominique's headache. But then, she'd always found her mind easily clouded by spirits. She decided against it.

"I was supposed to be in York," she said. "But then the invitation came and I had to ride hell for leather to make it here in time."

"Any inkling why we've been summoned so urgently?" Red was leaning forward, eagerness dripping from her. She'd been too long without a quest.

"You shall find out presently," Jane said calmly.

Dominique heard the footsteps before the others, and was already half turned to the door when it swung open to admit the Duchess of Guilford.

The duchess had hardly changed in three years—she was equally as beautiful and intimidating. Her gaze flicked around the room, passing over each lady knight in turn, before she settled into the open chair and fixed her gaze.

"Red."

The eagerness melted from Red's face.

"Your mother is insufferable." The duchess sighed, rubbing at one temple. "Pass me that flask." She held her hand out to Jacquetta, who did not try to hide her smile as she passed it over.

The duchess drained the flask before passing it back to Jacquetta. "Your father has fine taste."

Dominique smiled to herself. Jacquetta had so many talents; it was endlessly entertaining that she often put them to use nicking her father's expensive liquor.

"We have a shared love." Jacquetta grinned. "My sister will

be looking for me soon. Why are we here, Matilda?"

Dominique suppressed her shudder. She'd never be able to address the duchess so informally. Perhaps it was her own status and upbringing, but the woman always seemed a cut above the rest. Dominique respected her deeply—and had feared her, at times.

"I do not know. I was not the one who called this meeting," the duchess said. Dominique followed her eyes.

"I was," Jane said.

Jane was significantly less intimidating. Dominique had no qualms about fixing her friend with an expectant stare. "Let's have it."

"Grayson Thane is back in London," Jane said.

Jacquetta nearly jumped out of her seat, while the duchess's face remained unreadable.

"When?" Jacquetta demanded.

Dominique followed the conversation with half an ear. Jacquetta was like a terrier—when she became fixated upon something, there was no shaking her. Grayson Thane had been her fixation for months, and now she was finally to have her chance.

Despite the danger it would entail, Dominique was glad her friend would finally have some satisfaction.

But it did not answer why *she* had been dragged away from York.

"Even captivity?" Jane's voice cut through Dominique's musing.

All the Lady Knights were at attention now.

"I am to be his captive?" Jacquetta asked, eyes already working.

Heavens above, she is actually going to enjoy this...

"If we decide to go forward with this, we put it out that you've stumbled upon the secret of Thane's falling-out with his family all those years ago," the duchess explained.

"And that is somehow related to his master?" Jacquetta said.

The duchess and Jane exchanged a look. "Our sources say yes."

"Then what?" Jacquetta asked, but Dominique could tell from a quick survey of her peers' expressions that they all knew what was coming.

"Then he will take you."

"My quest, then, is to remain in his dubious clutches long enough to find out the identity of his mysterious employer," Jacquetta summarized, looking to the duchess for confirmation.

"And not get yourself killed in the process," Red inserted unhelpfully.

But Dominique's mind was already turning. If Jacquetta was to be a prisoner, she would need to have many methods of escape at her disposal. Which meant—

"If I am to break free of his prison, I shall need you to teach me a thing or two about picking locks," Jacquetta said sweetly.

Dominique's hands began to itch with eagerness—not to tear away her cap, but for the roll of slender, gleaming implements secreted in the deep pocket of her skirt. "It will be my pleasure."

The table erupted into side conversations, quick updates, and exchanges of information. "Dominique, a moment, please, before you begin," the duchess said, lifting just one finger from the table.

Red had already slipped back down to rejoin the ball. Jane departed in the opposite direction. Although she and Red were social acquaintances, outside of the Lady Knights, they were careful not to appear too friendly. It was safer if Society did not connect them to one another. It was an easy enough ruse; boisterous Ethelreda McGovern had little in common with the quiet wallflower—at least on the surface.

Jacquetta lingered, though her attention had turned inward. Thane had been in her sights for months. Dominique was unsurprised to see her friend so sharply focused.

Dominique resisted the urge to loosen the white lace cap on her head. She'd pinned it too damnably tight. But just as she was about to curl her fingers in her apron to keep her hands busy, she had to stifle that impulse as well. The duchess's servants were known for their perfectly proper appearance at all times. Mussing herself was a juvenile error she would not make.

"Has there been any more direction on the Tippleton matter?" Dominique asked the duchess, forcing her palms flat in her lap.

She'd been looking into Mr. Tippleton and his questionably legal business enterprises for the last few months, only awaiting word from her superiors on when to make her move, such as obtaining a bit of incriminating evidence.

But the duchess shook her head. "I'm afraid not. Tippleton has been shelved for now. Your talents are required elsewhere."

Dominique did not quite frown, but she was aware of the slight smile she'd been wearing fading away. She was always aware of her expression, even in safe quarters such as the round table. It had saved her life on more than one occasion since she entered the queen's service.

"Of course," she said plaintively. She was disappointed, but she tempered it. It was not her place to be disappointed. If the Crown had decided to divert her energies elsewhere, it spoke enough to the importance of one matter over the other.

"I cannot give tell you the full brief now—I will be missed below," the duchess said, standing. Sure enough, several notes of music floated through the partially open outer door. "We will meet at your rendezvous point in two days at the usual time."

Dominique nodded, filing the information away.

She would have to send a note to her mother begging off supper that day, but it was of no consequence. Her mother was used to that sort of thing after all these years.

Their rendezvous was always the flat where the duchess had first recruited Dominique. They always met in the early evening, when their carriages could easily be mixed in with those of the other *ton* socialites on their way to their evening entertainments.

"I shall see you then," the duchess said, not waiting for a response before tossing a nod in Jacquetta's direction and taking her leave.

Once the door was firmly shut, Dominique turned to Jacquetta and drew her well-loved brown leather roll from the pocket of beneath her gown. Untwining the leather strap, she laid out the implements on the round table between them.

The golden-haired young woman eyed them with interest. "I cannot deduce whether you plan to teach me or torture me," she said.

"A bit of both." Dominique winked, selecting the first narrow blade.

CHAPTER THREE

I N THE FIVE minutes David had been away in the retiring room, the ball had changed entirely. The crowd had swelled to at least double. It was not quite the "crush" he'd heard young women yammer on about, but it far exceeded the country dances of Hampshire.

The dancing had begun in earnest, pairs of elegantly dressed ladies and gentlemen no more than colorful blurs. David ground his teeth. He was a passable dancer if he had a competent partner. The only time he'd ever felt truly comfortable on the dance floor was when he'd whirled across the ballroom of Wartham Grange with Dominique Beauchamp in his arms.

David stumbled over the threshold from the corridor into the ballroom.

Dominique had always had a way of knocking him off balance. Even now, when she was nothing more than a memory.

A cherished memory.

His eyes roved over the crowd as he edged around the dance floor to rejoin his cousin. He searched the twirling mass for dark hair and olive skin adorning a svelte, womanly body. She'd been lovely and lush even at seventeen. She must be even more beautiful now that she'd reached full womanhood.

David always looked for her.

Once he emerged from his initial grief at her loss, he'd cast his net. Every time he delivered a commission, he scanned the faces of the townsfolk as they strolled the street. He traveled often to visit his cousin in Derbyshire—even before the deaths of his father and brother—simply hoping he might catch a glimpse of her somewhere along the journey.

By the time David reached his cousin's side, he'd resigned himself to the reality that she was not in attendance tonight.

Of course she wasn't, he admonished himself. London was the very last place Dominique and her mother would have fled. If the ridicule of a small country village had been so harsh, the *haute ton* would surely be unbearable. The most likely location was France… an eventuality his heart ached to consider.

"Stopped off for something stronger, did you?" Geoffrey said.

David frowned, remembering the snifter of brandy clenched in his hand. He held it up to his cousin.

"For you," David said. "You know I cannot stomach the stuff."

Geoffrey accepted the brandy with a nod of thanks. "I thought perhaps this lot had finally driven you to drink."

"Not yet." David forced a smile.

If losing Dominique had not sunk him into his cups, he doubted anything would. He had not taken a drop of liquor while he mourned his father and brother. Surely, he'd already lived through the worst life could offer.

"Gird your loins, cousin. The onslaught is about to begin," Geoffrey said.

David followed his gaze, sighting the quartet of women approaching them with just enough time to wipe the surprise from his face.

"My lord," the eldest of the group said to Geoffrey, dipping a graceful curtsey. "How pleased we all are to have you returned to town!"

"You are too kind, Lady Brandon," Geoffrey said, bowing. "I have brought my heir, Mr. Grisham."

Lady Brandon's eyes sparkled with intent as they raked over

David.

Lord, have pity upon me.

"I heard from the Duchess of Hereford that the future of the earldom had shifted somewhat of late. How fortunate for you, Mr. Grisham," Lady Brandon said.

David pressed his lips tightly together and forced himself to nod and bow politely.

Lady Brandon motioned the three young women on her flanks forward. "Do allow me to introduce my daughters and niece. Miss Brandon, Miss Evalina, and Lady Martin."

In unison, the three young women curtseyed.

In response, David suppressed a groan. He felt Geoffrey shaking with silent, carefully contained laughter beside him.

"I am most pleased to greet you, Miss Brandon, Miss Evalina, Lady Martin." David nodded to each of the young women in turn. He smiled.

Geoffrey nudged him in the ribs.

"May I have the honor of partnering each of you for a set, if your dance cards are not already full?" David smiled charmingly.

In truth, it was not so hard to slip into the persona he'd always worn. He *was* kind and smiling and jovial by nature. It had just been a bit difficult to summon those sides of himself after the year he'd endured.

Lady Brandon clapped her hands in unrepressed excitement. "How lovely, Mr. Grisham!"

"I do not see your card, Lady Brandon," David said. He caught the older lady's eye and cocked a half-grin. She blushed effusively.

"I am at your disposal, Mr. Grisham," she said.

David was vaguely aware of the current set nearing its end in the periphery. Best to get on with it. He reached for the dance cards of each of the young women in turn.

"Your penmanship is quite elegant, Mr. Grisham," Lady Brandon said, catching her eldest daughter's hand to glance at her dance card.

None of the young women themselves had said a word. David glanced at Lady Brandon; he imagined it was hard to get one in with this imitable lady as their chaperone.

"I thank you for the compliment," David said.

He darted a glance toward Geoffrey, who was watching him closely. They had not explicitly discussed whether or not he should keep mum about his profession, but David was smart enough to deduce that a working professional would not earn the same interest as a future earl.

"Will you do me the honor of this dance, Lady Brandon?" David asked.

Lady Brandon blushed again and nodded. One of the daughters tittered. David ignored them as he led the older lady to the dance floor.

He'd come to London to learn about what would be expected of him as a future earl. He had no intention of taking a wife. Not now, not yet.

But as he and Lady Brandon took their places on the dance floor, David could feel the eyes of the other guests—particularly the female ones—burning into him.

He may have no intention of looking for a bride, but that would do nothing to stop the matchmaking mamas of London from trying to foist one upon him.

⟫⟫⟫⟪⟪⟪

SHE SPENT FIFTEEN minutes demonstrating the rudiments of lock picking to Jacquetta, but with only the two internal locks between their meeting room and the main upstairs corridor, there was not much to cover. Those locks were relatively straightforward, and after a few minutes of instruction, Jacquetta unlocked them both successfully, if not very quietly.

It might be all they had time for before Jacquetta went to Exeter to bait her trap. Who knew what Dominique's new mission from the duchess would entail?

To learn more about Tippleton, she'd posed as a flower girl in the square outside his Trafalgar offices. From there, she'd been able to note the comings and goings throughout the day, and even follow Tippleton discreetly a few times.

But instinct told her that whatever it was, it was grievous.

Dominique's orders had come in many forms over the years. Once, the duchess had handed her a letter addressed to her own mother, Madam Beauchamp, while Dominique posed as a maid at a ball very much like the one happening that night. Inside had been listed three names, addresses, and the direction to avoid being seen at all costs.

On another occasion, she'd been handed a dossier as thick as a Bible detailing the exact role she would assume, down to fake details about her parents and grandparents before them.

Which would it be this time?

She descended the servant staircase, keeping her eyes carefully downcast as two other maids and a footman bustled past her. She fought the urge to glance back over her shoulder to see what had caught their attention on the upper floors. With a ball in full swing, the staff were usually completely occupied on the main level.

But ultimately, it was none of her concern. Following and entangling herself would only make her stick more firmly in the full-time staff's memory—something she'd been careful to avoid over the years.

The duchess always brought on extra staff for major events, such as balls. Sometimes, Dominique was among them. Other times, she was not. Her excuse was that she could not always be spared by the family whom she was employed by during the daytimes. Thus far, the ruse had worked well.

Her sturdy black boots hit the landing, and she turned for the kitchen to resume her place ferrying items up to the ballroom. Footmen would carry the actual dishes out to the refreshment tables. A loud grandfather clock clanged the time; soon the guests would be invited in for the lavish supper, to be followed by yet more revelry into the wee hours of the morning.

Dominique straightened her apron. It was going to be a long night of hard work. But she was suited to it. She fixed a smile on her face and joined the other maids.

Ten minutes later, she wound her way through the maze of hallways, a laughing young maid named Geraldine at her side.

"Have you managed a peek into the ballroom?" Geraldine whispered.

Like Dominique, the younger girl had been brought on just for the evening.

"No, and neither should you," Dominique advised. But she smiled at the younger woman. She understood the attraction, the desire to see the glamour firsthand—though Dominique herself had no such desires.

They rounded a corner, both sidestepping wide around two other maids retreating back toward the kitchens.

"However," Dominique whispered conspiratorially, "if you can get away, the second-floor gallery overlooks the ballroom."

Geraldine's eyes sparkled with excitement, swinging immediately toward the other end of the hall where the sweeping main staircase awaited.

Dominique nudged her shoulder gently, urging her down the corridor to their destination.

"Ach, how can these folks eat such grand food before the meal is even served?" Geraldine rubbed at her shoulder as she handed off the heavily laden tray to a footman.

The footman gave the young woman a long-suffering look, but Dominique interceded with a bright smile for the staid footman and an arm around Geraldine. She massaged her shoulder as she turned her back down the hallway.

"Where are you bound next?" Dominique asked.

Geraldine sighed heavily. "Linens for the retiring room."

They paused at the servants' staircase—the less ornate sibling to the one through the swinging door a few yards ahead of them.

Dominique darted a glance around, but for one blessed moment they were alone.

"Go on, then. Scurry up to the gallery and have a look. I'll see to the linens," she said.

Geraldine's mouth dropped open, then spread immediately into a blinding grin. "Are you certain?"

"On with you, before I think better of it," Dominique said, giving her shoulder a little push. But she winked broadly.

It was all the encouragement Geraldine needed; she disappeared up the stairs like a shot.

Shaking her head, Dominique laughed softly and wound her way to the scullery to fetch the linens. She was still smiling, picturing the look of joy on Geraldine's face when she took in the grandeur of her first ball, as she nudged the swinging door open with her hip and stepped into the main corridor, where the gentlemen's retiring room waited at the end of the hall.

Only to have her heart drop clear out of her body.

THE PUNCH MUST be laced with liquor.

It was the only reasonable explanation.

There was no other way that Dominique Beauchamp, the woman who haunted his dreams, could possibly have just stepped through the door from the servants' quarters dressed as a maid, taken one look at him, and run away.

Point number one—Dominique was not a servant. The scandal… Well, it certainly had made her life difficult, whatever it was now. But Dominique would not serve as a maid to a lady of the *ton*—she abhorred the peerage.

Point number two—she had no reason to run away from him. They had parted on amicable terms. Devastating, yes. But not because of anything that had occurred between them. She'd been so sure of his devotion she'd left a note… He preferred not to think of that.

Point number three—he'd drunk an awful lot of punch. It was the easiest way to avoid talking or dancing. It also meant he was on his third trip to the gentlemen's retiring room. The ladies in attendance were bound to think he suffered from a weak constitution. Perhaps that would work in his favor for fending them off.

It must have been the punch that had him taking a step not toward the retiring room, but toward the door through which the maid had retreated.

A maid who was not Dominique.

A maid who must have borne a resemblance to her, no doubt.

But it was surely his own desire—and the punch—that had manifested Dominique before his eyes.

Perhaps he would just pop through the door, just to be certain—

The door swung open suddenly, and a dark-haired maid came through, nearly colliding with him.

David fell back instantly, bowing reflexively. "I beg your pardon."

"Not at all, sir." The maid curtseyed and then scurried around him, arms full of linen.

She must have been the one—dark hair, carrying linens, in that starched uniform. Her resemblance to Dominique was no more than a passing one. It was all no more than the delusions of a fool.

DAVID WAS IN London.

Why, oh why, was David in London?

How had he found her after all of these years?

But he had not found her, she realized as she sped back

through the door and lodged her heel against it to prevent it from swinging inward—an instinctual action, to prevent anyone from following her.

The expression of shock and disbelief on David's face had matched her own. She could feel the strain of her eyes, so wide they were watering. Her mouth was opened in an *O* as her chest heaved, desperate for air to fight the racing of her pulse.

He had not expected to see her.

Of course, there was no way he could have. First of all, he did not know she was in London. Even if he managed to locate her mother's flat or contact her, her mother did not know where she was this evening.

Which left only one plausible possibility—David was a guest attending the ball.

Dominique's stomach twisted painfully. Once, she'd dreamt of dancing at a ball such as this. Her eyes had been just as starry as young Geraldine's. And there was only one young man she'd ever wanted to share it with.

But dreams were just that—figments of the night.

This was her reality. And David Grisham had just reentered it.

She rocked forward, taking her heel from the door and reaching for the wall for support.

"Are those for the ladies' retiring room? They've plumb cleaned us out," a regular household maid huffed, shoving through the door.

"The gentlemen's," Dominique managed, though she failed at mastering the strangled note of her voice.

"The menfolk can wait. It's the ladies who will have my job," the maid said. She grabbed the pile right out of Dominique's arms and disappeared with a frown.

Dominique blinked twice. She forced her feet to move, back down to the scullery to retrieve another set of linens. She dawdled, setting aside one that had a miniscule tear no one would ever notice, trading it for another from the line that had not yet been folded. She refolded it twice.

After five long minutes, she could delay no longer without endangering her likelihood of being invited back for the duchess's next ball. It was by far the easiest way for the Lady Knights to meet all together, and Dominique refused to be the one to ruin it.

When she reached that swinging door again, her stomach turned over. Thank goodness she'd resisted the temptation to sample any of the delicacies down in the kitchen. If she saw David again, she might very well retch them up all over the floor.

But when she finally ratcheted up the nerve to press her shoulder into the door, the corridor was deserted.

Relief crashed through her.

Deep in her gut, a ripple of something else made itself known, tiny and dangerous—disappointment.

CHAPTER FOUR

1807
10 years ago
Wartham Grange, Hampshire

"I CANNOT DO it!"

She threw down the ribbon in frustration, her mahogany brown hair falling loose to her shoulders, shaking with frustration.

Dominique chuckled softly. "Here, sweet, allow me."

She retrieved the ribbon with one hand, deftly tucking it into the bodice of her gown while the other hand swept up the long brown hair. For a few moments, she simply ran her fingers through the long, silky tresses, soothing and stroking.

Amelia's shoulders began to ease, her scowl softening.

Dominique began to plait her hair in an elegant French style.

"I shall never be as elegant as you." Amelia sighed heavily.

Dominique bit her lip. It would be unkind to laugh—her younger sister was completely earnest.

"You have some years yet, sweet. By the time you reach full womanhood, I doubt I shall hold a candle to you." As she spoke, Dominique flicked the ribbon loose from her bodice and tied it at the end of the plait.

Amelia caught the end of the plait in her hand, dragging it

forward to examine the neat, elegant coiffure. She shook her head in disbelief.

"Can you show my maid how to plait my hair in the French style?" she asked, turning her round, bright blue eyes up to her elder sister.

Dominique's throat tightened. She inhaled sharply and forced the air down.

"I think it best we save this for when we can be together," she said, patting her sister's shoulder. Amelia opened her mouth to protest. "Your mother would not be pleased," Dominique added.

Amelia frowned, but nodded. Even at fourteen years of age, she was wise to the world. Dominique was often impressed by how seriously she regarded even the smallest problem or conflict. Her heart tightened, just as her throat had moments earlier. Always, these moments with Amelia were bittersweet.

She caught a loose strand of hair at the temple and tugged it loose from the braid, curling it around her finger to frame her sister's sweet face.

"Mama will not be home until Tuesday. Perhaps you can stay with me tonight!" Amelia's eyes brightened.

Dominique stepped back. If her heart constricted any further, she might swoon. "Perhaps," she said.

"I shall ask Father!" Amelia hopped to her feet, her pale pink dress falling into place around her.

Such a lovely little thing she was. Her bright energy never failed to lift Dominique's spirits. Lady Wartham was away until Tuesday. Perhaps she and Amelia could steal a night together. They would be no sleeping, of course. It would be all giggling and teaching Amelia to braid in the French style and answering questions about the village boys.

Warmth spread through Dominique's chest as she followed Amelia to the door and out into the corridor. She did not know where her father's quarters were; she'd so rarely been allowed upstairs at Wartham Grange. Only when her stepmother was away. Only when she could be snuck in without the villagers noticing.

Even tonight, though she'd spent the afternoon primping with her sister, she would play her part. Once the village guests began to arrive, she would be nothing more than Miss Beauchamp, a guest like all the rest.

She shoved down the sadness that threatened. This time with her father and sister was precious. She would not spoil it.

Amelia skipped around the corner, leading the way to their father's rooms.

Dominique nearly toppled the smaller girl over.

She'd come to a standstill. A second later, Dominique realized why.

She felt the moment Lady Wartham's eyes landed upon her. Her gaze burned through Dominique's body like lightning, right down to her toes tucked into her silk slippers.

She braced herself, desperately trying to be ready for the words that would follow.

But Lady Wartham turned away instead, swinging open the door in front of her without a knock and storming inside.

Perhaps she would be reasonable. Perhaps after all these years, she'd finally decided to stop fighting the love between her and Amelia and let them be happy—

Then the screeching began.

"How dare you! I come home early from my visit to my mother's sickbed, feeling tired and ill myself, only to find that... *that girl*... in my house!"

"My dear, please do not make yourself ill—"

"I am already ill! It takes no more than her and her mother's presence to make me so! How can you visit this hell upon me? Upon your daughter!"

Her father's heavy sigh echoed into the hall. "They are both my daughters."

"As I am constantly reminded by their presence here in Winleigh. It is bad enough that I must see them every time I go into the village. Now I find you are secreting the girl into my house when I am away. Do you have her mother tucked in your bed as well?"

Dominique lurched forward. She could weather the hateful words Lady Wartham threw at her, but to hear her mother blasphemed so cruelly—

A soft hand closed around hers. Not enough to hold her back, to force her. But a gentle reminder, to say, *I am here. I love you.*

"I have never given you cause for such allegations," their father said. Hope surged inside her. Was this it—the time when her father would finally, truly take her side? He sighed again. "The dance is set for seven o'clock. Guests shall begin arriving soon. No one will notice Dominique. It shall be like every other time…"

Dominique turned away. She did not need to hear her father consoling his wife.

LADY WARTHAM PLEADED illness and did not attend.

Nor was Dominique's mother, Madam Beauchamp, in attendance.

When they'd first come to Winleigh, her mother had looked long and hard at Wartham Grange. Dominique could still recall the wetness shining in her eyes and the tight set of her mouth. Her mother's declaration had never been spoken aloud, at least not to Dominique, but she understood it clear enough.

Her mother would never set foot in Wartham Grange, the place where the man she loved had married another. She would come to the village so that her daughter might know her father. She would accept the pension paid to them each month by that same father. She would keep her own identity and her daughter's secret. All of that, she would do for love of Dominique. But crossing the threshold of Wartham Grange was one step she could never take.

To repay her mother's love and kindness, Dominique answered every summons to the grange, be it a personal invitation while Lady Wartham was away or a general invitation received along with the rest of the village. She told herself she did it for her mother and for her sister. But she also did it for herself.

She loved her father.

Despite his inability to defend her or claim her as his own, she loved him.

But why?

This was the question seventeen-year-old Dominique Beauchamp pondered as she stood in the corner of the small ballroom at Wartham Grange, sipping her punch and generally being ignored by the other guests. She did not have many friends in Winleigh; being the beautiful, exotic French girl had earned her the attention of most of the young men and the ire of all the young women.

Amelia lingered with their father near the doorway from the entry hall. She was the perfect little hostess in her proper pastel-pink dress and matching bow, dipping curtseys and smiles to all who entered. It would have made sense for Dominique to hate her. But from the moment she met her younger sister, and Amelia had wrapped her chubby arms around her older sister's legs jubilantly, there had been nothing but love between them.

Matters with her father were less straightforward.

For the first seven years of her life, he'd been a biannual visitor to their home in Paris. Then she and her mother moved to Southampton, and eventually to Winleigh—at her father's behest. She had not really understood the what or why of it all.

A decade later, Dominique knew three things. The first was that she was a bastard.

The second was that the secret of her birth must be kept at all costs.

The third and most devastating was that the peace in her life was entirely at the mercy of Lady Wartham. It was for Lady Wartham's benefit that her connection to her father was kept secret. It was Lady Wartham who had finally granted permission for her mother and her to be moved to Winleigh. While her father had grand arguments with his wife—today's was not the first she'd witnessed—Dominique knew the truth. If Lady Wartham decided, she and her mother would be abandoned.

"You can scowl as hard as you like, but it shall only deter them for a few minutes more," a voice said into her ear, the warmth of it tickling down her neck.

Dominique rolled her shoulders as a shiver snaked through her, a smile already climbing her lips even as she turned to look at her newly arrived companion.

"You have not seen my glower. I have been practicing it in the mirror," she said.

David laughed, loud and jovial. Several surrounding eyes swung toward them, but he grinned at her as if he did not notice anything but her. Dominique felt that unusual fluttering in her chest… the one only David seemed able to conjure.

"Let's have it, then," he said.

She straightened her shoulders and turned to face him fully. Lifting her chin, she narrowed her eyes until her brows nearly touched and her lips were so tightly compressed they all but disappeared. As a final touch, she let a low growl slip from her throat.

David's smile slid from his face, blank surprise taking over the handsome planes. Then he burst out laughing.

"Christ, Dominique, now you're actually growling at suitors?" He slapped his thigh.

"I haven't any suitors," she said fiercely.

David blinked, his mirth fading as he straightened.

He'd struck a painful spot, and he knew it.

But Dominique could not stay upset at him. He reached out to place his hand upon her arm, a simple act of comfort. But a quick glance around the room and he thought better of it.

Dominique let out the breath she'd been holding. She wanted him to touch her, she realized. But not now. In her father's ballroom, she could be nothing less than perfect.

"My mum's gone to the retiring room. Let's nip out of here," David said.

Dominique quickly scanned the crowd. Mrs. Grisham was indeed out of sight. "What about your father?"

David waved his hand dismissively. "He's speaking with Lord Garrity. They'll be discussing the odds at Newmarket for at least the next quarter hour."

Dominique bit her lip. There was no one to monitor her own movements. Lady Wartham usually watched her like a hawk, but the woman was safely above stairs. Amelia and her father were playing the gracious hosts; not that they would pay her any extra attention in any case.

"Yes," she said, nodding sharply.

David leaned forward, a half-grin tugging up one side of his wide mouth. A lock of his overlong gold hair fell across his forehead, casting his face in rakish shadow. It would have been quite dashing, except that, even at three years her senior, David was the farthest thing from a rake.

And he is dashing, her mind corrected Dominique as her eyes tracked his movement around the perimeter of the ballroom and out the side door. She lingered a few minutes more, sipping her punch and ensuring no one was watching her. She caught a few wishful glances from the young men of Winleigh, but it was the middle of a set, and most of them were engaged with other young women. This was her moment to slip away.

The hallway was darkened; clearly the servants were not expecting any guests to wander this way.

Dominique quietly closed the door behind her, muting the sounds of the ballroom as well as its bright lights. She squinted, trying to find—

"Ah!" she yelped, stumbling backward as David jumped from a shadow.

He caught her elbow to keep her from falling, and this time there were no eyes upon them. Dominique did not push his hand away.

His touch was so warm, she could feel the imprint of each finger even through her elbow-length silk gloves. The hallway was cool by contrast to the swirl of warm bodies back in the ballroom. That must account for how acutely aware she was of his touch—and for the warmth spreading up her arm and through her chest.

There was that fluttering again.

"Are we going to linger here in the hallway, or did you have some other location in mind?" she breathed.

She knew in that moment she would follow him anywhere—good sense be damned.

David blinked—once, twice. His gaze fell to where their bodies touched and lingered there. She watched his chest heave. Was he as deeply affected by their proximity as she?

Then he pulled his hand away from her elbow.

Disappointment keened through her… until his fingers closed around her own.

"The orangery," he said with a wink.

Dominique did not protest as he led her through the hallways of Wartham Grange, winding through them toward the rear of the house. David had grown up as a guest in these halls, longer even than Dominique herself. The Grisham family had been in Winleigh as long as the Warthams.

He paused outside the door, glancing around, presumably to ensure they were still unobserved. Then he tugged her into the glass enclosure, tonight illuminated only by the moonlight overhead.

"I bet you've never been in here," David said proudly, leading her between the rows of potted citrus trees.

The orangery was her father's pride and joy. Few villagers had been invited in to the sacred space, for Lord Wartham's fear they might breathe wrong upon his precious fruit trees.

The irony was not lost upon Dominique.

"My father was invited last month to take tea with Lord

Wartham. He brought Thomas and I along, since we are to be his apprentices," David continued.

She did not tell him that she'd once played hide-and-seek amongst these trees with a six-year-old Amelia. Or how Amelia had run her forehead into one of the pots, earning two black eyes. It had been almost a full year before Lady Wartham permitted Dominique to visit again. After that, most of her visits were contained to when the lady of the house was away.

David knew none of that. He only knew her as Dominique Beauchamp, daughter of the elegant French widow who lived on the outskirts of the village.

The widow who was not a widow.

But when David stopped in the middle of the orangery, the scents of citrus all around them, and took her other hand into his, Dominique forgot to worry about all of that.

"It's lovely, isn't it?" he asked, eyes meeting hers. The bright blue of the ballroom was muted to a softer, darker hue in the moonlight.

"You're lovely," she breathed.

David's warm chuckle filled the air around them.

A flush climbed her cheeks with alarming speed. "I meant… Oh bother—"

"Hush," he said softly, leaning closer. Dominique's heart threatened to stop beating altogether. "It is only proper to accept a compliment from a beautiful woman."

There. It had stopped entirely.

"Now you are the one complimenting me," she said.

"I would compliment you every day for the rest of our lives, if you would let me."

Just as the depth of those words sank in, he leaned in and brushed his lips against hers. She gasped for air, completely overtaken. But all she found was David.

His kiss was tender and gentle. She'd seen the tongue-tangling ferocity of others' stolen kisses and had expected such from her first kiss. But it could not have been more different. The first brush was so light that she might have imagined it. The second lingered, and they shared the air between them for a breath before he slanted his mouth and kissed her again. His kiss was a question, and her body knew the answer, even if her mind did not.

She parted for him without realizing what she was doing, until she felt the tentative touch of the tip of his tongue against her lips. It ought to feel repulsive, to do such a thing. But she wanted David closer, was leaning into him even now, as she welcomed him into her mouth.

He tasted of tea and cinnamon, a soothing libation she wanted to drink down to the last drop. He slipped one hand free, sliding it up her arm to her shoulder. The touch of his fingers against her bare shoulder sent a bolt of sensation ricocheting through her body.

The shock of it sent her reeling back, the warm air that rushed in between them cool against the heat pulsing through her body. That fluttering she'd felt in her chest had turned to an overwhelming pulse, a throbbing need for one thing—*David*.

"Dominique, I did not mean to take advantage of you," he said quickly, stepping forward.

He reached for her hand again, and though the wise thing would have been to step further away and maintain the distance she'd put between them, Dominique did no such thing. She let him hold her fingers, clasping them between his own. She was grateful for the thin silk of her gloves. It was the only thing keeping her mind in some semblance of order.

"You do not need to apologize," she said.

She lifted her eyes to his, meeting them across the two feet of heavy space now separating them. The space was nothing, not when she felt their hearts beginning to join.

"I was surprised," she said, her breathing still labored. "But not… I just… I do not know if I am ready," she managed.

Instead of stepping forward to take her again into his arms, to try to convince her, David raised her hand to his mouth and kissed her knuckles gently. "Of course," he murmured.

The sweetness of it was so overwhelming, she knew that if he tried to kiss her again she would be powerless to stop it. But instead he released her hand and stepped back.

In the distance, a door closed sharply—a reminder that while they might be unseen at the moment, they were not alone.

"I ought to return to the ballroom," she said quietly.

He nodded. "I shall linger here a few minutes more."

Not trusting herself to speak any more, she gave him a small smile and turned away, forcing herself to take each step back toward the melee.

"I will wait as long as you need," she heard David say, his voice a promise on the orange-scented breeze.

CHAPTER FIVE

1817
Present Day

THE THEATER WAS not as glamorous as one imagined.

The Theatre Royal's four statuesque white pillars might gleam in alluring invitation for the wealthy patrons who filled the rows and boxes inside. But for the working Londoners putting on the show, the glamour was severely lacking.

The atmosphere was not improved by the glares Dominique garnered as she wound her way through the narrow corridors to her dressing room. She'd arrived an hour earlier today than yesterday to avoid those very glares; apparently that still was not early enough.

Cora in particular fixed her with a scowl fit to wither even the hardiest of plants.

"Good afternoon, Cora," Dominique chirped. She paused beside the two overturned crates where Cora and her companion, a chorus girl whose named eluded her, were lounging.

"Is it?" Cora said, face unmoved.

"I rather thought so. You were brilliant yesterday; that ovation was all for you," Dominique said. The compliment was genuine. Cora was a skillful actress—which was precisely why she hated Dominique.

"Perhaps someday I shall know what it feels like to bask in such attention," Cora bit out.

"You shall, very soon. I am certain of it." Even as she spoke, Dominique dug into the satchel tucked under her nondescript black cloak. She pulled out the wax-paper-wrapped parcel and offered it to the other woman.

"What is it?" Cora eyed her suspiciously.

"It's a Chelsea bun. From a shop near my mother's flat. I recalled you were fond of them, and these are the best I've found in London," Dominique said, offering a smile along with the wrapped treat.

Cora was unconvinced. "Is it poisoned?"

Dominique repressed her sigh of exasperation. "What would I gain from such a thing? It is a kindness, Cora, nothing more."

The other woman's nostrils flared, but she did reach out and accept the parcel.

Dominique did not wait for a "thank you." Not only did she doubt that it would come, it was immaterial to her purposes. She needed to befriend Cora, not make her grovel.

She ignored the feel of the other women's eyes on her back as she made her way down the corridor to her dressing room. Shifting her satchel back over her hip, she reached for the handle. The damn thing was sticky…

No. The damn thing was locked.

She shoved her hand back inside her cloak, refusing to give Cora and the chorus girl the satisfaction of watching her try the handle for a third time. Dominique knew what a locked door felt like; she'd spent the last three years coaxing even the most complicated ones into opening for her.

But Cora and the others could not know that.

Her fingers itched for the slender brown leather roll safely in the hidden pocket of her gown. She kept it on her person at all times, not even willing to store it in the satchel.

And there it would stay, she reminded herself.

She took a moment to compose herself before turning back

down the corridor. She ought to be surprised and embarrassed. This was a trick meant to make her feel like an outsider. The jest was on them; Dominique had spent her entire life as an outsider. Now she'd made a profession of it.

Cora thought she was the better actress—that she deserved the role that had been given to Dominique instead. Cora knew nothing. Dominique had been playing a role since the first time she stepped over the threshold of Wartham Grange as a child. She was so accomplished, she now played the part for queen and country.

When she turned, her step was slow and hesitant. She let her lower lip quiver and fought down the blush she'd summoned to her cheeks moments before. She wanted to appear embarrassed, but managing it well. Let them feel some satisfaction and some regret.

"My dressing room is locked, but the stage manager neglected to give me the key," she said, stopping before the two women. She flicked her eyes to the unopened bun still in Cora's hand.

Cora followed her gaze, regret flashing in her eyes for a moment. *Good.*

The chorus girl suffered no such circumspection. "Keys are earned, Miss Beauchamp," she said.

Ah, so that was it. Receiving the key to one's own dressing room was a rite of passage, and Dominique had swept in with no prior company experience and taken a primary role in the production.

"I shall do my best to be worthy," she said. *Is there a key to your shared chorus dressing room?* she did not let herself ask. Instead, she smiled at Cora. "Enjoy the bun."

The guilt written on Cora's face was exactly as potent as Dominique had intended.

She sidled past the women and back toward the rear of the theater where she'd entered. The stage manager was wary of her as well. Dominique suspected he was Cora's lover, which would account for how they'd managed this jape to begin with.

When the duchess had given her this quest, she had not anticipated the malice Dominique would find among the theater cast and crew. Leading actresses visited Covent Garden frequently, staying on for a month or two before moving on to another lucrative production. It was perhaps more unusual for one of the company to be promoted to a leading role. But those actresses were famous names, hired for the recognition. The duchess had seen a few accolades added to Dominique's background, but they were all French. Even more cause for the company to keep her at a distance.

Even so, Dominique smiled brightly at each person she passed. She would not be here long. A month, maybe two. As many allies as she could make in that time could only help her cause.

Luckily, her closest ally was monitoring the stage door and munching on a pastry of his own.

"Is it to your discerning satisfaction, Charles?" she asked, unable to stop herself from smiling at the burly man tasked with guarding the rear entrance.

"More than," he said, flakes of buttery pastry peppering his chin and chest.

Dominique chuckled. "I shall bring you another tomorrow," she promised. "If you can assist me today."

"Anything, Miss Beauchamp," he agreed, swallowing and licking his lips.

"The stage manager seems to have neglected to give me the key to my dressing room."

Charles frowned. "It should be in the room waiting for you."

"I doubt that. Unfortunately, the door is locked."

He rolled his shoulders, impressive bulk clearly on display. There was no doubt in Dominique's mind as to why Charles had been hired to guard the stage door. "Those harpies—"

She waved him off. "It is of no consequence. But I do need to gain entry."

"Shall I rip the door of the hinges for you?" he offered. She had no doubt he could.

"Perhaps a subtler solution is in order this time," she said.

Charles stared at her hard. She'd won him over with the pastry and a bit of kindness. Most of the company probably thought the brawn to be below them, but she knew he had a wife and seven children. Tomorrow she would bring pastries for them all.

"Stay here," he finally said.

He lumbered off down the hall, through a door at the end that she knew was the office. The door closed with a ghastly slam, but she supposed that was better than hearing the yells or cursing taking place within. Less than a minute later, he emerged, key in hand.

"You tell me if there's any more trouble," he said.

She most certainly would not. "Thank you, Charles," she said, rising to her tiptoes and pressing a kiss to his cheek. The man was old enough to be her father, and a happily married man, but he blushed nonetheless.

Dominique smiled to herself as she made her way back to her dressing room. Cora and her friend had thankfully cleared off, so her way was unimpeded.

She took the opportunity to carefully examine the layout of the backstage corridors, noting which rooms were occupied and where viable exits might be. It had been another reason for her early arrival today: she needed to better know the physical layout of the place she'd be spending so much of her time over the next few weeks. A lady knight never knew when a hasty exit might be in order.

Her graceless exit two weeks before at the duchess's ball sprang immediately to her mind.

Dominique cringed.

She still did not know for certain what David had made of her presence. She'd seen recognition on his handsome, achingly familiar face. But had she moved quickly enough to convince him it was his imagination playing a trick upon him?

In the intervening weeks, she'd tried and failed to fill in many of the blanks of David Grisham's life in the ten years since they'd parted. He still lived in Winleigh, which meant that reports were hard to come by without prying more directly, which was not a risk she was willing to take. She would not endanger her mother's peace, even for David.

But she had managed to glean some details. In particular, the reason that David was now in London. He was the heir to the Earl of Danby—which meant his father and brother were both deceased. Her heart ached for him; the Grisham family had always been tight-knit. Memories of his mother's kind face flashed in her mind. Where was Mrs. Grisham now?

Was there another Mrs. Grisham?

No, no. She'd found that answer as well. It was the talk of the *ton*—the Earl of Danby had a new heir, one who was in want of a wife.

She shivered despite her thick cloak.

Fitting the key into the lock, she pushed in the door and entered her dressing room. At first glance it all appeared to be in order, but she needed to check it over. If Cora and her company were willing to play one trick on her, they would not be above another. She would be unsurprised to find a toad in the drawer of her dressing table.

David had once snuck one into the vicar's desk drawer. The memory of the man's face during the Eucharist still had her chuckling.

A voice called across the corridor. The door was still ajar.

Dominique admonished herself again as she turned and locked it with the key, then fixed the bolt in place as well. She could not allow herself to be distracted—even by the handsome, kind, laughing face of David Grisham. Distraction led to mistakes, and mistakes could mean discovery, injury, or even death.

David was in London. But he was being toasted by the *haute ton*, while she was tasked with seducing and investigating a member of Parliament with a penchant for actresses. It was unlikely they would meet again.

She approached her dressing table, cautiously opening the top drawer. No toad. But there was something else.

The quarto was partially unfolded and a bit wrinkled; a casual onlooker would surely dismiss it as a bit of trash. But Dominique knew better. She carefully finished unfolding it, spinning it to better see the scrawled sentence near the bottom. The last word was cut off, but she knew it was intentional and understood nonetheless.

Do not miss the mark at stage le—

Dominique crumpled the paper and tossed it into the bin, relegating it back to the rubbish it appeared to be.

Her dubious parliamentarian would be in attendance tonight.

Let the quest begin.

CHAPTER SIX

DAVID TUGGED AT the waistcoat, wishing he'd forgone one entirely. Geoffrey, however, had informed him that was not an option. His shirt was rubbing as well. Geoffrey's laundress was overly fond of starch.

The contrast between London and the country was stifling. Every evening, there was a different entertainment. Be it musicale or ball, the follies or the opera, their attendance was expected somewhere each night of the week. Since that first ball when he'd been announced as Geoffrey's heir, it felt like he was being tailed by a coterie of hopeful debutantes and their less-than-subtle mothers.

David had never spent more than two nights in London. Long enough to receive or deliver a commission and then travel home to Winleigh. It was not that he did not enjoy it, precisely. But it was so at odds with the quiet life he'd led. His evenings mostly consisted of supper with his mother or an occasional pint at the local pub.

Winleigh was a far cry from Covent Garden, where he sat in his cousin's dedicated theater box waiting to watch a wildly popular new production from Joanna Baillie.

"Between the acts, we shall be expected to socialize," Geoffrey said quietly into David's ear as he paged through the playbill.

"Must we?" David sighed. He'd already spotted—or been

spotted by—several acquaintances the last few weeks.

"If we linger here, they will only seek us out," his cousin said without looking up at him.

"Why did I come to London?"

Geoffrey smiled into his program. "For the culture, most definitely." He nodded toward the stage.

David wrinkled his nose. "I have never been much for theater," he admitted.

"Then take a nap. That is what I intend to do." Indeed, as candles and lanterns were doused, Geoffrey raised the program to his face and effectively shielded himself from everyone and everything.

David stifled his laugh, though it was an appealing proposition. He could not discuss the play with overeager young ladies if he had not seen any of it. Perhaps he would even dream of—

Dominique.

There, at center stage.

This time, there was an entire theater with their eyes riveted upon her.

She was real.

⫸⫷

BY THE TIME the curtain fell, Dominique was dripping sweat, and the cosmetics she'd applied were threatening to run off her face. She fantasized about the clean linen towel and ewer of water awaiting her in her dressing room. The most she'd ever applied in her ordinary life was a bit of rouge. But on stage, the more she could alter her face, the better.

She became an abstract, mysterious creature. The thing fantasies were made of—in particular, the fantasies of one Roderick D'Terre, the parliamentarian she needed to seduce. He'd been seated exactly where the duchess had indicated. Between the acts, amid sips of tea and a few dry biscuits, she'd sent a note to his box.

Now she only had to beat him back to her dressing room.

Weaving around the other cast members, in particular avoiding Cora and her contingent, she moved as quickly as was possible without garnering any extra notice. If they thought her a prima donna, retreating to her dressing room rather than fraternizing with the rest of the cast… it was unfortunate, because there may be a time when she needed their help. But for the moment, it could not be avoided. She'd set her trap—she must be present in order to spring it.

Luck was with her—the corridor was empty. She slid the key from her bosom and into the singular latch she'd fastened.

The performance had been well attended, which meant D'Terre would have to weave his way through the throngs of noblesse and well-off Londoners that filled the theater. Dominique counted continuously in her head, tracking the minutes as she stripped away her costume. Her hairpin snagged on the lace-trimmed shift she replaced it with.

"Heavens," she muttered, tugging the offending pin from her hair and tossing it onto the dressing table. An errant wave of dark hair fell to her shoulder, but she supposed that would only add to the effect she was trying to achieve.

She snatched the scarlet dressing gown from over the back of the chair and strode to the door. There was so much noise in the back of the theater that it was difficult to distinguish footsteps. Her best chance of a warning would be if she was near the door.

Her intuition was correct—a few breaths later, she heard a pair of heavy, unhurried steps. D'Terre was a large man who moved with confidence through the world—assured of his position, powerful within the House of Commons.

Even more so because he was blackmailing a dozen of his colleagues. Allegedly. She'd been tasked with seducing him and finding the proof that would put an end to his reign of tyranny in the lower house of Parliament.

She loosely tied the waist of her dressing gown, purposefully putting her full body on display. D'Terre had a penchant for taking Covent Garden actresses to his bed; she was to be just another conquest.

The sharp knock at her door sent her back across the dressing room on silent feet. She checked her reflection in the mirror above the dressing table, bit her lips to give them a bit more color, and sauntered across the thick carpet like the courtesan she was supposed to be.

She opened the door slowly, letting her scarlet dressing gown appear first as she stepped into the gap. Starting at his booted feet, she drew her eyes up his body with an openly appraising gaze meant to give him time to do the same.

When she finally reached his cravat, she glanced up through her eyelashes and dragged her tongue over her bottom lip before speaking.

"Bonjour, monsieur…" She trailed off and inserted a heavy breath that drew his eyes down to her bosom.

"Roderick D'Terre," he supplied, bracing one fist upon the doorframe—already taking a proprietary stance meant to convey a message to anyone who passed through the corridor.

"*Bonne,*" she purred, accentuating the French accent she did not truly have. "I was hoping you would accept my invitation."

"I was pleased to receive your note, Miss Beauchamp. Your performance was magnificent," D'Terre said, wasting no time in plying her with compliments. He was already looking past her, assessing gaze on her dressing room.

Had he already bedded one of her predecessors in this very dressing room? Dominique fought the urge to recoil.

"I have been told you are a most ardent connoisseur of the theater, monsieur." She rocked back on her heel, cognizant of just how close D'Terre had already positioned himself. If she took another step, however, he might very well follow her into her dressing room.

"I am a connoisseur of beautiful things," he said. The low rumble of appreciation in his chest as he got an unobstructed view down the front of her dressing gown confirmed that if she permitted it, he'd have her on her back before the night was out. But Dominique needed more than a quick romp—she had to gain access to his home.

"I would appreciate your notes on my performance. But a gentleman as important as yourself must be very busy." She dropped her voice an octave and pouted out her lower lip. "Perhaps you will favor me with your presence again soon?"

D'Terre drew his eyes very slowly up from her bosom, pausing at the dark lock of hair she'd left to fall forward. Without warning, he snaked his hand forward and caught it, toying with the end, rubbing it between his fingers—all while holding her gaze.

"Tomorrow."

She chuckled. "I am onstage tomorrow, monsieur. But the day after…"

"Where shall I collect you?" he asked without pause.

Perfect—eager, but willing to play the little game she'd set into motion.

"Spencer's Confectionary," she said readily.

He quirked a coppery brow.

"I have a penchant for all things sweet," she confessed. A truth, mixed with all the lies. "Allow me to share my world of decadence with you."

The drool was nearly falling from his mouth. "It will be my pleasure."

She tugged her hair back, matching the motion with a playful smile. "Until then."

"Goodnight, Mademoiselle Beauchamp," D'Terre said with an accent that had even Dominique's ancestors cringing.

He did not bother to sketch a bow, but did flick his proprietary gaze over her body once more before pushing off the door frame.

"Adieu, Monsieur D'Terre," she purred, leaning against the doorframe.

He sauntered halfway down the hall before pausing and

glancing back at her. By which time, she'd allowed the arm of her dressing gown to fall down over her shoulder, revealing a generous expanse of olive skin and her lace-trimmed shift beneath. D'Terre rewarded her with a hungry smirk.

She pretended to realize the disarray of her garments and pulled them back into place with a small, secretive smile. D'Terre's hands tightened at his sides, but he turned and continued on. She'd offered him a promise of what might be to come, but still keep the chase alive.

He rounded the corner, and she heard Charles's voice, her indication she could tighten her dressing gown and retreat inside. But then another voice floated through the corridor. Dominique caught the door to her dressing room just as it was about to close, her curiosity getting the better of her as she glanced out and her heart stopped.

David Grisham rounded the corner a second behind his voice, and this time when his blue eyes landed upon her, she knew they would not let her go.

CHAPTER SEVEN

"I CANNOT BELIEVE it is truly you standing before me after all of these years," he said. His breath came in hitched, rasping wisps.

He cleared his throat and forced down a gulp of air, lest he expire on the floor of her dressing room.

"David, I..." She tugged her dressing gown tighter around her, the only sign of unease. Her lovely face was calm and unlined. "Ahem." She pressed a hand daintily to her bosom and smiled. "Do excuse me. I am quite overwhelmed."

If she truly was, she did not look it. Meanwhile, David knew he was one more shock away from keeling over.

"You were never given to the vapors." He grinned.

"Nor am I now," Dominique countered. "Do come in—it won't do to have you lingering in the corridor. It might give someone the wrong idea."

She beckoned him in, then bustled around him and closed the door herself, setting the bolt firmly into place. David was not sure what to make of that.

"One would think locking yourself in with a man would be the sort of thing that gave the wrong idea," he said. Then he winked broadly and grinned again. Even as his heart strained in his chest.

Dominique laughed, her eyes gleaming.

He was in such trouble.

"You have not lost your knack for making me smile, it seems. I am so very glad to see you, David." She flexed her hands as if she would reach out and touch him.

His skin began to tingle.

"I thought, perhaps, given your note…"

"Of course." She nodded. She did touch him then—a soft graze of her hand on his arm. There was no realistic way he could have felt it through the layers of his tailcoat and shirt. And yet…

"My life is very different than it was then," she said, pulling her hand back.

"The life of an actress," he mused.

He glanced around the dressing room, thinking it would tell him who exactly Dominique was now. But it was sparsely adorned.

A cloak hung in the corner alongside a row of costumes. Its ownership was made obvious by the contrast of the black velvet with the bright, jewel-toned frocks he'd seen her wear across the stage.

But there were no trinkets on the dressing table or extra sets of shoes or clothing. It was all quite minimal. It struck him as odd. Dominique had always exuded a sense of warmth and kindness—of home.

Yet her dressing room could have belonged to anyone. There was nothing marking the space as hers or denoting the vibrant layers of her personality.

Had she changed so greatly in the years they'd been apart?

"Among other things," she said, drifting to stand beside the dressing table.

What did that mean? She was not ordinarily an actress? He knew little about the theater, but somehow it seemed unlikely that anyone other than a professional would be cast in a leading role at Covent Garden.

But he did not ask any of those questions. They were secondary to the most important ones.

"Are you well? I have not stopped thinking of you since…" He trailed off, wanting to punch himself. "I have often wondered after your well-being." It was a modest improvement on his prior attempt at making sense of himself.

But Dominique, always graceful and kind, seemed to understand his awkwardness twined with excitement. She smiled openly, her eyes creasing as she chuckled at him.

"I am well," she said. From the slight dimple in her cheek, David found himself believing it. "And you?"

He frowned then. The sight of her had allowed him to forget why he was in London. "Some would say I am lucky," he began. "I have my health. And my mother's as well."

She caught the significance of his words. It was evident from the smile as it slipped away from her face. But she let him continue.

"My father and brother were lost in a fire at the foundry last year," he explained as stoically as he could manage. "I find myself suddenly without half my family and in line to inherit my cousin's earldom."

When she reached for his hand, David forgot to be sad. He felt only warmth and desire where her fingers touched his own. He thanked his uncouth manners, which had urged him to stuff his white gloves into his pocket as he'd wound through the crowd to find her. Because now their skin was touching, their bodies connected for the first time in a decade. It sent thrills of excitement down his spine and directly to his heart. More than anything, it felt like coming home.

"Thank you," he heard himself saying.

"I did not say anything," she murmured back.

When she touched him, no words were needed. "Thank you, nonetheless."

He glanced up from their joined hands to find her eyes watching him. If her touch had been a comfort, her intense, dark eyes upon his were a lightning strike. How had he survived ten years without her? Even as her familiar scent filled his nose, he could not imagine how he'd ever managed to breathe without it.

For a moment, Dominique's composure broke. Her eyes flashed, betraying the emotion that simmered just beneath the surface. She was as affected as he, David realized. It was only that she'd become an expert at hiding it.

"It is late," she said, stepping back suddenly. "You have caught me about to leave for the night, I'm afraid." A patent untruth, given that she wore a dressing robe. But David did not contradict her.

"Allow me to see you safely home," he said.

She was going to refuse. She ought to refuse—it was highly improper. But David could not let her go. Not yet, not when he'd just found her again. A loud, vociferous part of him warned that if he let her out of his sight, she might dissolve into the daydream she'd been for the last ten years.

"Yes," she said, her brow furrowing as if she'd surprised even herself with her answer. But as quickly as it had appeared, the frown was gone. "Allow me a few moments to dress and I will join you," she added.

David nodded, retreating to the corridor, but not a step further.

⧎

"Maid, actress… what else have you done these past years?" David asked, attempting to be casual and making a horrible job of it.

Dominique could see the strain in his shoulders, hear the hopefulness in his voice. He was like a starved man who'd stumbled into an oasis. She was the drink of cold water.

She was not much better, she admitted to herself. The wise thing would have been to put him off at the theater and then avoid him forevermore. But when David stepped into her dressing room, he'd reawakened a piece of her she'd thought long hibernating. Try as she might, she was drawn to him with the same unquenchable thirst.

Which could be the only accounting for why she not only allowed him to escort her home, but then said:

"I also help my mother with her dance lessons. An unmarried woman's place in the world is precarious," she said. That sentence, at least, was pure truth. "Would you like to come up for a spot of tea?"

"Of course," he said. She was already nodding toward the stairwell.

As she climbed the stairs to the first floor, she could feel David's eyes upon her. The contrast to D'Terre earlier in the night was so stark. The parliamentarian's gaze was that of a conqueror surveying his conquest. But when David looked at her, it was as if he was trying to absorb every detail.

The landing was too small for the both of them, forcing him closer to her than was proper. His hand brushed against her sleeve—she'd traded her risqué dressing gown for a modest, long-sleeved mauve gown—and lingered a few seconds longer than could be passed off as accidental. But she did not brush him away.

She worked through lock after lock in the long column that guarded her door. Only years of experience and training kept her hand steady. With David mere inches behind her, every nerve she possessed was tingling.

It had always been like this between them. When they were teenagers, she had not fully realized what it was. Not until they'd snuck off to the orangery and shared that first kiss. What would it be like to kiss him now?

You will not be finding that out, her inner voice admonished her. In truth, the voice sounded less like her own and more like that of her fellow lady knight, Jane.

Finally, she got the door free and moved inside, inviting him into her home. While David walked in easily, eyes sweeping over the flat, Dominique felt unease creeping in her stomach. Few others visited her here. Her mother, of course, and occasionally one of the other Lady Knights. But she did not have friends or guests to invite to tea. Her chosen profession rather precluded it.

And she had never entertained a gentleman here.

But as he slowly looked around the room, eyes floating from the neatly arranged sideboard to the bookshelf stacked with thick volumes, a smile pulled at his face. He glanced toward her, and her cheeks burned immediately.

"What is it?" David asked, grin firmly in place now.

"I do not have many visitors," she said.

"Your home is lovely," he said warmly. She could tell from the tilt of his head and the sparkle in his blue eyes that he meant it.

She swallowed past the lump in her throat and turned quickly so he would not see her expression. For a woman who'd just acted on London's most famous stage before hundreds, she was having a damned hard time holding herself together in David's presence. Dominique had made artifice into an art form; yet with David, it all came apart with frightening ease.

"Tea," she murmured, moving for the kettle and the direction of the hearth.

As she touched the handle, a loud thump rang out above their heads.

"Oh!" she exclaimed, handing him the kettle. "Be a dear and put that on," she said, bustling to the sideboard.

She rustled through the cupboards, and it was only when she straightened again that she noted the perturbed look upon his usually ruddy, grinning face.

Usually. As if he'd been a constant fixture in her life for the past decade, rather than a cherished memory.

She held up the parcel. "If you will excuse me a moment, I just need to dash up to Mrs. Fletch's flat. I do a bit of shopping for her, on the days her son cannot make it here. She is quite elderly."

Something flickered in David's eyes as he watched her. She thought it was understanding, though that made no sense. He rubbed at his chin, at the invisible stubble that must be there, and the understanding in his gaze was followed quickly by relief. Which was an equally baffling emotion, given the situation.

"I will just pop up to her flat," she said, stepping toward the door.

"Go on, then." David's face erupted into a blinding grin. "I'll manage this fine."

Shaking her head at how she could be so completely attuned to and confused by someone who'd been back in her life for all of an hour, Dominique climbed two flights of stairs to deliver the parcel of food.

By the time she returned to her own flat, the kettle was whistling merrily and David was setting the tea on to steep.

"You've made yourself rather comfortable," she teased, mostly for her own benefit. The way her heart lurched when she saw him in her flat, among her most treasured possessions, was decidedly unnerving.

"Your set is lovely," David said, ignoring her comment and nodding toward the teapot and matching cups he'd retrieved from the sideboard and set out for them. It was decorated with blue and gold fleurs-de-lis cleverly twined with an emerald and gold vine motif.

"It was a gift from my mother." She smiled fondly as she poured her tea.

"Is your mother well?" David asked, eyes fixed on his own cup.

Dominique nodded. "She teaches dancing lessons to wealthy, social-climbing families hoping to marry their daughters into the peerage," she said with a sigh.

David quirked a brow. "You do not approve?"

"I cannot help but approve. My mother's ingenuity built us a comfortable life from nothing." She did not need to say more than that for David to understand—and that was the most disconcerting thing of all.

Despite the undeniable attraction between them, it was the

ease with which they related to one another that shook her. Suddenly, even though they'd been apart for ten years, the relationship between them felt deeper than ever before. The secret of her birth was no longer between them.

Though one crucial secret remained.

Dominique was not an actress. At least, not in the conventional sense.

But if inviting him up to her flat had been foolish whimsy, telling David anything about her status as a lady knight of Her Majesty's Round Table was utterly unthinkable.

The silence stretched between them until David cleared his throat. His tea was empty. She could offer to refill it or she could send him into the night, no more than a memory.

"It is quite late," she forced herself to say, though her stomach turned over and her heart protested within her chest.

"Indeed. Geoffrey will wonder where I've gotten to," David said.

Her eyebrow rose, separate of any control she'd once had over her body.

"My cousin," he explained, moving toward the door.

Relief. She ought to be feeling relief. He was going to leave without a fuss. There would be no disruption to the life she'd carefully crafted, nor to her quest as a lady knight.

So why did it feel like one of her limbs was being torn from her body? Again?

She followed him to the door, catching the solid slab of wood as he opened it and stepped onto the landing.

"It was an inexplicable pleasure seeing you tonight," David said, chest heaving with obvious emotion. "I cannot describe how it felt to see you on that stage."

And yet he was going to walk away. It was no more than she deserved—no more than she had done all those years ago.

Perhaps she could touch him one last time. Just the brush of her hand against his would be enough, would *have* to be enough. She leaned forward on her exhale, only slightly. Not enough for him to perceive it.

"How often do you perform?"

She blinked, surprised. That was not a farewell.

And now, she was very close to him—leaning forward, her bosom trembling, her lower lip trying desperately to match it.

"Four nights of the week," she managed.

"Tomorrow?"

"Yes."

"After that?"

"No, not for the next three days."

"I've heard tell there is an orangery at Kensington."

Her heels hit the floor suddenly. Dominique had not even realized she'd risen onto her tiptoes, leaning forward into a kiss that her body had known was coming even if her mind had not. But his mention of the orangery knocked her back toward reality. Or, at the very least, nudged her in its direction.

"It is too public," she said. Before he could argue or ask what she meant by that, she countered, "Temple of the Muses, in Finsbury Square."

"In two days," David breathed. He looked as unsteady as she. The grin was gone, replaced by open-mouthed breathing that indicated he was struggling as much as she to control himself.

"Midday," she added, taking a full step back. "Goodnight."

She closed the door with a sharp click, but her hands paused above the column of locks that defended her flat from intruders. Through the thick wooden panel, she assured herself it was no more than her imagination that heard the words: *Until then, my love.*

CHAPTER EIGHT

THOUGH THE SUN was shining, it was as much a ruse as the revealing neckline Dominique sported as she circled the sweet shop. It was nearly June, but London was still grasped in the cool winds of spring. Gooseflesh pebbled along her bare arms as she cursed D'Terre under her breath. He was not due for another quarter hour, and already she was shivering.

She'd arrived early to reconnoiter the location, marking the exits and any nooks well suited for hiding. The shop was not busy, by intent. It also was not her favorite sweet shop; that was Hartley's in Piccadilly. But she did not intend to risk her favorite source of lemon drops on a quest that could easily go awry.

Convinced she'd given the place an adequate inspection, she retreated into an alleyway across the street to watch for D'Terre's arrival. Caught in the shadow between buildings, she was essentially invisible to the street. But she was also hidden from the feeble sunlight.

The shivers were coming in relentless waves now.

Think of Bath in the summer. Imagine the wind as nothing more than a seaside breeze.

The mind tricks she'd been taught as a lady knight had never worked particularly well for her.

Instead, she decided to think of the sweets lining the counters inside the shop. There was a promising arrangement of chocolate.

They had rows of beautifully molded marzipan, which was her favorite. But nothing compared to the lemon drops and sugar-plums at Hartley's. Perhaps she would take David there, after the library.

The memory of David standing in her flat pouring her tea spread through her, warming her with the efficiency of any cloak.

That was apparently what it took to keep her warm on a frigid London afternoon.

It was too bad she would never tell the ever-composed Jane about that particular trick.

Before she could dwell on that thought, a carriage pulled up across the street. She recognized it instantly from the description in the brief the Duchess of Guilford had given her upon assigning Dominique this quest.

Interesting. Most of the shop's patrons strolled on foot, de-termined to enjoy the sunshine even if it was cold. Londoners were starved for it after a long, wet spring. But D'Terre chose a closed carriage instead. Seeking to hide his identity or to make a show of it?

The footman jumped down to open the door, and a second later, Dominique had her answer.

Roderick D'Terre was dressed like a king. At least, in compar-ison to the modestly colored frocks and coats dappling the street. His double-breasted tailcoat was bright turquoise, with a collar of sapphire velvet and gleaming gold buttons. The bottle-green waistcoat beneath was flamboyantly embroidered with gold and green thread in an eye-catching feather pattern. Her eyes did not know where to look first. He most certainly wanted to be noticed, which was less than desirable for Dominique. She would rather have maintained her anonymity—a feat that would be next to impossible on D'Terre's arm.

She began to modify her goals for the day as she circled the back of one of the buildings she stood between, careful to appear she was arriving from the opposite direction of the street rather than lurking in the shadows. She'd meant to keep this interaction entirely public, to whet his appetite. But if D'Terre insisted on being so obvious, then perhaps it was better to adjourn to his residence sooner. Though she'd have a challenge extricating herself from it without some sort of physical offering...

Dominique pushed that thought away and instead slid an easy, half-cocked smile onto her face, pouting her lower lip out just enough to be noticeable. When she reached D'Terre, she sank into a low curtsey that was entirely unnecessary, given their respective lack of titles, and also highly effective at flattering the man's ego, which she saw the instant she rose.

D'Terre was licking his lips, barely getting his eyes from her bosom to her face by the time she straightened. Though Dominique doubted he'd felt the need to make much effort.

"*Bonjour, mon paon,*" she said.

"Good day, Miss Beauchamp," he said, not even bothering to incline his head in her direction. "You must excuse me, but my French fails me just now. *Paon?*"

She would never have excused such a man anything, but she merely widened her smile and laid her hand on his arm. "It is not fit for public discussion. Perhaps I will tell you when we are alone."

His eyes narrowed on her mouth. Dominique swiped her tongue slowly over her upper lip and blinked up at him through eyelashes darkened with kohl.

Though he looked as if he'd rather take a bite of her than entertain a trip into the sweet shop, he curled his hand possessively over hers on his arm. "We shall see to one hunger first. Then later, another."

"*Oui,* whatever you desire," she purred, angling her body so her breast brushed against his gloved hand as he negotiated her around other patrons and into the shop.

Dominique was spared much conversation once they were inside. The shop itself was more crowded than it had been during her initial turn of the place, which left them not much room to do anything but place an order. D'Terre paid for the expensive chocolates Dominique selected, and she brushed her body against his a few times as the moved through the crowded space.

By the time they returned to the street, the footman and driver appeared thoroughly bored. Another item of note for Dominique's expanding profile of D'Terre. If his hired help were not on alert, they either did not know of the nefarious activities of their master, or she was not considered any sort of threat. Either possibility was beneficial to Dominique and could be exploited for her cause.

"I have a claret in my study which will pair perfectly with these." D'Terre referred to the parcel of chocolates in his hand, though his eyes never left Dominique's mouth. "It is but a short carriage ride."

She was about to start shivering again, but she determinedly forced the physical impulse down. Instead, she smiled brightly. "It is such a fine day. May we walk?"

D'Terre frowned, eyes finally leaving her lips and bosom to glance in the direction of his carriage. He'd had aspirations for the carriage ride, clearly enough, however short he claimed it to be. But Dominique needed access to his home. If she let him kiss and pet her in the carriage, she risked the interlude ending without her having been invited in to inspect the interior of his residence.

"It is rather cold. My carriage would be more comfortable."

Dominique slid her hand in the hot crevasse between his arm and his chest, drawing herself near to him until she was pressed firmly to his side. "I promise to keep you warm, *mon paon*."

She took a half-step down the street, gambling that he would follow.

"I shall hold you to that promise," D'Terre said, eyes clouding with lust as he anchored her close to his side.

Dominique smiled when she'd rather flinch. She could endure a few passing touches to reach her goal.

"I HAVE NEVER seen so many masterpieces in one place," Dominique gushed as she hung off D'Terre's arm. They were in a glorified hallway masquerading as a gallery.

The collection was impressive—if they were real. That sort of thing was not her area of expertise. The doors he'd led her past, most of them outfitted with Barron-style locks, had her hands itching for the roll of picks carefully secured to her thigh. She had her two favorites secured in special slits inside the boning of her bodice for quick access. But by the way D'Terre was hanging on her, she doubted he would leave her unattended for long.

He seemed intent on parading her through the entire ground floor of the house. He'd even paused at the stairwell, but she feigned interest in the wall of paintings before he could suggest showing her his bedchamber.

"There was almost nothing here when I bought the place. I have curated the collection entirely myself," D'Terre rumbled. He rubbed a sweaty palm over her hand where it rested on his arm.

"It is magnificent. I am quite overwhelmed by the beauty. Is there somewhere we might have a quiet respite?" she said, putting her hand to her bosom for effect.

She was not given to the vapors and, by the darkening of lust in D'Terre's eyes, knew he saw it for the thinly veiled invitation that it was.

"You mentioned a particular claret?" she added, nodding to the parcel of chocolates tucked under his arm.

"Ah yes, this way." He nodded toward a set of doors at the end of the hallway.

Closed, like all the others they'd passed by. It had made mapping out the footprint of his residence rather challenging, but at least she had a sense of the main arteries. But when he spoke of the claret, he'd referred to his study.

Satisfaction curled through her as he opened the doors— unlocked with a skeleton key from inside his tailcoat—and led her into the very room.

Perfect. The study was lined with books on either side, culminating in a wall of windows that overlooked the generous inner courtyard. In the center of the room, a large desk commanded the attention of anyone who entered.

She capitalized on the feeling of success flowing through her to pad the smile she offered and infuse the ease of her limbs as she disentangled herself from D'Terre and wandered around the room in apparent amazement.

It was a striking arrangement, with the double-height windows bathing the interior in sharp sunlight and shadow, and the commanding desk at the center. She walked to the windows and appeared to study the view. When she spun around, her gaze lingered only a second on the desk before landing back on D'Terre watching her awe with satisfaction.

But one glance at the back of the desk was enough.

It was old, likely inherited from whomever had owned this house before D'Terre bought it. She spied five drawers, each with a lock. But one stood out. The lower-left drawer's lock was different, the brass gleaming. A double-acting tumbler.

Simple.

Now she only had to get him out of the study long enough to pick the lock.

Lips still parted in open-mouthed admiration, she swanned to the sofa and delicately lowered herself to the edge. Placing one hand on each side of her to frame her breasts, she stared directly at D'Terre.

"This place... it has such a... *je ne sais quoi,*" she said, voice just above a whisper.

"We can linger here as long as you'd like," D'Terre said.

She was ready for him to join her on the sofa, expected as much, but instead he turned for the sideboard. *Ah, yes, the claret.*

The claret.

He carried the bottle with him as he walked, setting it upon the low-lying table before the sofa. Then he handed her the full glass.

"What shall we toast to?" she asked, eyes meeting his over the crystal rim.

"To new pleasures."

Dominique executed the next three moves simultaneously. She lifted her glass to toast, causing D'Terre to lift his as well. But instead of clinking their glasses together, she leaned in as if for a kiss. Last, she caught her foot on the hem of her skirt, jostling the table.

Wine went everywhere. So did her breasts, nearly spilling out of her bosom. It was difficult to say which was responsible for the drastic widening of D'Terre's dark eyes.

But the effect was instantaneous. He leapt off the sofa to avoid the wine, as did Dominique. She might have let it spill on her—a soaked gown was a painfully easy tool of seduction. But she did not want to risk dripping wine across the floorboards and leaving a trail when she went for the desk.

"I beg your pardon, monsieur. I have ruined your lovely sofa." She fell to her knees, playing at searching for something to mop up the spill.

Instead of coming to her aid, D'Terre rang for a servant, exactly as she'd expected him too. She stepped to the side and allowed the maid to bustle in and tidy the mess, while looking sheepishly at the ground and attempting to appear embarrassed.

When the maid finally left, she shot a glance over her shoulder at Dominique that spoke loudly about her opinion of her employer's new would-be mistress.

Dominique marked the young woman's face so she could make a point of avoiding her.

"How shall I ever redeem myself?" She sighed, drifting to the armchair.

D'Terre was not the type to offer comfort. But he was the sort to take advantage. He circled around the furniture, coming to stand behind her. He did not take her in his arms, but he laid one hand on either side of her, enclosing her in the space between his body and the back of the chair.

"I can think of a few potential avenues," he murmured, his breath sticky and hot against her neck.

Dominique tilted her head back, letting him breathe in her scent before she said, "If only there was even a drop of claret left, to calm my nerves."

He rumbled with frustration. She was balancing on a knife's edge. But she had to get him out of the room, if only for a few moments. So she lifted his hand, dragging the fingertips over her lips, then down her chin, and skimmed them over the curve of her breasts. A tease, a promise.

D'Terre shifted toward her, and she felt the telltale press of his desire against her back. "Monsieur," she rasped, willing her voice to sound scratchy and parched.

He sighed heavily. "I will fetch a bottle of claret from my cellar. Do not move an inch."

"Of course, *mon paon.*"

He cursed under his breath, but strode away from her and out of the study, closing the doors behind him.

She had to be quick. He might encounter a servant anywhere and send them to fetch the bottle. Though usually, the wine cellar was the purview of the butler. But if D'Terre encountered a maid or footman, he might very well send them after the butler so he could return to his attempts to paw at her.

Dominique had the picks out of her binding in a flash, and was already bending to the lower-left drawer. She could have had the other four open in a heartbeat, simple ward mechanisms that they were. But this was the lock that demanded her attention. It had been updated to the more modern Barron-style lock while the others were untouched. Whatever D'Terre stored here, it was worth protecting.

She had to position the two picks just so, applying pressure with one while the other moved—

Click.

She didn't bother to hide the smirk that came to her face as the drawer jumped open. If he truly wanted his papers secure,

D'Terre would be better off with something in the style of Bramah or Chubb—the true visionaries of modern locksmithing. Though she could get through those as well.

It was paper inside—but Dominique knew better than to be fooled by the lack of something more obviously sinister. Words were often the most dangerous weapons. But what she saw were not words, at least not solely.

Interspersed with the documents, letters with names she quickly tried to commit to memory, were several charcoal drawings. They were brilliantly rendered, with minute details, down to the types of trees lining the background. She frowned, scanning them for clues, then flicking back to the letters. It seemed like normal, aboveboard parliamentary correspondence. Nothing to do with the sketches attached. She skimmed the first letter, to Lord Hawley. It made no mention of Carlton House, the building depicted in the drawing enclosed with it. There were six sets in total, but Dominique only managed to look over three of them before she heard D'Terre's unmistakable heavy footsteps.

She shoved the drawer closed with her foot even as she stood. There was no time to get the picks into their narrow sleeves sewn into the inside of her gown, so she stuffed them into the thick pile of curls atop her head and prayed that he would not look too closely.

Her bum landed on the velvet armchair as the door swung open and D'Terre stepped into the room, a new bottle of claret tucked under his arm.

"My last one," he commented, fixing his eyes on her immediately.

Dominique plied him with a smile, forcing her lips to say something leading and her head to tilt mysteriously. But her mind was already miles away, planning. Seducing a man like D'Terre took only a fraction of her attention; stealing from him would be another matter entirely.

CHAPTER NINE

D AVID HAD COUNTED the hours—would have calculated the minutes if he thought the number would have done anything other than depress him. Two days seemed an eternity to be parted from Dominique, having only just found her again.

Especially after seeing her flat.

If her dressing room had been a puzzle, her flat had helped the pieces begin to fit together once more. The personal touches that had been missing from her sparse room at the Theatre Royal were everywhere in her flat. The parcel she'd insisted on running up to her neighbor was proof that the kind woman he'd always loved was still there, if now hidden beneath the exterior of an actress. And a maid.

There was more that Dominique was not telling him. He'd had two days to mull it over, and still had not landed upon a satisfactory answer. The most important fact was that she was not engaged with a gentleman… but then, he did not really know that for certain either.

The bare hour he'd been able to spend with her had left him with more questions than answers, really. But still, the warmth in his heart told David well enough that whatever and whoever Dominique was now, he was still very much in love with her.

Back in Winleigh, all those years ago, he'd been all but certain the feeling was reciprocated. Now, he was not so certain. There had been emotion in those compelling, dark eyes of hers, sure enough. But love? They hardly knew one another now.

But he would see to that. Today, they would begin to reacquaint themselves. The only hurdle being that Dominique had chosen a library for their meeting.

David had agreed out of hand when she mentioned the Tower of the Muses. He'd actually had no idea what it was—though his mind had dreamt up something much more scandalous than the bookseller and circulating library Geoffrey described to him when asked.

Perhaps Dominique knew something more about the establishment than he did. She had suggested it, after all. Or perhaps she'd suggested it because it would preclude any substantive exchange of words, and thus allow her to conduct the encounter with all due politeness before making her excuses and disappearing once again.

David did not know that he possessed the fortitude to let her go.

If she turned him away, he would respect her wishes, of course.

But he would also likely stand across the street from her flat and stare longingly for the rest of his days.

He was spared having to debate the pitifulness of that prospect by the appearance of the massive four-story building as he rounded the corner and entered Finsbury Square. Standing in front of it, framed by one of the wide arches, waited Dominique.

She looked every inch the graceful gentlewoman he'd known she would one day become. She wore a short-sleeved white muslin dress, edged in Brussels lace that teased the ground as she swayed from side to side with the breeze. Only the barest inch of her olive skin was visible between the edge of her cap sleeves and her high lilac gloves, but somehow the covering made that sliver even more appealing. The ruffled neckline framed her face, her dark curls piled atop her head and fixed with a white bonnet that was decorative rather than useful. It would not have done a thing to shade her face from the spring sun. But it was not meant to; it was meant to draw attention to her lovely face, as if anyone seeing her would be able to look away.

In the night, she'd been an achingly beautiful memory, a shade who might vanish with the shadows. But in the bright of day, she was his dreams come to life.

And if he did not rein in his enthusiasm, he would scare her away.

"A library. I ought to have known. You always were the schoolmaster's favorite pupil," he teased, the grin following naturally as her eyes lit upon him.

"It is not my fault that you and your brother were rather more interested in japes," she countered, smile lighting her face.

"Japes are more enjoyable than maths," he insisted, noting the slightly crooked bow of her lips, now even more lush than he remembered.

Instead of lingering on how it would feel to kiss them, he offered his arm. "Shall we go in?"

She took it, leading him back through the arch where she'd been perched. "This is one of my favorite places in all of London," she confessed as they stepped into the atrium.

The wall of windows facing Finsbury Square bathed the cavernous room in gold. Or it would have been cavernous, he amended, were it not stuffed to bursting with books.

She steered him past the circulation desk, behind the tall stacks of books that towered toward the double-height ceiling. He tried to pause, but Dominique's pressure on his arm was insistent. David's eyes flicked back to the round desk, crowned with the atrium above. Was there someone there she was avoiding?

But no one looked their way, and Dominique's footsteps slowed once they were behind the sky-high double-sided bookcase. There were other patrons, of course, but the space was large, a veritable labyrinth of tomes. Privacy and quiet reigned here.

"Are we allowed to speak?" David whispered, making no

show of considering the books. He enjoyed reading, but Dominique was the reason he'd come.

She, however, was running one hand lovingly over the spines as they drifted along.

"Yes," she said with a soft smile, eyes still upon the books. "But it is polite to speak quietly," she clarified, nodding toward a staid-looking man at the end of the aisle, nose buried in a book heavy enough to do harm if lobbed with any amount of malice.

"I have my favorites." She nodded toward the end of the aisle, indicating her usual direction. "But what might interest you?"

It was a gentle, easy way of reacquainting themselves with each other, and David was able to admire the artistry of it. Even if he wanted to ask her a thousand questions instead.

"A great many things." *You.* "Have they any collections of etchings?"

"Etchings?" Already, though, her scanning eyes had changed directions.

"Yes. I'd like to see if any of mine have made it in."

Dominique stopped scanning, frowning at him directly now. "Your etchings? Do you not work at the foundry?"

David pushed past the tightening in his throat. "The foundry is gone. The fire that took my father and brother… It was a near total loss. The premises were not fit for use. I suppose the bank might have offered me a loan to rebuild, given the strength of the family name. But I'd no desire for it. I have not worked at the foundry for years. And my mother is already off in Derbyshire at Geoffrey's country seat."

Dominique's grip on his arm tightened. "I apologize. I ought to have thought…"

"There is no way you would have known."

A strange shadow passed over her face. Regret, David thought. An emotion adjacent to sadness, but that did not quite fit the situation.

"What do you do now?" she asked, moving forward once again, presumably toward whatever etchings they might find.

"I'm a forger."

It was a jest, of course. But Dominique's eyes widened instantly. She tried to cover it, feigning a cough and averting her eyes.

It was David's turn to squeeze her arm reassuringly. "Only the legal sort, of course. I create charcoal and line reproductions of paintings, so they can be transferred to silver and manufactured as etchings. It is an increasingly popular way for painters to supplement their income, but most do not lower themselves to creating the line versions themselves. I've made rather a good job of it, surprisingly."

Her smile had returned, soft and sweet. There was a hint of color in her cheeks. Embarrassment? Certainly not. "Not surprising at all. I remember your drawings in the back of your schoolbooks," she teased, nudging him in the ribs.

"Yes, well." He blushed. "I do not know how much longer I shall go on with it. After this sojourn in London, I will be permanently relocating to my cousin's estate in Derbyshire. I have much to learn about running an earldom."

As they browsed the stacks, he slowly composed a picture of his life over the last ten years. He spoke of the fears he'd felt striking out on his own and of his family's unconditional support when he left the foundry.

Dominique seemed content to listen, rather than speak of herself. But he did manage to urge a few details from her.

"My mother brought us directly to London, where she'd styled herself Madam Beauchamp, the dance instructor to social-climbing hopefuls. She started with one student, then that girl's cousin joined in. After that, it all happened rather quickly."

"And you were her assistant?" he asked, hoping she would share something more.

"For many years," she offered, but nothing more, before turning the subject away from herself.

She did not ask after her sister or father, and he would not mention them. Not yet.

"After the fire, my mother went to Derbyshire. I think the memories in Winleigh were too painful for her," David finished, around the time they reached the bottom of a staircase. He flicked his gaze upward. "More books?"

Dominique laughed. "Not precisely." She nodded up the stairs, and David, of course, escorted her up.

They stood in a lavish hallway, festooned with flowers and a thick emerald carpet. Sunlight flooded into the corridor from two open doors.

"They keep the more precious books up here," Dominique explained, leading him through the first door.

It was a spacious apartment of sorts, with sofas and chairs and a sprawling view of Finsbury Square. There were glass cases carefully positioned throughout the room, centerpieces to the tableau. Dominique tugged him along to a magnificently illuminated copy of Grimm's fairytales.

David's breath caught in his throat. As an artist of sorts himself, he could appreciate the care and time it would have taken to render the breathtaking work. As a human, his only articulate thought was that it spoke to his soul, as all great artworks did.

"It is quite literally breathtaking," Dominique said quietly.

David realized that she was looking at him, rather than the book. Had she noticed the way his breath caught? Did she see the way his pulse pounded now in his throat above his cravat, just from being so near to her?

They were quite alone, the only other patron having drifted out the door moments ago. Suddenly, her hand on his arm felt like an invitation. The press of her fingers seemed to be drawing him down. But he could not, would not, without invitation. Still, he moved closer, until they shared breath, fractions of inches apart.

"David," she said softly, her breath ruffling his hair.

He wanted to kiss her. But he wanted no passing touch. He dreamt of gathering her into his arms and holding her while they kissed one another with all the pent-up desire of a decade spent apart. If he kissed her now, it would be a sorrowful shadow of what his heart yearned for. And yet he could not bring himself to step away.

Instead, his mouth moved past her lips, along the column of her neck. There, where her pulse was beating every bit as wildly as his own, he skimmed his lips against her pebbled flesh. The low moan was unmistakable.

David was about to throw all caution to the wind when hushed voices dragged him back to reality. Two young women, accompanied by an elderly matron, entered the room. Dominique slid back onto her heels; he had not even noticed she'd risen to her tiptoes. While he was huffing and struggling to manage himself, her cool exterior was back in place. She offered a subtle nod of acknowledgment to the other patrons.

He stared at the illumination before him until his pulse slowed to a manageable pace and he was certain his complexion was ruddy rather than flushed. Dominique must have noticed as well, for there was the pressure at his arm once again.

"Let us go down now," she said gently.

"Of course. Would you like to have a look in the other room?"

"Another time, perhaps. I have an appointment this afternoon that I must honor."

Disappointment surged through David, rapid and cold. His hand went to where their arms were joined, a reflexive need to hold her closer. That was when he caught a glimpse of her dark eyes, right before they stepped into the dim hallway. Full of emotion, just as his had surely been.

She might hide it better, but she was as shaken as he. If they must part, then he would treasure that realization until they were reunited once again. But Dominique paused at the top of the landing, holding him back.

"David, I would…" She glanced around them, though David had no notion what she was searching for when her eyes landed back on him. "I would like to ask for your help with a bit of work

I've taken on. It calls for an artistic eye, and I am vastly lacking in that quality myself."

"What sort of work?" What need did an actress or a maid have for an artist?

"I cannot tell you just now." She glanced around again, seemed to notice him watching her, and then continued down the stairs as if nothing were amiss. "I have my appointment this afternoon, you see, and it takes rather a bit of explaining."

It was damned strange, but David still heard himself saying: "Of course. Whatever it is, I am at your disposal."

In every way that mattered.

CHAPTER TEN

1807
10 years ago
Winleigh, Hampshire

"Have you anything else for the wash, Maman?"

"No, darling. Bella saw to it yesterday before she left for London," Collette Beauchamp called from the upper floor of the cottage.

Dominique frowned, looking around the kitchen with an assessing eye, scanning for abandoned clothes left on a countertop or stuffed in an apron on the peg. But she found nothing. Bella was nothing if not industrious, doubly so when she was planning to be away for a few days—which was why Dominique currently held the basket of washing.

Not that Dominique minded. It was lovely that Bella was able to get away to attend her sister's wedding in London. She and her mother could certainly manage for a few days on their own. Though, as she hefted the basket under her arm, Dominique felt a surge of affection for the maid her father's monthly pension paid for.

She cast an appraising gaze over the apron hanging on the peg, and decided to leave it. As it was, what she had in her basket would occupy most of the afternoon. She'd thought she was being kind, sparing Bella from her heap of laundry yesterday when the maid was already busy with preparations for her journey. Now she regretted being quite so ambitious.

"Maman, are you occupied?" she called up the stairs. "Perhaps—"

A sharp knock sounded at the front door of the cottage, followed almost immediately by her mother's quick footsteps on the staircase. Dominique sighed in resignation and made for the kitchen door. Whoever was calling would want to speak with her mother—which meant she would have to get the washing started on her own.

At least the day was fair.

"Mr. Grisham—a surprise as fair as the day!" Collette exclaimed, her voice carrying right across the cottage and out the door that Dominique already had ajar.

"I apologize for not sending word, Mrs. Beauchamp," David said, bowing respectfully and removing his hat.

The cottage was tidy and well apportioned but simple. The first floor was one room, the sitting area sharing space with dining table and the kitchen set up in the corner. Upstairs was only marginally more complex—a small landing and two modest bedrooms. But it was more than adequate for Dominique and her mother.

Of course, that meant that David had seen her from the moment her mother opened the door. Dressed in her oldest, dingiest gown, poised by the kitchen door with a heap of dirty laundry. Good grief.

And, of course, David simply looked over her mother's shoulder and smiled broadly. "Good afternoon, Miss Beauchamp."

"Good afternoon, Mr. Grisham." Dominique dipped her head, shifting her basket to the side as unobtrusively as she could. "I apologize for my attire; we were not expecting visitors."

David's gaze flicked down to her gown, the threadbare yellow linen that had faded to a pale butter color. "You shine as brightly as a ray of sunlight," he said with complete sincerity.

Dominique flushed; David did too, probably realizing what a lovesick fool he sounded. But thankfully, Dominique's mother had more presence of mind than either of the young people before her.

"Has your father sent some message for me, Mr. Grisham?" Collette asked.

David's father was a parish councilman, in addition to owning the foundry. Although Dominique and her mother lived a mostly quiet life, Mrs. Beauchamp had slowly gained respect for her wise eye.

"No, nothing of that sort." David shook his head. "I wished to speak with you on my own behalf, Mrs. Beauchamp."

If Collette was surprised, she did not show it. She merely nodded and motioned to the chaise and armchair arranged by the front window to catching the afternoon sun.

"Please, make yourself comfortable. Dominique, set that aside for now and put on the kettle for tea," Collette said, not even sparing a glance for her daughter.

Dominique cringed. Her mother was not going to let her escape. Her mother knew precisely how she felt about David; there were no secrets between them. But instead of letting Dominique retreat, embarrassed by her plain gown and half-pinned hair, her mother kept her in the room. A lesson in moral character, surely. Sometimes, Dominique wished her mother was not so determined to make her into an upstanding young lady.

"How is your mother? I had heard she was stricken with fever."

"She is much recovered, Mrs. Beauchamp. I shall tell her you asked after her."

"Thank you. She has always shown my daughter and me such kindness."

Dominique listened to the bland exchange of pleasantries as she set the kettle over the hearth and stoked the embers to life. While the water heated, she retrieved a tray and sorted through their small cupboard. David adored raspberry tarts... If she'd known he was going to call, she'd have run into the village this morning. Drat him—the next time she had him alone, she would—

"... concerning your daughter."

Dominique crushed the petite scone she'd been about to set on the serving tray.

"I am listening, sir," her mother said smoothly, voice unruffled.

"As you know, I have had the pleasure of Miss Beauchamp's friendship for many years. She is kind and clever, a credit to your upbringing, no doubt." David's voice was a bit strangled. He sounded as if he'd rehearsed this speech.

Bless him.

"Thank you, Mr. Grisham."

"Now that I have left school and taken my position at the foundry, I have ample income to support myself and a household. My family—"

"I am well acquainted with your family," Collette interjected, voice gentle but firm. Dominique bit her lip, staring at the pile of crumbs in front of her, terrified and thrilled as she waited for what would come next.

"I would like to ask your permission to court Miss Beauchamp."

The teakettle began whistling shrilly.

Dominique swung away, knocking the crumbs to the floor—crumbs she would have to sweep up later. She pulled the kettle from the hearth and reached for the teapot on the shelf, but gentle hands closed over her shoulders.

"Dominique," her mother said softly. "I shall see to the tea. Join Mr. Grisham. He has something he would like to ask you."

She blinked, staring into her mother's expressive, dark eyes—the mirror of her own.

Collette smiled, nudging her shoulder. "The decision lies with my daughter, Mr. Grisham. You may put your request to her."

David was standing now, pretending not to watch the tender exchange between mother and daughter but at the same time unable to tear his gaze away from Dominique. She could feel the caress of his soft blue eyes as she drifted over to join him. Behind her in the kitchen, her mother made an inordinate amount of noise retrieving teacups from the cupboard and assembling the tray.

"Miss Beauchamp," David began.

A soft chuckle fell from Dominique's lips. "David," she murmured.

This time, David blushed, his gaze flicking down to the rug beneath their feet. But when she paused before him, he looked up and caught her gaze with his own.

"Dominique," he breathed, her name a prayer upon his soft, inviting lips.

Had it really been weeks before that she'd kissed him in the orangery at Wartham Grange? How could it be that she could still feel the tingling in her body?

"I would like to court you," he said.

"I heard," she responded. She watched his eyes widen; surely the thought that she might reject his suit was passing through his mind. But as much as she enjoyed teasing him, she could not even entertain the thought. "Yes. Yes, of course," she whispered.

David's grin was blinding. He lurched forward, surely to take her into his arms. Dominique felt her body begin to melt, reaching for him as surely as he was for her.

The clang of the tea tray on the countertop set them both jerking back.

"Tea is almost prepared," her mother called innocently.

David's eyes flashed, the pale blue darkening the way they had in the orangery. Desire, Dominique realized. The same intense feeling flooded her own veins. Suddenly, she was desperate for his touch. She held out her hand, hoping—

He grasped it tightly in his own, lifting it to his lips. He pressed a kiss to her flat, folded fingers, then to her knuckles, and then the back of her hand. Heat radiated up her arm. Oh, that his mouth would follow the path of that heat…

But even if she wanted to throw caution to the wind, David was a perfect gentleman. Always. He lowered her hand and pulled his away, even as his eyes caressed hers.

"May I come tomorrow, to take you for a turn about town?"

"After our Sunday devotions," her mother put in from the kitchen.

Dominique's heart surged. She began to mentally tabulate the hours.

"But first we shall have tea," her mother said, nudging her daughter aside with her hip. "The three of us," she said pointedly.

But it did nothing to diminish the heat that surged through the air. As she perched on the armchair across from David, Dominique thought that for the first time in her life, she might be truly happy.

SHE BRUSHED OUT her waist-length hair until it shone, gleaming in the sunlight from the window she'd shoved open. The air was a bit cool, the first tinges of autumn floating through Hampshire. But the slight nip was helping to calm the jagged edge of her nerves.

Why was she nervous? She'd spent hours in David's company over the years. They had made faces at one another over their Bibles in church as precocious nine-year-olds. On many a market day, they'd played with the other children on the village green. They'd attended the same schoolroom until Dominique transitioned to a private tutor.

But then David kissed her in her father's orangery.

Everything had changed.

Or perhaps it had been there all along—that thread between them that allowed them both space to grow and mature, but kept them close. Her eyes always drifted back to David. More often than not, she found his eyes upon her as well.

And now they were courting.

She heard quiet footsteps on the stairs. A moment later, a soft knock on her door followed.

Her mother appeared, a silk shawl draped over her arm. "I thought you might like to wear this," she said.

"Grandmère's shawl?" Dominique blinked. It was the closest thing they had to an heirloom—a precious remnant of their family in France.

"I knew you would wear the lavender gown today." Collette smiled. "And the color complements it so nicely."

She *was* wearing her lavender muslin gown. It complemented her olive skin, several shades darker than the pale bloom of the village girls. Her mother draped the deep amethyst shawl over her shoulders, deepening the contrast between the pastel gown and Dominique's dark hair and eyes. They both stared into the looking glass, regarding the effect, until Dominique caught the glint in her mother's eyes.

She spun on her stool, grabbing her mother's hand. "Maman, what is it?"

Her mother frowned. For the first time since David had declared his intentions, she looked worried. Collette took a deep breath, and Dominique knew what was coming next.

"I worry for you," her mother said, holding her gaze. She blinked away the tears that had threatened, replacing them with steely resolve. "This courtship with Mr. Grisham could be… precarious."

Dominique swallowed. "If he finds out about my status."

"Yes." Her mother squeezed her hand. "I suppose your father will make provision for your dowry. He has never said so explicitly, but he has provided for us well."

Dominique could tell how the words pained her mother. Her parents did not speak to one another, not really. She had a few vague memories of her father's visits to Paris, before he married

Lady Wartham. Her mother had been a ballerina then, her father a minor English lord originally appointed on a diplomatic mission. The result of their liaison was her.

To her father's credit, he'd never shirked responsibility for her. In Paris, he'd visited annually and provided for them financially. Then he'd moved them to England, where he furnished them with the cottage and a monthly pension. Every time her mother wrote with a request, it was granted. When most young girls left the village school to join the domestic workforce, Dominique's father had provided private tutors to continue her education at home.

So she supposed that if she did ask for a dowry, her father would provide it.

But it did not change the fact that she was illegitimate.

"I will not lie to David," Dominique said. Then she bit her lip. She had already lied to David—to everyone. "If he should propose marriage… I will tell him. I cannot trick him."

Her mother nodded, understanding. She always understood.

Love surged through Dominique. She surged to her feet and flung herself into her mother's arms, suddenly so grateful. Her father had provided for them. But her mother had given her the one thing that truly mattered—unconditional love.

Collette stroked her hair and held her tight, offering no words of condolence—what could she say? They were at the mercy of everyone else's kindness and always had been.

The terrible truth of that nagged at Dominique.

"Should I have turned him away?" she asked, her voice trembling.

Her mother kept stroking her hair, rhythmic and soothing. "I cannot answer that for you, *mon coeur*. I have made the best decisions for you that I could, but the future is yours."

"But it would be so much easier if you made this one."

Collette laughed softly. "Follow your heart. Yours is whole and perfect and lovely. It will not lead you astray." Then she tugged gently on a lock of her hair. "Sit up—I shall plait it for you."

Dominique settled herself onto the stool again, facing the mirror. But instead of admiring her gown or the shawl, she watched her mother plait her hair. She hoped she had inherited a small fraction of her grace and strength.

DAVID WAITED IN the churchyard, his best tailcoat meticulously brushed and his heart in his throat. The service had dragged on longer than usual, the priest attacking the sermon with unusual vigor. Nearing eighty years old, the old man was known for nodding off during the hymns. But not today. Of course, on this day of all days, he seemed to have gained a renewed verve.

David had contented himself with going over every detail of the stolen minutes in the orangery with Dominique. The diversion had passed the time pleasantly, even if he had had to shift his Bible in order to cover the growing need in his trousers.

The things she did to him.

Dominique was his first thought upon waking and the last name he mumbled in his prayers before drifting off to sleep. On the nights when he could not restrain himself a moment longer, he called her name into the darkness as he stroked himself to release.

He watched as the patrons slowly filtered out of the church, talking idly and exchanging gossip. Mrs. Bradbury had snagged Dominique and her mother; the woman could talk the ear off a sow. If Dominique did not appear in five minutes' time, he would go and rescue her, he decided. It would make his intention abundantly clear to the rest of the village, but David supposed there was no harm in that. They would all know soon enough.

He would marry Dominique Beauchamp. It was only a matter of time.

He'd known since he was fourteen years old, old enough to

understand the meaning of such things, that he was in love with her.

Since then, it had only been a matter of moving through the required steps.

He'd finished top of his class in school and then moved into the foundry with his father and brother, taking up a position. In the intervening two years, he'd established himself and saved away a good amount of money. He did not waste his earnings on ale or fripperies. He saved every penny for the cottage he would buy for himself and Dominique. He'd even spoken to Widow Westerly, who planned to move to Bristol to live with her daughter and grandchildren sometime in the spring. He would purchase her cottage, a lovely little place with honeysuckle that grew over the doorway.

It was less than a half-mile from the cottage Dominique shared with her mother, and a short jaunt from the foundry where David worked each day.

Now that she'd accepted his request to court her, everything was proceeding splendidly.

After a respectable amount of time, he would propose. The banns would be read, they would marry, and David would spend the rest of his life endeavoring to make Dominique blissfully happy… as happy as she made him with every smile and touch.

It was perfect.

She was perfect.

God himself seemed to approve of the direction of his thoughts, letting through a beam of pure sunlight to frame Dominique as she stepped into the churchyard.

He watched her searching, wide, dark eyes looking for him amongst the families and friends chatting with one another in the early autumn sunlight. A few of them glanced her way, but finding nothing of interest, they resumed their conversations. More than one young man's gaze lingered upon her. How could they not? She was like Persephone come to life, blooming in the courtyard while the rest of the world turned to gold and brown.

But then her eyes alighted on him and the rest of the world fell away.

David was not sure if she crossed the churchyard to him or if it was his strides eating up the space between them—only that suddenly they were separated by mere inches rather than yards.

It took every bit of strength inside of him not to pull her into his arms and kiss her there in front of the entire village.

"If the priest sees that glint in your eyes, you shall have to intercede with the Lord himself," she said, her own eyes glinting.

"You've no business looking so beautiful," he stammered, reaching for her hand. He lifted it to his lips, wishing he was pressing them to her mouth instead.

"You have always been bold, but this side of you is completely disarming," she admitted. Was her lower lip trembling? That could only be a good thing.

At least, he hoped it was a good thing.

"Do I offend you?"

She shook her head, the end of her plait sliding over the silk shawl and begging him to toy with it. "On the contrary, I find myself waiting eagerly to hear what lovely and ridiculous thing you will say next."

She flicked her plait of her shoulder and smiled sweetly.

He promised himself he would twine those silky locks around his fingers before the day was over. They would take a turn around the village, and then he would tug her into an alley and steal a kiss.

"Shall we be off?" he asked, not waiting for a response. The glow in her eyes was answer enough.

His thumb swiped over the inside of her wrist as he settled her hand in the crook of his arm. The jumping of her pulse matched his own. The knowledge woke a deep satisfaction inside of him.

"I think you have made your intent quite known to everyone assembled," she teased. "We may as well enjoy our walk now."

David did not hold back his grin as he led her out of the

churchyard. He nodded to various personages as they walked by, but his smile was for her alone. Dominique blushed, dipping her head under the intensity of his gaze. He did not mind. He intended to worship her for the rest of their lives; she would get used to it eventually.

As they rounded the oak tree that marked the end of the churchyard, a quick movement in his periphery caught his attention.

Lord and Lady Wartham stood in the shade of the tree, speaking quietly with the priest while their daughter toyed with a posy of wildflowers. The older gentleman was speaking animatedly, but the girl glanced up to them and stilled. She watched Dominique, David realized, not him. Unsurprising; so many of the village girls admired—and envied—Dominique's Gallic beauty and quiet grace. It was no surprise the young Miss Amelia Wartham did as well.

As he watched, another set of eyes landed upon them.

Lady Wartham's hand landed on her daughter's shoulder, yanking her back.

Rage flashed in her eyes.

But then it was gone, replaced with placid indifference—the lady's usual expression.

The look was gone so quickly that David thought he must have imagined it. What ire could the preeminent lady of the county bear toward him or Dominique?

On his arm, Dominique seemed oblivious to the family. She held his arm tightly, leaning against him as they walked. The feel of her soft curves molded against him was enough to rob him of all other thoughts.

CHAPTER ELEVEN

1817
Present Day

HER LONG-SLEEVED GOWN, covered in a fashionable, close-cropped pelisse, provided her ample warmth as she made her circuitous approach of D'Terre's residence. But it did not stop her from shivering when she recalled the way David's lips had felt on her neck.

Nor from yawning, since she'd gotten little sleep while mulling over the wisdom of allowing David to consult on her quest. And if she thought of David and of her bed, the distraction practically created itself.

But she could not afford to be distracted.

Every second she spent in David Grisham's company, the more her feelings for him grew. Or perhaps the more they emerged from the carefully hidden cabinet she'd kept them in for the last ten years. Being with him was so damnably easy.

She'd struggled to make any close friends in Winleigh as a child, always carefully guarding her secret. In London, her focus had been upon helping her mother build up her clientele of dancing students to support them financially. When finally she'd stepped out on her own and become a lady knight, she found a cadre of like-minded women. But even then, they were rarely all together. More often than not, they were scattered to the winds on whatever quest they had each been assigned.

But with David, friendship had always come naturally. As an adult, she realized why—their souls spoke to each other. There was an underlying attraction that fueled their friendship, and the friendship enabled the attraction in turn. Since their meeting again in London, it was if the thread had been seamlessly picked up.

Friendship, she could allow.

Romance and attraction…

She was not so sure.

Her time to consider was quickly coming to an end, however. For as she turned the last corner, she spotted David waiting outside the flower shop, precisely where she'd told him to be.

"You are still quite punctual," she said by way of greeting.

"My father would be proud to hear it," he said. Sadness flitted over his face at the passing mention. Dominique waited a moment to let him feel it before nodding toward the alley.

"This way," she said.

She did not wait for a discussion, but she noted the surprised look upon his face. There would be no avoiding an explanation, at least some small one, but she'd rather give it in privacy than on the busy street.

Dominique walked down the alley with purposeful steps before reaching a T and turning right. David followed at her heels—so closely that when she stopped midway down the alley, he nearly toppled her over.

She bit back her laugh and held up a hand to indicate he should stay where he was while she turned her eyes to the other end, where the busy street was visible.

"Why are we loitering in an alleyway?" he asked, glancing at the rubbish lining the ground.

"We are waiting for the right moment," she said, eyes still fixed ahead. "When I move, follow me and keep quiet."

He moved with exuberance, and she doubted he could actually keep himself from being detected, but the house was unoccupied, so it ought not matter. They were only waiting for the street to be clear so no one would spot her picking the lock at the rear door.

There was a break in the flow of people on the street. Dominique clucked her tongue to alert David, then moved to the door on their right.

"Block me from sight with your body," she said.

She withdrew the worn leather roll from her pocket, crouching down to examine the lock. The more time she had to look, the better chance of her selecting the correct pins and making quick work of the lock. She'd gotten lucky with D'Terre's desk, but it was better to prepare for it to take longer than to assume her own speed. Another reason having David along was helpful—his body provided a shield. Now she was crouched by his bottom… his well-muscled, decidedly grabbable bottom.

Forcing herself to focus on the lock in front of her, she selected two picks and inserted them smoothly into the lock. She had to apply quite a bit of force to get at the detainer that kept the bolt in place. But after a few moments of finessing, the bolt sprang free.

"Come quickly," she murmured, slipping inside even as she replaced the picks in their role and secreted them back into her pocket.

But she was not fast enough for David to miss the action. His eyes were wide as he watched her, but his mouth was silent. For the moment, at least.

"We need to get as high as possible," she said, nodding toward the stairwell.

They were in the kitchen of the townhouse. A small stairwell led up into the main building, then a long hallway and another set of stairs. It was a modest dwelling in comparison to the luxurious townhouse D'Terre maintained across the street. Though it was fortuitous, because if it had been grander, it certainly would have been rented for the season.

Then she would have been faced with breaking into an occupied house or finding a more conspicuous way to watch D'Terre's comings and goings. As it was, she'd had a run of good luck on this quest.

Though she was not sure how David figured into that run—an additional bit of luck or a bad omen.

He followed her up several flights of stairs to an upper bedroom without question. Only when she'd opened the curtains and dragged a chair over to the window, dropping herself into it, did he finally open his mouth to speak.

Dominique preempted him. "I suppose you have questions."

David barked out a laugh. "A few."

"I will not be able to answer them all."

"Should that prevent me from asking?" He sounded curious, rather than offended. As if she might ask him to go along with her breaking into a house without her giving a single explanation, and he might actually do it.

"Ask. I will answer what I can."

"May I sit?"

Dominique did not look at him—her eyes were fixed on the front of D'Terre's house—but she did chuckle. "Yes, of course."

David disappeared from the room, returning a few minutes later with a wooden chair that he set next to Dominique's. She may be watching the street, but there was no mistaking the feel of his eyes upon her.

"When did you learn to pick a lock?"

So it began.

She folded her hands in her lap and adjusted her seat so she was comfortable for observation and interrogation. "Three years ago."

David hummed to himself. "*Why* did you learn to pick locks?"

"It is required for my profession," she said, her voice holding steady.

She could not see it, fixed as her eyes were on D'Terre's townhouse, but she could imagine the bushy golden brow rising.

"What profession requires you to pick the lock of an empty house and stare out the window?"

It was a well-phrased question. She'd asked him to help her with her work but had given him no information on what that might entail. He'd agreed anyway. Would that change once he had his answer?

"Not an illegal one," she said. She could turn a phrase as well.

In her periphery, she saw David's golden head nodding. "Which means whatever your profession, it is lawfully sanctioned."

She chuckled soundlessly. In truth, Dominique had no notion about the legality of the Lady Knights and their existence. But she trusted the Duchess of Guilford implicitly.

"You can pick locks with startling speed." He had no idea. "You are adept at moving without detection." He'd noticed her soundless footsteps. "You are equally comfortable as a maid at a ball and an actress at Covent Garden." As well as a dozen other roles she'd assumed over the past three years. "And now you are watching that house with the intention of a hawk sighting a mouse."

She darted a glance at him, long enough to see the way he raked his thumb across his chin while he considered how to form the words.

"Out with it, then," she urged, her voice a near whisper.

"You are a spy."

"I prefer the term lady knight."

The feet of David's chair scraped across the floor as he leaned back abruptly. "What the hell is a lady knight?"

Her mouth curved into a coy smile. "You are sitting with one now."

He chuckled, this time with that customary humor. Relief began to trickle through her. Asking for his help was the first gamble. This was the second.

She kept her eyes trained forward and the emotion from her voice, though inside she was quaking. "If you choose to work with me on this quest, you can never speak of it to anyone. Not your mother nor your cousin, nor your grandchildren on your deathbed. If you do, we will know."

"Dominique… is that a threat?" He sounded amused, thankfully, rather than offended.

"It is our job to know things," she said.

"If I agree, will you tell me why we are sitting up here?" he teased.

Teasing. Good heavens, he was *teasing* her.

"Do you agree?" Dominique forced herself to ask. She needed to hear his affirmation, spoken clearly. For her own sake, and for the justification she would have to make to the duchess later.

David did not hesitate. His voice was clear and true: "Yes."

The trickle of relief turned to a flood.

She did not realize her hand was trembling until his fingers closed around hers.

Though she tried to ignore it, David's touch sent warmth spreading from her hand and through the rest of her body. A warmth that threatened to turn to heat in certain areas.

"That is the residence of Mr. Roderick D'Terre, duly elected member of Parliament from the borough of Whadpole. We are watching his house to determine if there is a pattern to the movements of him and his servants." Speaking about the quest seemed infinitely safer than speaking about the emotions summoned by his touch.

"That pattern would be relevant because you intend to pick the lock of his house as well?" David sounded a shade less amused.

"Precisely. I have already scouted the interior, so I know where I am going and what I will be retrieving." As she watched, a maid appeared from the back of the building where the rear kitchen door was located. Dominique tugged out her locket watch to note the time.

When she flicked her gaze to David, she found him frowning. "When did you scout the interior?"

Ah. Not spy material—he was much too friendly—but a sharp man nonetheless.

"Mr. D'Terre invited me himself. He has something of a reputation for Covent Garden actresses."

David's grip on her hand tightened. "I see."

She swallowed, turning her eyes away from him reluctantly. It was because she needed to watch the house, she told herself. Not to avoid his gaze.

"May I presume that since you are investigating him, the... whomever you work for... suspects he is getting up to something untoward?" David asked, the tension evident in every clipped syllable.

"He is suspected of blackmailing his colleagues in Parliament to influence the outcome of important votes. But I do not yet know the *how* of it."

Across from her, David shifted in his seat. She expected him to withdraw his hand, but instead he scooted his chair closer so he could hold it more comfortably. That warmth he'd kindled inside of her seemed intent upon staying put.

"Where do I figure in?" he asked. He also stroked his thumb over the back of her hand.

She'd thought talking about the quest would distract her from David? Hardly. David was distracting her from the quest. Despite the internal admonishment she had given herself earlier in the day, she was no closer to managing the attraction between them than she had been since that first night.

"I had a look in his desk drawer. He's keeping a collection of letters and drawings secured in his study." She could tell from David's sigh that he understood how she'd illicitly gained that look. "I am certain the drawings and letters are related to the blackmailing scheme, but I cannot steal them without alerting him that someone's been snooping in his study. I need someone to reproduce them. As you are an artist skilled in reproduction..."

"I see."

"You're rather wearing the phrase out," she said in a feeble attempt at teasing. David rewarded her with a chuckle nonetheless.

He leaned back in his chair, rubbing at his chin with his unoccupied hand. "How will I be able to reproduce them? Are you planning on sneaking me in there with you?"

A sharp laugh burst from her throat. "Heavens, no."

"Ought I be offended?" he said, pinning her with his blue eyes.

She stared into them for several long moments before she realized she was no longer watching the house. Cursing herself, she turned back.

"Once I have established the ideal time of day, I will sneak in and take the drawings and letters. I will bring them back to my flat to copy, then I will return the originals before D'Terre notices they've gone missing," she explained.

Even with her eyes fixed below, she could see him nodding understanding.

"How long will you need to copy the drawings?"

He hummed again, considering. "I will have to look at them to be certain. But to make a decent approximation, I should think an hour or two would be enough."

"I will take a few, then, and we shall see how far we can get."

"Ah." David sat back again. This time when he did, his hand went with him. He laced his fingers together in front of his mouth. "I am not available this evening."

Dominique felt the frown that wanted to lodge itself upon her face, but she held it at bay, settling for a neutral line instead. "Oh?"

"Geoffrey has promised we will attend the opera with Lady Sharpton and her daughters," he said. He, too, was struggling to keep his voice carefully neutral. But Dominique could tell from the slight inflection at the end of his words that he was uncomfortable.

"I see."

"I rather thought I'd claimed that turn of phrase," he teased, an attempt at ease that was more successful than her earlier ones.

"It is fine," she said quickly. "It is best that I have several days of watching to establish patterns." She nodded toward the window for emphasis and tried to pretend that the feeling taking root in her chest was not hurt.

"Well enough," David said slowly.

They stared out the window in silence for long enough that Dominique began counting the time silently in her head. But she had not even made it to twenty before the unwelcome thoughts began swirling in.

David was attending the opera with eligible young women. He was dancing with them almost nightly at the various balls and soirees his cousin took him to, bent upon introducing his heir to the *haute ton*. David was handsome enough without a title. Add the earldom to his broad shoulders, sparkling blue eyes, and raffish smile, and he'd have debutantes swooning wherever he turned.

"Ahem," David said. "You are going to damage the chair."

She released her hands immediately, but the damage was already done. Her nails had scored deep lines in the velvet. She had not realized she'd been gripping the arms so hard. Heavens, was she destined to lose control of herself every time she was in his presence?

"Are you courting one of the Misses Sharpton?" She hated that she let herself ask.

She refused to look at him, not trusting herself to keep the emotion from her eyes. But she heard the shifting of his chair once again. "Any closer and you'll be sitting in my lap," she said sharply.

"I would rather you sit in mine," he said. The last word was half swallowed, as if David had surprised even himself with his forwardness. "I am not courting the Sharpton girls. Nor any ladies of the *ton*."

Dominique did not respond. When he reached for her hand once again, she did not pull away. But she certainly was not expecting him to make good on his desires and pull her from the velvet armchair and right into his lap.

"Are you jealous?" he murmured into her hair, her face still determinedly facing the window.

"Ought I be?" she whispered breathily.

David caught her chin with his forefinger. Though she knew she should keep watching, that it was part of her duty, she did not stop him as he turned her face and met her lips with his.

He tasted like a memory.

Her body and her soul seemed to recall exactly how their lips fit together. When his tongue nudged at her lips, she parted them instantly and welcomed him in with the curl of her own. Everything about the kiss was perfectly synchronized, like the dances she adored. She thrust her bottom lip out, and he caught it gently between his teeth. She tilted her head to taste him deeper, and he moaned against her mouth to intensify the sensation.

If she'd been warm before, now her body was aflame. Her breasts ached, eager for his touch. Between her legs, need pooled so demandingly she had to wriggle against him or else she might perish.

As David curled one hand into her hair, she mirrored him with her own touch. She slid her fingers through his long, silky locks. She'd thought his longer hair made him look boyish? Oh no, no, no. Having something to hold on to while she made love to his mouth was utterly intoxicating. She'd never allow him to cut it.

He tugged on her hair, his own fingers tangled in the curls, until he could kiss her throat. That same spot where he'd only teased the day before, now he covered in searing kisses.

My breasts, now.

But he continued to caress her collarbone, and she realized she'd thought the words rather than spoken them aloud. Which was for the better, she realized, as she slowly descended from heaven back into reality. She was supposed to be on watch, not making love to David in a deserted house.

Gently, regretfully, she pulled away. David lifted his mouth from her throat but did not let her go, instead shifting her in his arms so she was facing the window but still firmly situated in his lap.

"Never," he rasped against her hair.

It was only then that she remembered her question from minutes before.

No, she had no reason to be jealous. Her worries where David was concerned were *so* much bigger.

CHAPTER TWELVE

S PY. LADY KNIGHT. Love of his life.
Dominique was all of those things, but he had yet to make sense of any of them. In all the years they had been apart, David had imagined many possible futures for Dominique. With her impeccable manners and excellent French, she'd make a suitable governess. Her grace and poise could have easily earned her a career in the ballet like her mother. Once, on a visit to his cousin in Derbyshire, he'd spotted a young woman in a flower shop with Dominique's dark hair and a svelte build. For weeks after that, he'd dreamt of Dominique's face framed in roses.

But this was a future he'd never predicted. Did some tangential part of him suppose such people existed? Well, yes. Seeing Dominique in the role…

On some fronts, it fit. She'd always been a bit of an enigma. It was only after she was gone that he'd realized it was because of the secret she'd guarded. But for someone who'd spent their entire life guarding secrets, perhaps a life of secrecy was not so wild a notion.

Lady knight she may be, but she was also the same warm and kind woman he'd fallen in love with a decade ago. It was evident everywhere around her flat, where he now sat waiting for her to return with the drawings he would copy.

He tried to subdue the anxiety of knowing she was at that

very moment sneaking into D'Terre's home by studying the details of her flat.

There was another parcel on the worktable, identical in size and shape to the one she'd delivered to her elderly neighbor that first night. A heavily worn armoire stood in the corner, doors neatly closed. It would be snooping to open it up, but perhaps...

No. She trusted him enough to bring him into her quest and to leave him alone in her home. He would not betray that by sneaking through her drawers.

He was also a bit afraid of what he might find. A pistol hidden beneath her gowns? A letter from a past lover tucked in among her books?

David swallowed hard, unable to push that question fully away. She had not outright said that she was seducing Roderick D'Terre, but she'd implied it sufficiently: *A taste for Covent Garden actresses.*

The words had haunted him ever since she'd spoken them.

He hated himself for wondering how many men she'd been asked to seduce for king and country.

Did she enjoy it?

He hated himself for wondering that even more.

The thought of her with D'Terre made him physically sick. Yet it had been Dominique who'd needed comforting when he mentioned attending the opera. She was unable to keep her jealousy hidden. David found that a worrisome comfort. If someone as adept at disguising themselves as Dominique could not control the distasteful emotion, how could he hope to?

I must find a way, he told himself as he sat down at the worktable and rearranged his charcoal for the third time. Dominique had asked for his help, and he would deliver upon that request even if he bit a hole through his tongue in the process. He would not allow his own petty jealousy to compromise her quest, which was obviously of importance to her.

If he was to convince her that they could be partners in all things, then this was his opportunity to prove it.

Not quite all things, he amended. He had no intention of becoming a knight of any shade. An unexpected earldom was quite enough for David.

AS SHE WOVE through alleyways and down darkened streets, Dominique slowly ascended from the place of cool, collected calm that she always delved into when moving in secrecy. When she was working in darkness, trying to remain undetected, every breath was measured and every movement calculated.

Two letters and their accompanying drawings were tucked into the wide white apron she wore over her starched black dress. Her outfit did not precisely match the one she'd seen on the maid who'd cleaned up the wine she spilled in D'Terre's study, but it was near enough in the dark.

After nearly a week of watching, she knew that by the time D'Terre left for his evening entertainments—and there was always something he was up to in the evenings—his staff on the premises was reduced to just three members: the butler, a maid, and the senior footman.

Avoiding them had been stunningly easy. With D'Terre out of the residence, the maid and footmen went up to their attic rooms. Dominique had waited in the rear courtyard until candles lit two of the tiny windows near the top of the house. The butler was more difficult to predict, since he would be the one waiting up for D'Terre. But she'd seen no sign of him as she snuck in, stole the papers, and snuck back out, picking and then re-locking doors behind her.

As she walked, she subtly began to alter her appearance. She unpinned the top half of the apron and shoved it into one of the deep pockets sewn into her dress. By the time she'd rounded the next corner, her hair was loose around her shoulders. She paused in the next alleyway, and when she emerged it was braided down her back and she wore a sapphire-blue cape over her shoulders.

Any observers on the three previous blocks would have seen, respectively, a sharply dressed maid, a woman of loose morals, and finally a middle- to upper-class young lady dressed for the cool weather.

But any woman alone on the streets at night was vulnerable. Dominique stayed in the shadows, choosing her route carefully to avoid unsavory stretches, before finally arriving back at her flat. Her gaze went to the window of her flat by habit; she always checked it before entering the building.

As expected, the inside was well lit. David would need thorough lighting to ensure he captured every detail of the drawings in his reproductions. She paused in the vestibule long enough to retrieve the hidden key before climbing the stairs to her door. She could have picked the locks easily enough, but it would take time she did not want to spare.

Besides the fact that her locks were nearly unpickable—to anyone but her.

David leapt out of his chair, knee hitting the table with teeth-clenching force and the chair itself hitting the floor with a crash.

"Heavens, David," she cried, though she was perfectly steady. She paused a moment in the doorway, waiting to see if Mr. Pritchett had been awoken by the commotion.

After several moments of blissful silence, she locked the door behind her and turned back to David.

"How did you get in so quietly?" David demanded, gripping the back of the righted chair.

"The key," she said with a slight smile, tossing it down on the table.

"You left me the key." He frowned as he reached into his pocket and withdrew it, appearing worried he'd somehow misplaced it when he had not even taken a step out of the flat.

"There is a key hidden beneath a floorboard in the vestibule. I will show you later," she said dismissively. "We must hurry. I want to get these in place before D'Terre returns from the follies."

"How do you know he's at the follies?" David asked, though he looked immediately as if he regretted it.

Dominique cocked an eyebrow. "You are expecting something nefarious, such as intercepting and reading his correspondence. But most information is gathered simply by listening—he told me a few days ago he'd received an invitation to the follies tonight with Lord Ingraham."

Relief flashed in his blue eyes, along with a much stronger emotion she dared not name or acknowledge. Forcing down that ever-present lump in her throat, she drew the sheaf of papers from the pocket of her apron. "We'd best begin."

SHE FLITTED AROUND making tea and tending to other mundane household chores. First she tidied away the laundry that had been delivered that morning. Then she began on her writing desk—David had opted to spread out over the larger worktable. But her flat was small. While that was usually a comfort, cozy and easy to care for, now she longed for a floor to mop. Instead, she was forced to settle into the armchair before the hearth, book in hand, and pretend she was not staring at David's profile while he sketched.

It was not until the book dropped into her lap, heavy and unattended, that Dominique realized how utterly she'd failed. She could not recall a single word she'd read. But she was aware of the slight indent midway down David's nose. It had been perfectly straight ten years ago. He must have broken it since. She wanted to know all the details of his life since their parting.

"Are the drawings remarkable in any way?" she asked instead.

David's gaze did not flicker from his work. "Only in that they are quite detailed," he said.

"Too detailed?"

He grinned, hand still moving steadily across the paper. "Not for me."

As his concentration deepened, his tongue was visible just between his lips. Dominique's heart quickened traitorously in her chest.

"Quite sure of yourself," she teased in a light voice, allowing herself to come stand beside him. Her breath caught in her throat. Not at the drawings—they were fine enough. He'd finished one and was in the beginning stages of the other. But the care and accuracy of his reproduction was stunning. They were identical.

"I had no notion you were this talented," she breathed, reaching for the finished work to compare it to the original more closely.

He did glance at her then. "I hope you did not bring me along on your quest solely for my handsome face and charming repartee," he said with that irresistible grin.

She wanted to kiss the smile from his face. The drawing she'd been examining floated back to the table. If she had not released it, she would have crumpled it beneath the tension in her fingers.

Shoving her trembling hands into the folds of her skirts, Dominique stepped away for fear she would lose complete control of herself. If she let herself touch him now, she did not know if she would be able to stop.

"You should transcribe the letters," David said, cutting through the fog of attraction consuming her. "I do not think I will have time to copy those as well. I'm not as good with handwriting, in any case."

Dominique seized the excuse to shuffle around in her desk for a fresh sheet of paper and a quill pen. "As long as I can transcribe them, that will do well enough."

David paused in his work long enough to reach back over his shoulder, the two letters in hand.

There was a smudge of charcoal on his forehead where he'd pushed back his long hair from his brow. Dominique wanted nothing more than to reach up and wipe it away. Instead she took the papers from his hand, careful not to let their fingers touch, and hummed to herself to try to distract her mind for the next hour of torture.

⇶⇷

"THAT WILL HAVE to do," David said, pushing back from the worktable. Despite his hedging, he was damn satisfied with the work he'd done.

Dominique moved to stand behind him, her scent floating over his shoulder. She reached for the completed copy at the same moment that he shifted in his chair, her fingertips skimming over the collar of his shirt and grazing his neck. David understood why she'd avoided touching him all night. The instant their skin touched, it was as if lightning crackled across the room.

She jerked her arm back as if burned, though the expression on her face was beatific rather than pained. David swiped the two originals up and handed them to her carefully, avoiding her eyes, worried that if he met them he'd have her in his arms, and damn the Crown's quest.

"Thank you," Dominique murmured, turning away to tuck them into the apron she'd donned once again. "I shall be quick; less than an hour."

"I shall wait here until you return," he said.

Her eyes widened slightly, but it was all the surprise she let show.

"To ensure that you have made it in and out safely," he added. *And to have a few precious moments with you without this specter hanging over our heads.*

"I will use the spare key again," she warned, already halfway to the door.

"You may take this one," David said, reaching for the one he'd abandoned on the table earlier. "I am not going anywhere."

The words gave her pause. When she had every reason to

hurry, Dominique turned in the doorway and stared at him, eyes so dark with swirling emotions as to be nearly unfathomable.

Even as she disappeared into the night, David knew the truth. He would never truly be able to let her go.

CHAPTER THIRTEEN

THE NERVES AS she stepped back into her flat had nothing to do with the small mission she'd just completed and everything to do with the man waiting inside. She'd had the entire walk back to contemplate how she would respond to him. But when she stepped over that threshold, all thoughts and intentions were swept away on a phantom wind.

At first, she thought he'd left after all. The candles and lamps had all burned down, casting the dark flat in a soft golden light that hid the corners in shadows. On silent feet, she crossed the floor, fighting the disappointment blooming in her chest. There was not even a note on the worktable.

Had she been so wrong in her estimation of him? Where were her lady knight's instincts now?

Then she heard a soft snore from the shadows near her bed.

A few more steps confirmed—not only was David still in her flat, but he'd fallen asleep in her bed.

Not precisely *in* her bed, she amended. But most certainly on it.

He was sitting up, head resting against the headboard and legs stretched out before him. He'd at least had the courtesy to remove his boots, rather than setting the ruddy things on her clean coverlet.

It was the sight of his stockinged feet that tugged at her heart.

It ought to have felt rude and presumptuous. But seeing David there, casual and comfortable in her home, made her feel other things entirely.

Desire, of course. She wanted nothing more than to wake him with a kiss and then tug him down on top of her. But along with the desire was a heavy dose of longing. She knew herself well enough to recognize it—the longing for a normal, easy life. The life she'd naïvely imagined they would have when he'd asked to court her all those years ago.

Heavens, how she wanted him. In every single possible way.

Thinking herself strong, she raked a knuckle along the tender sole of his foot rather than brushing her lips against his.

David gave a start, leg jerking and eyes flying open. Much darker in the night than their usual clear blue, his eyes landed on her immediately.

"Rather presumptuous, falling asleep in a woman's bed," she said, willing her tone to be light and teasing.

"Ahem." He cleared the sleep from his throat and shifted his shoulders so he was sitting more upright. "I thought to tread upon our long friendship."

He did not get up, did not look even a bit regretful. Dominique's stomach flipped over in warning, while simultaneously heat began to pool between her legs.

"Friendship," she said quietly. "Is that what it is between us?"

"It was once," David said, watching her closely. Her hands were twirling in the folds of her cloak—a telltale sign of unease that she did not bother to tamp down.

"We are not the young people we once were."

"Nor are we old." David chuckled. He caught her hand, pulling it from her cloak and turning it over in his. He stroked down each fingertip, tracing the barely visible lines of her palm. Gently. Reverently. "See? Not a single wrinkle."

She tried to swat his hand away, but instead he caught her wrist and lifted it to his mouth, placing a kiss against the sensitive skin and sending a shiver all the way down her spine.

"What are we now?" Dominique could not keep the tremble out of her voice.

David unbuttoned the sleeve at her wrist and slid it up so he could access her forearm. "What do you want us to be?" One kiss on her arm. Then another.

She sighed heavily, her body quickly clouding her thoughts and any ability to think reasonably. "Can we simply *be?*"

"We can be anything you want." With that declaration, he leaned forward and took her lips.

But instead of the expectant demand she'd accustomed herself to from men like D'Terre, David's caress was a gentle invitation. He swiped his tongue across her lower lip then retreated, keeping the kiss light until she chose to deepen it. Freeing her other hand from her cloak, Dominique cupped his head of golden hair and dove into him.

She drank in the taste of him like a fine wine, determined to savor every nuance. He was familiar and new all at once. The man she'd known and loved was still there in every touch and taste, but there was a new element of spice and experience.

The hand that had held her in place while he showered her with kisses now slid up her arm, underneath the cloak to circle her waist and draw her closer. She slid into his lap, eager to feel the full warmth of his body.

Heavens, he was blazing with heat. And there, pressing up urgently against her bottom, was the hot, hard length of his manhood. Dominique ground her hips against him, glorying in the moan that ripped from his throat and reverberated between them.

Suddenly, the world was spinning. David used his grip on her waist to lower her to the bed and roll on top of her, one knee outside of her hip and the other urging her knees apart. The shower of kisses began again, this time from her lips, along her chin, and down her neck.

She tugged her hands from his hair so she could rip open the clasp of her cloak. A grunt of frustration from one of them—no telling who—and she was ripping away the maid's fichu as well.

David drew back for a moment, eyes snagging on the delectable expanse of skin now visible above her neckline. His blue eyes were unreadable in the dark, but the low growl of need in his throat was telling enough.

He lowered his mouth to her bosom, his tongue drawing wicked circles along the curve of her breasts where they swelled above the starched black fabric. He nipped at the fabric, as if he would rip it away with his teeth. A nervous laugh bubbled up in Dominique's throat, quickly silenced as he cupped her breast through her gown and thrust his hips insistently against her.

She arched upward, hooking one leg around his hip, desperate for the contact.

It was all happening so quickly, like a fuse lit and ready to explode. She was losing all ability to think, caught instead in a never-ending cascade of emotions. She wanted him, she longed for him, she lo—

Dominique silenced the thought ruthlessly. She forced her focus back to the attentions of his mouth, now climbing back up her throat. She felt her lips tremble fiercely, begging for his touch and reeling with the feelings she did not dare acknowledge.

IT WAS NOT only her lips. Her hands were quivering, her arms shaking delicately even beneath the warmth of his body.

Was she cold? Or worse, afraid of him?

But when David drew back, the hunger in her eyes dissuaded him of that humbling notion. She was not afraid of him—she was afraid of what this might mean. Those gorgeous, mysterious dark eyes of hers were clouded with indecision. While he wanted her more than life itself, and could feel her willingness in the way she clung to him, he would not take her like this. He'd waited most of his life for the moment they would finally be joined together. He would not allow it to be tinged with regret on either side.

He kissed her again, softer this time. Slowly, he eased her head back onto the bed, untangling his hand from the riot of dark curls spread over the white bedsheet. When he finally found the fortitude to pull himself away from her lips, he rested his forehead against hers.

"We can be anything you want," he reiterated. "And I will be right here when you're ready."

Dominique opened her mouth, and David expected her protest. But her eyes searched his, and finally he felt the slight dip of her chin in acknowledgment.

They lay there for several minutes, pressed together and breathing each other's air. Somehow, it was even more intimate than the fervent touches of moments before. Only when her breathing had slowed and her limbs were relaxed did David push himself off the bed and reach for his boots.

"Thank you for your assistance with the drawings," she said quietly, following him across the flat.

"Of course. What do we do next?"

She hummed softly behind him. "I will study the letters and the copies, see if there is a coded message somehow hidden there. I might need to retrieve more, to determine any meaningful patterns."

David paused at the door, nodding and thinking. They would have more time together. He could wait for her to be ready. He'd been waiting for years.

He leaned in and kissed her forehead. "Goodnight, Dominique."

She answered with a smile so small, he almost missed it. But the emotion it held, paired with her wide, dark eyes, was more than enough.

"Thank you for waiting," she murmured as he disappeared down the stairs.

"I would wait forever to you," David whispered back, though he knew the words did not quite reach her.

CHAPTER FOURTEEN

1807
10 years ago
Winleigh, Hampshire

"REMIND ME WHY we are venturing into the village on a day like this?" Collette Beauchamp bristled, pulling her cloak tighter around her shoulders.

"Mrs. Quill's two little ones have taken ill, and she's unable to make it into town for provisions. The least we can do is see the dears have some fresh meat. It is only neighborly," Dominique said, trotting ahead on the road.

"Where is Mr. Quill?" her mother mumbled.

"Best not to dwell upon that," Dominique advised. Mr. Quill was a known reprobate who hardly attended to his own well-being, let alone that of his young family.

Collette muttered an unintelligible string of French curses.

Dominique bit her lip to stop herself from chuckling at her mother. It was brisk—the season had turned and autumn had fully taken hold of Northern England. But even if the wind was biting, the sun was shining and the crisp air in her lungs made her feel fully alive. Granted, she'd been humming with excitement perpetually for the last four weeks. Since that moment when David asked to court her, she'd been only tangentially tied to reality.

"I will be speaking with Mrs. Grisham while we are in town," her mother warned. "Not about you and your gent—about Mr. Quill."

Dominique cocked her head to the side. "What good will that do?"

Her mother raised her eyebrows and cleared her throat—the clear indication that what she was about to say was important and Dominique would do well to lend an ear. Her mother was always imparting little lessons in this way; she was determined not to *tell* Dominique how to be a worthy young lady, but show her.

"Mrs. Grisham and I may speak casually. Our children are courting, after all. If I happen to share a bit of neighborly news, and she happens to mention it to her husband, no one will think a thing of it." Her mother paused, watching her expectantly.

Dominique considered. "Mr. Grisham is a leading member of the parish council."

"And the owner of the foundry," her mother inserted.

"As the owner of the foundry, he frequently does business with the quarry where Mr. Quill is employed." Understanding flashed in Dominique's mind. "He could arrange for the foreman there to see what could be done about getting Mr. Quill home to his family at the end of the workday instead of off to the pub with his mates."

"*Bonne.*" Collette nodded sharply. "And all of it without embarrassing Mrs. Quill and her young ones."

"You are very crafty, Maman."

"Kindness takes many forms, Dominique. It can be as simple as bringing fresh bread and meat to ailing children or as strategic as ensuring the right words make it to the appropriate ears."

Dominique considered that as they continued the walk into the village. Her mother's point was clear. While her own good deed would ensure the family was fed for the next few days, her mother's might change the course of their well-being for months or years. She had much to learn still, despite edging ever closer to her majority.

Smiling to herself, she linked her arm with her mother's as they entered the village. She would happily spend the rest of her life learning to be as kind and graceful as her mother.

They walked companionably to the butcher, purchasing a side of pork that could be stretched across several meals, as well as cheaper, tougher beef that could be added to stews.

"What else do you have in mind?" Collette asked as they stepped back out into the brisk afternoon.

"Bread, of course, but Bella can spare a loaf of that easy enough, though she mentioned needing more flour. Perhaps some apples. Maybe a few biscuits for the girls." As she spoke, Dominique's eyes tracked around the village to where they would procure each item on her list.

She spotted Mrs. Wright in the doorway of the baker's shop. She raised a hand in greeting, thinking they would go there next. The woman saw her, but instead of waving back, she turned abruptly and closed the door behind her.

How odd.

A few doors down was the stall where Farmer Jones was selling his crop of apples. She would buy some for herself as well. They'd always been a favorite… Her eyes slipped past that to the town green, full of leaves over the wet grass.

At the end of the street, a group of young people she'd been at school with were laughing. A few younger children played with a ball on the town green a few yards away, in the charge of their older siblings busy socializing.

Her mother nudged her shoulder.

"Go on, then. Your David might be among them," she teased lightly. "I will see to your list and fetch you after I've spoken with Mrs. Grisham."

Before Dominique could protest, her mother was off in the direction of the baker.

The excitement that lingered just below the surface of her skin bubbled to life, flooding her with a dizzying warmth as she started down the street. She counted six heads in the group… Maisie, who was in the same year as Dominique, and her younger sister Anne. Tom and Joseph Bolton, twins of an age with David. Tom was courting Elizabeth Brenton, who stood beside him. And beside her, a familiar crown of gold hair.

David.

She cut across the town green, ignoring the squelch of her boots in the muddy grass. She was much too excited for good judgment. When would this feeling in her stomach go away? Would she look at David in ten years and still feel this overwhelming flood of joy?

"Arrgh!"

"Good heavens!"

She kept from slipping, the grace inherited from her mother keeping her on her feet, but that was not her primary concern. The poor little boy she'd nearly trampled was.

She caught him on the shoulder, steadying him and keeping him from feeling the damp of the leaves around them. His ball, half buried in leaves, was a few feet away. He must have been running for it when they collided.

The brown-haired lad turned his eyes up to her, and she recognized him immediately.

"Are you well, young Master Brenton?" she asked, her brow wrinkling with concern. He seemed well enough, though a bit muddier for the encounter. Dominique supposed that was the punishment they both earned for mucking around the town green in such a condition.

His eyes widened. He snatched the ball from the ground and lit in the opposite direction, disappearing around the skirts of his elder sister at the end of the street.

Good heavens, had she hurt him?

There had been no hitch in his step as he retreated, but perhaps she'd knocked the wind from his stomach. But the Brenton lad was not known for being skittish.

Still frowning, Dominique closed the last few yards to the

group waiting on the other side of the green.

David stepped out immediately, a smile lighting his handsome face. But Dominique only nodded in his direction, instead searching out Elizabeth Brenton's gaze.

"Is your brother injured, Miss Brenton? I must apologize—I was not watching well enough where I was walking," she said, searching for the boy. The top of his head was just visible behind her skirts.

Elizabeth frowned, glancing behind her. She curled an arm around her brother and held him a little closer. "He is fine, Miss Beauchamp."

David arrived at Dominique's side; she could feel the steadying warmth of his presence. But something in Elizabeth's face kept her from relaxing.

"Really, it was an accident," Dominique said earnestly.

"I am certain it was," Elizabeth bit out. She turned to Tom Bolton. "I hear my mother calling. Will you escort us, Mr. Bolton?"

"Of course." Tom Bolton nodded, offering his arm to her.

He exchanged a glance with his twin brother, Joseph, then led Elizabeth and her brother away. The look he shared with Joseph… Unease twisted in Dominique's gut.

She watched them retreat, trying to deduce what in the heavens she'd done. She did not have any close friends among this set—except for David—but they'd always been friendly.

Dominique turned to Maisie and Anne, the two young women who remained. "Have I done something to offend Miss Brenton? It truly was an accident."

Anne stared at her, eyes round—and uttered not a word.

Maisie cleared her throat awkwardly, opening and closing her mouth as if not sure what to say.

Dominique felt David shifting his weight beside her, then the touch of his hand at her elbow. A silent show of comfort.

"What is it?" he said.

Neither girl responded.

"I shall not allow you to be so rude to my—"

"Your what, Grisham?" Joseph Bolton interrupted.

David jerked back in surprise, looking at the other young man. Dominique did too. The revulsion on his face speared through her, driving deep into her soul as she realized what was coming next.

"You are well aware that I am courting Mis Beauchamp," David bit out.

"Oh yes, the whole town is aware." Joseph snorted. "But unlike you, the rest of us do not want to sully ourselves with the bastard get of a French whore."

No.

Not like this.

How, how, how had this happened?

"Have you taken leave of your sense?" David gasped.

"Have you?" Joseph replied. "Lady Wartham herself—"

Dominique spun away. If David reached for her, she did not give herself time to find out. If he had words of retort, of disbelief and betrayal… she could not hear those now either.

She flung herself toward the nearest alleyway and ran like hell.

She would not allow herself to look back.

⟫⟫⟩⟨⟪⟪

"WHY WOULD YOU say such a thing?" David demanded.

"Because it is true." Joseph shrugged. Shrugged—as if he had not just torn another person's life asunder.

Then David did something he'd never done in his entire life.

He intentionally harmed another person.

He planted a facer to Joseph's jaw with enough force the other man went sprawling backward in the mud.

David did not hear the startled cries of the townsfolk witnessing the spectacle.

He was already running after Dominique.

⟫⟩⟩⟩✦⟨⟨⟨⟪

SHE HEAVED OPEN the door of the cottage, flying over the threshold in a swirl of velvet cloak and tangled hair.

She needed to throw something, to scream and curse the world. She grabbed the first thing she saw—not really seeing at all—and flung. It was not enough. She grabbed again.

There was a terrible crash. Whatever it was exploded over the floor.

Above her head, a woman screamed in surprise.

Bella.

Heavens, what am I doing?

Dominique barreled past the shards of clay pottery and out the kitchen door.

She had to get away… had to go somewhere without the judgmental looks, without the snickering laughs. She felt the burn in her thighs, the only indication that she was climbing. Up, up, up, no real awareness of where her legs were carrying her.

Then the burning stopped. A gust of wind whipped over her, throwing back the hood she'd pulled up to hide her face as she fled the village.

She was in Farmer Jones's orchard.

She stumbled forward a few steps, grabbing a tree trunk for support. Then she sank down against it, unable to stand any longer.

The anger was the past. All that remained now was devastation.

The sobs rose in her throat, burning her chest. She let them come.

She dragged her fingernails up over her scalp, pulling loose the strands of her perfectly coiffed French-style plait.

The bastard get of a French whore.

No one had ever dared to say such a thing to her or her mother—not the servants at Wartham Grange, not even Lady…

126

Lady Wartham.

She was the one who'd told.

After a decade of harboring her husband's secret, lamenting the shame of it at every opportunity, the vile woman had had enough.

The look she'd given Dominique and David in the churchyard sprang to her mind.

Lady Wartham had done this.

She'd always resented Dominique and her mother. Not just their existence, it seemed, but their happiness as well.

So now it was all destroyed.

A fresh sob rose in Dominique's chest, stealing the breath from her throat. She felt as if she would die, alone in an apple orchard, unable to breathe. Perhaps it was for the best. Her mother could return to Paris, get away from this torrid mess…

"Dominique."

She thought her heart was broken. But, of course, there was David. She was not the only one hurting. She'd lied and betrayed him.

"David," she whispered, unable to look up at him. "David, I am so sorry. So very sorry. I should have told you before I accepted your courtship. I should have told you years ago. I was such a coward—"

"Hush, hush." He sank down to the ground next to her.

He did not run away. He did not grasp her chin and force her to meet his eye while demanding answers. He pulled her into his lap and kissed the top of her head. "Hush, my love," he murmured into her hair.

Dominique sobbed against him, unable to form words.

David slid his hand inside her cloak, finding her bare arm. He stroked up and down it, over and over again, steady and soothing. She let herself focus on him—the scrape of his callouses from his work at the foundry, the heat of his body as it cradled hers. His breath lifted the hairs on the nape of her neck. When the heaving sobs finally ebbed to jagged breaths, she started to hear his heartbeat.

She had to say something now, to explain herself. She sucked in a breath, trying to find the words.

"Why didn't you tell me?" he said softly.

She pressed her eyes closed. She could make some claim about protecting her mother or her family. But with David, only the truth would do. "I was afraid you would not want me."

He sat up, catching her shoulders and shifting her so he could look at her face. Her heart clenched. But instead of rejection, she saw only love in his blue eyes.

"How could you think so little of me?" His voice cracked.

"This ruins everything, David. Your family will never accept me. I will be nothing but an embarrassment to you. Before, it might have been a carefully guarded secret, but now..." She broke off, unable to continue.

"This changes nothing," David said fiercely.

"David," she whispered. He was wrong. So terribly wrong. But the conviction in his voice settled into her chest.

"I love you," he said. Simple, clear. As true a declaration as one could make. "No one will take that away from us."

Before she could protest, he sealed his declaration with a kiss.

No longer shivering in an apple orchard, no longer alone, Dominique wanted with her entire being to believe him.

CHAPTER FIFTEEN

1817
Present Day

DOMINIQUE ARRIVED EARLY, determined to spend the time on the Bramah lock that the duchess had installed two months before. She was not supposed to visit the various sanctuaries unless explicitly instructed or necessitated by a quest, but Jane had mentioned it in passing. Ever since, the challenge had lain waiting in the recesses of Dominique's mind.

It was rumored to be unpickable.

She intended to prove that wrong.

Though she would be proving it to no one but herself and her fellow Lady Knights. She would never be able to come forward publicly and claim the prize associated with the challenge. A replica of this very lock sat in the window of the Bramah Company, waiting for some enterprising genius to pick it open.

Dominique pulled the leather roll of picks from the deep pocket of her gown and stroked it with almost loving reference. She'd collected the picks slowly over the last three years, even commissioning a few to her exact specifications. She knew the idiosyncrasies of every one. Sinking to her knees, she leaned in to consider the infamous lock.

She did not need the prize or the recognition.

But she would pick it nonetheless.

"We do not have time for that."

Dominique rocked back on her heels, blinking rapidly. Red had approached on near-silent feet. Deep as she'd been in the lock, she hadn't heard a single creak or footfall.

"How long have you been at it?" Red asked, laughter in her voice.

Dominique found her leaning against the wall on the opposite side of the landing. The Lady Knights owned the entire building, though only one flat was actively used. Which meant Dominique had felt relatively safe, sitting there alone immersed in her task. Foolish, to relax her guard.

"What time is it?" Dominique did not bother to disguise the subtle irritation in her voice as she slid the three picks she'd been manipulating back into place in her roll.

"Four o'clock," Red said, studying her nails.

Disappointment and surprise caught Dominique in their twin traps. "Two hours."

Red chuckled mercilessly. "And still you have not managed it? Has the master lockpick finally met her match?"

Dominique ignored her friend's teasing. "The duchess will be here soon."

Reaching into her other pocket, she retrieved the key to the flat and let herself and Red through the door. The hiss and click of the key in the lock mocked her with even more veracity than her fellow lady knight.

"I'm surprised Jane is not already here," Red said, glancing around the one-room flat—as if the most skilled lady knight might appear from the very shadows themselves.

"Unless she entered through a window, I think I would have noticed her arrival," Dominique commented, already moving to the hearth to start a fire for tea.

"Jane always has some new trick," Red murmured, going for the sideboard instead. She poured herself a glass of wine, then held the bottle up to Dominique in question.

Dominique shook her head, but Red did pour a second glass. For the duchess. Or for Jacquetta, on the small chance she'd already completed her quest with Grayson Thane. Though knowing Jacquetta, she'd snub the wine for the flask of cognac she habitually carried.

"You are jealous because she doesn't teach all of them to you." Dominique put the kettle on and settled into one of the armchairs surrounding the small, round table.

Hardly more than a side piece meant to stand beside a bed, it was symbolic rather than functional. They were the Lady Knights of Her Majesty Queen Charlotte's Round Table. Grace and intelligence reigned; friendship and equality were guaranteed.

"You do not have to say every thought that enters that pretty head," Red groused, dropping into a chair opposite from Dominique and taking a long drink of wine.

"Be thankful I do not."

"Where is this sass—"

They both fell silent as the key turned in the lock once again. Instinct had them each reaching for their weapons—Dominique the small knife secreted down her bodice, Red for her parasol resting with mock ease at her side. But the door swung open to admit the Duchess of Guilford herself, as they'd expected.

Someone might easily mistake the tall and dark-haired duchess for Dominique's close relation. She even had a slight tilt to her eyes that men and women had labeled as mysterious for Dominique's entire life. Some young women may have longed for it… to be the daughter of a duchess. Even an illegitimate daughter. But not Dominique. If there was one thing she was thankful for in her life, it was her mother.

Her relationship with the Duchess of Guilford was more than professional, but Dominique certainly would not call it maternal. The duchess was not given to shows of affection; perhaps it was her own lack of family. For not the first time, Dominique wondered at the older woman's history. She'd only ever been able to glean the bare facts.

"I am attending a dinner party with the Countess of Suffolk. We must make this exchange expeditious," the duchess said by way of greeting.

She flicked her skirts with expert grace, pooling them around her legs as she sat. Even her tightly fitted, military-inspired blue pelisse was perfectly arranged atop the dove-gray skirt beneath.

Red held up the second glass of red wine, but the duchess ignored it, turning her eyes to Dominique. "Report upon the D'Terre matter."

A direct command, though not an unkind one.

Dominique squared her shoulders. "I've gained D'Terre's interest. He has already granted me access to his residence in Mayfair. I have not been able to conduct a full search, but I have located several documents of interest in his study."

The duchess flicked her fingers. and Red promptly deposited the wine glass in her hand. "What sort of documents?"

"Letters to other members of Parliament, in both the House of Commons and House of Lords."

"Coded?"

Dominique tilted her head to the side, her own milder variation of a shrug. "One can only assume so. What is of more interest is that each letter is accompanied by a drawing. Detailed renderings of buildings around London, though I can deduce no pattern yet. I would like Jacquetta to have a look—"

"You will have to manage without Jacquetta for the foreseeable future."

Dominique's gaze jumped to Red, who was suddenly gripping her wine glass tightly enough to show the whites of her knuckles.

"What happened?" Red said, voice low.

Of the Lady Knights, Ethelreda and Jacquetta had known one another the longest. They had grown up around one another, and their mothers were once the best of friends. Dominique knew that Red, older by several years, saw Jacquetta as something of a younger sister—hers to protect.

"Jacquetta has executed her plan to allow herself to be kidnapped by Grayson Thane. However, we received a tip that she is being spirited away not to somewhere in England, but to the West Indies," the duchess explained calmly, apparently unruffled.

Red cursed under her breath, then covered it by knocking back the remainder of her wine.

Dominique ignored her, leaning forward intently. "What can we do?"

The duchess sipped her own wine daintily. "We can do nothing. Jacquetta is a highly trained and capable lady knight. She will manage well enough. I have sent Jane to provide whatever assistance might be needed once she lands in the West Indies."

Red's exhale was loud enough to account for them both. If Jane was with her, it would all come to rights. Between the two of them, they could manage. But Dominique knew that neither she nor Red would fully relax until they had a further report on their friend's status.

"If you must seek out a consultant in Jacquetta's absence, then do so. We need to know the significance of these drawings," the duchess said to Dominique.

An observer might think the stately woman was ignoring Red, but Dominique knew them both well enough to realize the duchess was giving Red the privacy to compose herself.

"I have already done so. Mr. David Grisham. I brought him on to help reproduce the drawings, so D'Terre would not realize they were missing," Dominique said quickly. She sounded authoritative and sure, but she was certain that meant little to the duchess.

"David Grisham? The heir to the Earl of Danby?" Though she phrased it as a question, the duchess's eyes flashed with recognition.

"Yes."

"Curious."

That one word felt like a challenge, and despite herself, Dominique was unable to resist. "He is a skilled artist. Before becoming the heir, he earned a living by creating reproductions of famous artists to be transferred to silver etchings and distributed for sale."

Another sip of wine. "He is trustworthy?"

The teakettle whistled its hot demand over Dominique's shoulder. "He is a childhood friend."

Even Red's eyebrows rose at that. But neither she nor the duchess spoke, the latter watching Dominique with careful consideration as she retrieved the kettle and set the tea to steep. She returned to the circle, though she lingered at the back of the armchair rather than sitting again.

"I trust him implicitly."

After several moments of careful consideration, the duchess inclined her head. "I trust your judgment," she said. "But make haste. The Excise Act will come up for a vote soon. We must have D'Terre firmly in hand before that happens. Use Ethelreda in whatever way you see fit."

"We have completed two exchanges already. I have four letters and drawings to work from. If there is a code embedded there, I will find it."

"Good." The duchess drank the rest of her wine and stood. "I must dress for the evening. Send word if you need additional assistance."

Red was on her feet and following the duchess in the next breath. "Miranda, I wish to speak with you about—"

"I do not have a quest for you at this junction, Ethelreda. I will summon you as soon as I do." The underlying rebuke in the duchess's voice was clear to both young women.

Dominique busied herself with pouring two cups of tea, while Red fell back, biting her lip.

"Of course," she murmured.

The duchess pursed her lips, face revealing nothing, then turned and left the flat. Red waited for the door to close, then followed and locked the door before joining Dominique.

She laid her head down on the wood-slab countertop and

groaned. "I made a mess of things and now I am being punished."

Dominique did not engage. Red's last quest... Well, it was something neither of them truly wished to speak about. "Tea?" she asked instead, already filling a second cup.

"If only I had some of Jacquetta's cognac to fortify it," Red said, propping her chin on her hand.

Dominique nudged the tea in her direction, and the other woman took a begrudging sip. Even so, Dominique watched her friend's features relax as the warm tea soothed her edges.

After several more sips, she straightened. "Tell me about these drawings."

CHAPTER SIXTEEN

"YOU TASTE AMAZING."

"You should not be here," Dominique protested halfheartedly against his mouth. Heavens, that mouth.

She'd had cause to kiss a fair number of men in her career as a lady knight, but kissing David did things to her that she could hardly explain. Was this what true desire felt like? She understood now why people made such foolish decisions in the name of lust and love.

"Tell me to go," David teased, massaging her breasts with his hand.

She wore only a dressing gown, all she'd managed to throw on before David's knock rung out on her dressing room door. He must not have even been watching the performance, but waiting at the rear stage door.

"Come back to my flat," she said without thinking. Dominique knew only that she never wanted this delicious burning inside her body to end.

"Miss Beauchamp, how forward," he teased, nipping on her ear.

"David," she groaned, arching against him.

Knock! Knock! Knock! Three sharp raps intruded rudely on her consciousness.

"Hold a moment!" she called. Had she remembered to lock

the door? Heavens, David was such a distraction that even her most basic precautions were suffering.

"Who is it?" he asked.

"Whoever it is, stay out of sight," she warned, giving him a playful shove behind the door while she opened it.

David did as she asked, standing out of sight. But the instant she opened the door, he began to unbutton his shirt. Dastardly man.

"Cora!" Dominique did not hide her surprise at all—she let it be a cover for the rapid rise and fall of her chest.

"Who is in here with you?" Cora demanded, standing on tiptoe to peer over Dominique's shoulder. Meanwhile, David was loosening his cravat and giving her an expansive view of his muscular chest.

"No one. I am alone," Dominique answered, willing her face to neutrality.

"I thought I heard voices." Cora fell back to her usual height, but the rising of her eyebrows said she was still unconvinced.

"You are mistaken," Dominique insisted.

Several loud laughs erupted from somewhere else backstage, drawing Cora's eyes. Was that worry in them? A shiver of unease pressed at Dominique's spine.

"You had better be speaking the truth, because Mr. D'Terre will be here any moment."

The unease turned to ice in her body. In her periphery, she saw David's hand freeze. "I did not see him in the audience tonight."

"He was a guest of the Duke of Marlborough," Cora said, glancing over her shoulder again. When she turned back, she noticed Dominique's attire, her gaze turning sharp. "At least you are already dressed the part."

"Cora—"

"Good luck, Miss Beauchamp." Cora turned on her heel and sped down the corridor.

Dominique caught herself before slamming the door, but this

time she did not neglect to lock it.

"You must go," she whispered urgently.

"Come with me," David said, already buttoning his shirt.

"I cannot. D'Terre is expecting me." She wished she'd put on a shift, but there was no time. She had to get David out.

"You have no arrangement with him for tonight," David insisted, reaching for the tailcoat he'd discarded on the sofa earlier.

"I *am* the arrangement, David. That is the entire point of this façade!" She grabbed his arm and reached for the door. But before she could touch the lock, another knock rang out.

Loud and demanding.

All of the blood drained from her body.

She turned to David, summoning the cool reserve of composure she'd been trained to draw on in moments such as these. "Hide."

Dominique did not turn to see how he managed; she could only pray that the sofa he was ducking behind would be big enough to hide that wide, strong body she'd come to adore.

"*Mon paon,*" she purred as she opened the door. At least the flush on her skin could be mistaken for excitement rather than terror. "I did not expect you this evening."

"I have brought you a gift," D'Terre said gruffly, stepping over her threshold without invitation.

Dominique's hands itched to pull her dressing robe tighter around her, but that would only draw his gaze. "A gift? I am honored, monsieur."

She caught his arm and brushed a kiss across his cheek, and the spiky stubble tore at her lips. When she drew back, she let her chin tremble and bit her lower lip. Kissing this man might repulse her, but he would never know it.

Dominique refused to think of David as she caught D'Terre's hands and laced their fingers together, drawing his arms around her.

"It must be quite small, tucked away inside your coat," she

purred, lifting his hand to her mouth and pressing a kiss to the side of it.

"On the contrary, Miss Beauchamp, it is quite large," he growled. "And tucked inside my trousers." He pressed his hips into her, his cock rigid and hard against her leg.

It took every bit of training to keep herself from jerking back. Disgusting. His gift was *himself*.

She forced her lower lip out in a petulant pout. "How cruel you are."

"How cruel? Here I thought myself most gracious." He disentangled their hands and slid his hands over her shoulders, dragging her fully against him. She did not have time to dodge before he roughly took her mouth, shoving his tongue past her closed lips.

Dominique lifted her tongue to meet his, counting to ten in her head while she prayed that David's head was ducked. There was no way he had not heard every word between them, but perhaps he would at least be spared the sight of D'Terre pawing at her.

Then she pulled back, heaving her chest for effect.

"Cruel, because I will not be able to appreciate it tonight." She watched his eyes darken, but she plowed on. "I am being fitted for new costumes, for our new production," she lied.

"Tomorrow," he demanded, hands an inch from her breasts.

"I have rehearsal tomorrow," she said, sending up a silent prayer he would not try to verify either lie she fed him. "The day after. Come for me here… I will be ready for you."

She infused her voice with every bit of invitation and cunning she'd acquired over the last three years. Relief coursed through her when D'Terre's hands fell away and he stepped back, already moving toward the door. It seemed that he was done attempting to woo her into his bed; he would have her physically or not bother with her at all.

"I will be waiting after you finish your performance, Miss Beauchamp," he promised.

"I will be here."

The dark desire that flashed in D'Terre's eyes as he paused in her door, raking one last proprietary look over her body, was laced with warning. The door closing ought to have been a relief, but even once she'd locked it behind him, the dread remained.

She would not be able to put him off much longer. Men like D'Terre enjoyed the chase, but only up to a certain point. If she did not deliver, he would take what he wanted and leave her to bear the consequences.

The thought of doing so made her physically sick, and her eyes searched out the chamber pot tucked away in the corner by reflex. But then the sofa shifted and David emerged, his dark expression a painful analogy to D'Terre's moments before.

"That man is a devil," David said, staring at the closed door.

"And it is my job to deal with the devil himself," she said softly. "I am sorry you had to witness that."

"So am I."

Her heart, which she'd stubbornly denied was involved, broke a little at his words.

"I will leave you alone to dress," David said stiffly.

Dominique waited for the offer to escort her back to her flat. But all she heard was the pounding of blood in her ears.

"I shall contact you when I have new information on the quest," she said. She managed to keep her voice from quivering, but only just.

She thought she saw David's chest cave in slightly, but it could have been a trick of her eyes. Or of her heart. If she had to stand here with him another minute, she would burst into tears.

"Goodnight, David."

He pressed his lips tightly together, as if unable to speak. Dominique could sympathize with the struggle. But it did not make it hurt any less when he turned and left her dressing room without another word.

CHAPTER SEVENTEEN

THE SOUND OF raindrops on her umbrella echoed the jumping of Dominique's heartbeat as she strode beneath the trees of Green Park. She did not think it had slowed since David's arrival in London. Jane would be appalled; of all the Lady Knights, she was known for her quiet implacability. She'd even devised breathing exercises to help them regulate their pulses in high-stress situations.

Dominique sighed, glancing around. She ought to do one now, so she was evenly keeled when Red arrived.

Instead, the slide of an errant raindrop down the back of her neck summoned the sensation of David's tongue, marking the same sensitive line from the base of her ear down to her collarbone. His lips were so soft against her skin, delicate and gentle when the world had been everything but with her. No harsh demands, only sweet and sensual worshiping.

But another memory stuffed itself rudely into her consciousness: D'Terre's stubble scraping across her cheek as he stole a kiss.

Not stole. She'd given it freely.

But had she, if it had only been in service of her quest as a lady knight? She'd become one of her own free will, had relished every minute of her service for the power it gave her to do good in the world, free of the constraints of her birth. So, it followed that any actions she took as a lady knight were also her choice…

Dominique let the umbrella teeter back on her shoulder so she could free one hand to rub her temple. Rain sluiced down the front of her gown, but she hardly noticed. These questions had kept her up most of the night. The pain and jealousy on David's face when he'd emerged from his hiding spot, D'Terre finally gone, haunted her every time she closed her eyes.

Last night would have been a damn good time for one of Jane's breathing exercises, she admonished herself.

Better now than never.

She fixed her eyes on a tree a hundred yards away. Starting at the base, she took a deep breath and held it as she traced her eyes upward to where the uppermost leaves touched the gray sky. Then she exhaled. She held her breath as her eyes slid back down to where the trunk met the grass, then inhaled again and repeated the process.

After four cycles, she could already feel her pulse quieting.

Why was Jane always right?

Her heartbeat jumped again. She forced her eyes back to the tree.

"Your gown is going to be quite transparent if you continue to hold your umbrella just so."

Even in the midst of her breathing exercises, Dominique had heard Red's approach. But then, she doubted the other woman was trying to be stealthy. Dominique knew her fellow lady knight's prowess well enough to know that if Red had truly wished to sneak upon her, she would have succeeded.

"Are you meeting with D'Terre after this? Wet and helpless is certainly one way to catch a gentleman's eye," Red commented, looking her up and down. "Or perhaps it is for the benefit of a certain Mr. Grisham?"

Dominique snapped her umbrella upright and glared at her friend.

Red appeared unbothered, adjusting her own parasol. While Dominique held hers with a tight hand, knuckles tense beneath her gloves, Red's grip on the handle was almost lover-like. But then, Dominique did not have a razor-sharp rapier concealed within hers.

"I do not have an appointment with D'Terre until after tomorrow evening's performance," Dominique said.

"Which means Mr. Grisham—"

"Shall we walk?" Dominique did not wait for a response before striding for the path.

Normally, they would have kept to the trees. There was more cover, and they were less likely to be spotted and remarked upon by *ton* socialites. While no one in polite society had any idea who Dominique was, Ethelreda McGovern was the eldest daughter of an old and respected family. She was an established spinster, which allowed her some degree of freedom, but did not exempt her from all speculation.

But it was pouring rain, they were in Green Park rather than Hyde, and the path was at least paved with gravel and less likely to ruin her boots than the squelching, muddy grass.

"Lovely weather for a stroll," Red commented, catching up with her easily. She did not protest their path, which meant she also judged the risk to be minimal. Still, the tension in Dominique's shoulders did not ease.

"I find it rather matches my mood," she said.

Red cut her a look, but Dominique did not meet it. "What is it?"

"It is nothing."

"It is Mr. Grisham," Red said, not bothering to mince words. No, she was too straightforward for her own good. Which was probably why she was a spinster.

Dominique's stomach dropped; it was an unkind thought. Red was a fiercely loyal friend and an accomplished lady knight.

She could not very well apologize for an unspoken thought, so she did the next best thing—she offered a truth.

"My feelings for him have complicated my quest," she said, the painful honesty of it more than she'd admitted even to herself.

Red said nothing, continuing to walk at her side. But she nudged her arm as they walked, a gesture so small it might have been a mistake or misstep. Except that Dominique knew her friend well enough to know otherwise.

"His artistic skills are exemplary—on that front, I have no qualms. The drawings Mr. Grisham has produced are indiscernible from the originals," Dominique continued, easing herself into the difficult bit, which came next. "But my seduction of D'Terre…" She could not even finish.

"Is D'Terre immune to your charms?" Red asked, her voice carefully even—no hint of judgment or reprimand.

"No, he's quite taken with me," Dominique said sharply. The bitterness in her own voice surprised her. She was supposed to be adept at concealing her feelings, but there with Red, alone in the rain, she'd lost all her finesse. "He's eager to consummate our relationship. I have no doubt he would install me in his townhouse should I only ask it," she said. "But I have not been able to bring myself—"

Red grabbed her hand, cutting off her speech and sparing her from having to voice the awful words.

"We shall find a way," Red said. "I have managed to complete every single one of my quests without so much as kissing a man, if you recall. I assure you, it can be managed."

"I was chosen for this quest because of my skills in seduction," Dominique said. That was the crux of it, really.

She was not a virgin. She'd seduced many men in the course of her work for queen and country, and allowed a handful to take her to bed. She had never felt an ounce of regret—only strength and pride in the dangerous, necessary work she accomplished.

Until David.

"You have many other skills, Dominique," Red said. She squeezed her hand even tighter. "Use them. And if need be, use me. The Lord knows I am bored out of my skull waiting around for my next quest." She heaved a sigh.

They passed the tree Dominique had stared at while mastering her breath. The sight of it infused her with a bit of calm, reminding her to keep breathing. She repeated Jane's exercise once.

It steadied her enough for her to ask: "Have you had any luck with the drawings?"

Red scowled, detaching their arms and shoving her hand inside her pelisse, fishing around until she withdrew a small packet. Dominique took it immediately, sliding it into the folds of her bodice to protect it from the rain.

"Not a single thing," Red declared, still scowling at the papers even as they disappeared from sight. "I pored over those damned drawings for hours, and not a single thing came to my mind. Is there any possibility they are *just* drawings?"

Dominique turned over the possibility for a moment, but rejected it almost immediately. "No, they mean *something*. There was one included in every communication of suspect. They are the only link between all the parties—the only physical link, that is."

Red nodded, her freckles darkened under the cloudy sky and even more so by the shadow of her knitted brow. "I wish Jacquetta were here; she'd crack it in a minute."

Jacquetta, with her uncanny ability to remember every detail of an image after only seeing it once, would no doubt have been able to unravel whatever codes or secrets were embedded in the images. But she was an ocean away, Jane with her. Dominique sent up a silent prayer for their luck and safety.

"I will have another look at them, and ask David as well. Perhaps he will see something the rest of us have missed with his artist's eye."

Red cut her a look at the use of his Christian name, but did not comment.

They'd reached the end of the lane, where they must turn or exit the park onto Grosvenor Place. Per their usual pattern, Red would continue through the park to where her family carriage waited on the southern edge, and Dominique would travel on foot along a circuitous route back to her flat.

But instead of bidding her good day or continuing down the path, Red stopped. She glanced around them, surely noting the park's sparse occupants. Dominique had already been tracking them—a pair of male riders, well-to-do enough to afford their own mounts but not well dressed enough to be nobility. There was a servant with a basket over her arm, hurrying through the park with her head down.

Red took a deep breath, and the pelisse buttoned up to her throat prevented Dominique from judging the staccato of her pulse. But her friend had other tells. She shifted her weight, raked her thumb across the inside of her other fingers—details most people would miss.

"What is it?" Dominique asked, unease pinching between her shoulder blades.

Red avoided her gaze, eyes fixed on the two men riding away from them. Dominique flicked her gaze to them as well, wondering if she ought to recognize them.

"I attended a musicale last night with my mother," Red said, shifting her weight again.

Red hated musicales even more than she hated being dragged around by her mother, who refused to accept her eldest daughter's spinster status.

"Unfortunate, but you will recover, I daresay," Dominique said with a smile, trying to lighten the leaden air around them.

"You have never heard the Marley sisters play the harp," Red said. She shivered with distaste. "But that is not what I have to report. There was a guest in attendance whom"—she paused long enough for Dominique's heart to clench—"whom I believe you know."

"Tell me."

"Amelia Wartham has come to London."

Dominique had thought the air thick and leaden? How wrong she had been. There was no air at all. Not in the park, not in the world. It had all been sucked away.

She clasped her eyes shut, then forced them open, turning on the spot until she found that damned tree again. She stared at it, forcing the breaths in and out in rhythm.

She felt Red watching her, probably aware of exactly what she was doing. She waited several breath cycles before speaking again.

"Dominique, we—"

"How long have you known?"

Red cleared her throat. "Since the beginning."

"All of you?" Dominique could not help her strangled voice, even with the breathing exercise doing its job—albeit slowly.

"Yes."

That single word, quite unexpectedly, did as much to calm her as the ceaseless cycle of inhales and exhales. Her friends knew—they had always known. And it had not mattered. Heavens, how had she gotten so lucky?

"It matters not a jot to any of us," Red said. The words of confirmation filled Dominique with warmth. Until Red continued. "But there is more."

An icy stone dropped into that warmth. "Tell me."

"Miss Wartham has come to town with her mother."

"Horrible woman."

Red chuckled. "It took me all of two minutes in her presence to ascertain as much. But that's not it." She reached out and laid a hand on Dominique's arm. "Lord Wartham is dead."

Part of her had suspected what was coming, but it did not lessen the pain that lanced through her. Pain, laced with confusion and anger, a kaleidoscope of emotions so powerful that no tree or breathing exercise could steady her. Only the touch of Red's hand, the silent offer of friendship and support, kept Dominique from going to her knees.

Her umbrella drooped, and the rain hit her dark hair and ran in rivulets down her neck and shoulders. Red nudged it back into place, holding it there herself for several minutes.

Dominique's father was dead. Amelia had not even bothered

to write. Amelia, who knew exactly where to find her. Amelia, to whom she'd sent letter after letter in the year after her and her mother's exile from Winleigh. Amelia, who had never sent back a word. The sister she'd loved so fiercely despite everything. The sister who had forsaken her. Now, Amelia was in London, probably seeking a husband, her horrible mother in tow. Without even a word to Dominique.

The pain that had speared through her narrowed to seething anger. She did not have time for this. Her world was complicated enough without her sister and Lady Wartham. How dare they float into London—which Amelia knew very well was Dominique's last place of residence—and upend her life even more.

No, she would not allow it. Lady Wartham had ruined her life once. Dominique would not allow her to do so again. She certainly would not let the harpy and her path of ruin anywhere near her mother.

Her hand tightened on the handle of her umbrella.

"I must get on. I have several errands to attend to." She turned back to Red, whose face was carefully blank.

Red squeezed her arm again, then eased her hand back. She would let Dominique handle this information in whatever way she chose. Dominique wanted to smile and offer her thanks, but if she did, the tight hold she had on her emotions might snap.

"Send word if you have need of my assistance," Red said. "On *anything*."

Dominique managed a nod.

"Good day, Miss Beauchamp," Red said.

"And to you, Miss McGovern."

Red did not hesitate, turning with a smart snap of her parasol and striding toward where her family carriage waited outside of the park. Dominique mirrored her efficiency, pointing her feet toward the street.

But somewhere between the edge of Green Park and Kensington she lost track of things, and when night fell, she found herself in the one place she truly ought to stay away from.

CHAPTER EIGHTEEN

"WHO WILL BE in attendance this evening?"

"It's a ball given by the Marchioness of Clydon, David."

David shrugged. He'd met so many marquesses, earls, and their troops of wives and daughter that most of their names had lost all meaning to him. But still, he repeated his question. "Of the women who have expressed an interest in courtship, who will be in attendance?"

Geoffrey frowned, the gray of his short-cropped beard catching in the dim torchlight of the carriage as he leaned forward and braced his elbows on his knees. "The Marchioness of Clydon is one of the most sought-after hostesses in London. There will be dozens of women you've met, and dozens more eager to make your acquaintance. But since when is it of any interest to you?"

"You've said it yourself—I must marry eventually." The words burned David's throat.

"That is not what I said," Geoffrey quipped, eyes still fixed on him.

David shrugged. "It's what you meant."

"Like hell it is. Marry one of the ladies you've met or take a wealthy widow as a mistress and remain a bachelor your entire life. There is someone far enough down the family tree to pass the earldom to," Geoffrey said. His frown deepened with each sentence.

"I have a duty to the earldom to marry and produce an heir," David said.

Geoffrey reeled back as if struck. "And perhaps you mean that Lily and I failed in our duty?"

Guilt snapped David's head from where he'd been gazing morosely out the window back to his cousin.

"I'm sorry," he said quickly.

"You are being an arse."

"I did not mean it." It was David's turn to lean forward, elbows on his knees, eyes begging his cousin to accept his apology.

Geoffrey held his gaze, his darker blue gaze searching David's. "I accept your apology," he said, sighing. "What has you so out of sorts, cousin?"

David rocked back against the seat. His impulse was to fix his stare back out on the darkened street and avoid the conversation altogether. But regret at the wound he'd dealt his cousin prevented him.

"There is a woman," he said.

Geoffrey held his gaze as his gray-blond eyebrows shot up. "Who?"

"You do not know her."

"So, not one of the women who we might find in attendance tonight."

"No."

"I see."

"You do not, and that is for the better, because I cannot explain it to you," David said.

He sighed himself, and then did allow his gaze to wander out past the curtains on the carriage window to the darkened street. Every woman they passed, he wondered if it was Dominique. Where was she now? What work was she doing? What danger might she be in?

The thoughts haunted him—had ever since he'd learned of her profession. Now, they were interspersed with images of her and D'Terre. He'd been able to ignore it, pretend as if she was not seducing another man, let himself think that she belonged to him. But hiding in her dressing room while that villain kissed her and ran his hands over her lush body was more than he could ignore.

"If there is another woman, then why are you interested in which ladies might be in attendance this evening?" Geoffrey asked, pushing through his internal monologue.

"I want a wife," David said.

The truth of that ground him in his gut. He shoved it away.

"And your mystery lady will not do?"

"You ask too many damn questions, Geoffrey."

Geoffrey chuckled under his breath—or he might have; David kept his eyes fixed out the window. The carriage was slowing; they were nearing the mansion home of the Marquess and Marchioness of Clydon, joining the line of other carriages in the sweeping, oval courtyard.

His cousin stopped asking questions as they waited. But by the time the footman opened the door of their carriage and the two men climbed out, David's focus had narrowed to one singular task—he would erase the image of Dominique and D'Terre from his mind, even if he had to dance with every damn woman at the ball.

HE WAS AN arse.

Dancing with no number of suitable young women would change the fact.

He realized it between the quadrille with Miss Dawson and the reel with Lady Stephenson. The waltz with Miss Dunn cemented the fact.

Miss Annabelle Dunn was the daughter of an earl, fashionably blonde and slim as a twig, and very sweet. She blushed when he smiled at her and held an intelligent conversation about the plight of wounded soldiers returned from France. Her kindness and goodness were evident.

But she was not Dominique.

And he was an arse.

"Are you well, Mr. Grisham?" Miss Dunn asked when he trod upon her foot for the second time in as many minutes.

"I am, Miss Dunn. I apologize for my mediocre form. I have always been more of an artist than a dancer," David said. Over her shoulder, he began scanning the crowd for Geoffrey.

"An artist? How fascinating," she squeaked. "What sort of art? Sketching, painting?"

"Etching," he answered, turning his eyes back to her when he failed to locate his cousin. "I create reproductions of paintings in drawing form, so they may be reproduced as etchings and sold as prints. By the artist's commission, of course."

"Have you done any I might recognize?" she asked, smiling eagerly.

"I…" David's breath caught in his throat at the hopeful, earnest interest in her blue eyes. She was a nice girl. Perhaps if he had not seen Dominique dancing across that stage at Covent Garden, Miss Dunn might have held his interest.

But in his heart, David knew it was not true. He had loved Dominique for more than a decade. Though ten years had changed them both, it could not change that.

With blessedly good timing, the last notes of the waltz rang out and the spinning couples around them slowed. David detached himself from Miss Dunn, leading her by her hand to return her to her mother on the edge of the dance floor.

"I thank you for the conversation, Miss Dunn," he said politely. "I hope that we meet again."

"Are you departing already, Mr. Grisham?" Lady Dunn said, tucking her daughter in at her side and imploring him with a hawkish gaze peculiar to the matchmaking mamas of the *ton*.

"I am afraid I must, Lady Dunn. I'm expecting an important correspondence from home this evening and wish to be there to receive it." The lie rolled off his tongue so easily, he wondered if Dominique's secrecy was having an impact upon him.

He nodded respectfully to Miss Dunn, noting the disappointment in her pretty eyes and feeling a stab of guilt. He'd started the evening intent upon dancing with as many beautiful women as possible. Dominique was kissing a crooked parliamentarian in her dressing room; he could damn well dance with as many young debutantes as he pleased.

But the earnest attraction in Miss Dunn's eyes reminded him of the truth his cousin had declared so aptly in the carriage even before they arrived.

He was an arse.

Dominique's involvement with D'Terre was entirely self-sacrificing. Rage and jealousy had burned inside of him as he watched, helpless, as she went from their shared passionate embrace to the rough caresses of D'Terre. But he had not thought for a moment about how Dominique might feel about it—how difficult the situation must be for *her*.

She, at least, acted for selfless reasons. Honorable ones. She was a lady knight on a quest for queen and country.

When he spun sweet Miss Dunn around the dance floor, it was for spite.

Lord, but he didn't deserve Dominique.

But he did love her. And loving her meant endeavoring to be better than he'd been tonight. The next time he saw her, he would apologize. He would beg her forgiveness. He would kiss her and not think for a second about anything other than the joy of having her in his arms.

He spotted Geoffrey sipping on punch near the doorway.

Perfect—it was time to leave.

IT TOOK EVERY bit of self-control he possessed to keep from

running to Covent Garden and waiting outside the stage door. The need to see her and touch her was visceral, overpowering. But he would not jeopardize her quest and all she had worked for. He would wait until tomorrow and go to her flat; he could slip a note under her door, if nothing else.

He declined Geoffrey's offer for a nightcap in his study and climbed the carpeted stairs, tugging at his cravat as he pushed open the door of his bedroom.

"I thought perhaps you'd decided to forgo your bed in favor of someone else's."

He froze, his fingers still tangled in the knot of his cravat. Her voice had come from over his right shoulder—the corner, the armchair tucked there. He wondered if she'd moved the shirts and trouser he tended to toss there, or if she'd settled in right on top of them.

But he did not turn to look. He hardly trusted himself to keep his voice steady as he spoke.

"There is only one woman I wish to have in my bed."

He was met with silence.

"How did you get in?"

Her soft chuckle floated through the air, caressing him. How long had he waited to hear that sound again? Every minute had been worth it.

He turned to face her as she lifted the small brown leather roll he now knew she kept on her person at all times.

"I am an accomplished lockpick, if you recall." Her face was in shadow, but he could hear the warmth in her voice. Warmth just for him.

"It is rather difficult to forget." He allowed himself a step in her direction. "You have a penchant for showing up in the places I least expect."

Another step. She uncrossed her legs and lowered her hand. "Such as?"

"The stage at Covent Garden, for one. My bedroom," he said. His voice was husky. He made no attempt to hide it. He ached for her and wanted her to know.

"It sounds more like I am thorn in your shoe that will not go away."

He paused, a heartbeat away from reaching for her hand poised on the arm of the chair. The delicate fingers were trembling.

His burning loins insisted it was only her desire, a fierce counterpart to his own. But the forced bravado in her voice…

"What is it?" he asked.

"An unwanted thorn is what I always was."

David grabbed her hand, sinking to his knees before her. He pressed a kiss to the inside of her wrist.

"I want you more than I have ever wanted anything in my life," he said truthfully. He did not mean just in the bedroom. He wanted every part of Dominique—her kind heart, her beautiful soul.

She leaned forward into the light as the first tear fell.

David reached, but was too late to catch it. He brushed it away with his thumb, then the next and the next as they began to fall in rapid succession.

"What has happened? I assure you, there is no one else," he said, pressing a kiss to her wet cheek. She was hunched forward, so that even on his knees he was able to easily reach her face.

She shook her head, a lock of her hair coming loose as his fingers moved over her face. Her hair was damp—she'd been outside in the rain. Why? For how long? His mind raced with questions, but he bit them back.

"It isn't that, isn't you," she managed to get out.

"I do not know whether to be relieved or worried," David said.

Dominique's chuckle caught in a sob as her chest rose and fell shakily. "How do you manage to make me laugh even when my world is falling apart?"

David repressed the sigh that rose in his own chest. "I've done so before. I always will." The promise was no effort at all.

Her bottom lip quivered as she drew her gaze up to his. She clamped her teeth down upon its sweet fullness, trying no doubt to still it. But to no avail. It trembled even as she spoke:

"Amelia has come to London."

He ought to have known. Dominique had been nothing but confident and strong since they'd reunited. He ought to have known the one thing that could so ruthlessly bring her low—her family.

"Are Lord and Lady Wartham with her?" He hated to ask, but if they were in London, his meeting them socially was almost inevitable. He'd rather be prepared—and he could better protect Dominique if he knew all the pieces upon the game board.

"Lady Wartham is here," she said.

David tried not to tense, knowing it would be no use to Dominique if he could not control his own emotions. But even though he'd met Lady Wartham socially dozens of times in the last ten years, he had never forgiven her. She'd not only ruined Dominique's life, she'd ruined his. While he might have eventually forgiven the latter, he'd never forget the former.

"Lord Wartham… My father…" Dominique heaved a mighty sob, her head falling forward onto his shoulder. David caught her, cupping her head and holding her tight. "My father is dead."

Whatever he might have felt paled as she collapsed into his arms. David drew her tight against him, down to the floor so he could hold her properly. He gathered her into his lap, vaguely noting that her gown was as damp as her hair, that the water was bleeding into his own clothing as well. But he hardly felt it—had concern only for the woman in his arms, her shoulders racked with sobs.

He didn't need to ask her to know how deeply she was hurting. Her relationship with her father had been fraught—naturally. For the first two decades of his life, David had not even known Lord Wartham was her father. When she and her mother fled Winleigh, it had not been to get away from David and their wreckage of a courtship. It had been to escape the vicious gossip, the hateful stares... to escape the Wartham family. But Lord Wartham was still her father.

As he rubbed wide circles across her back, the memory of his own father and brother's loss flooded David's mind.

Sitting at the dining table with his mother, sipping tea and laughing over a biscuit. His mother asking him about his latest commission—he'd stopped working at the foundry a few years prior. Then the sharp knock at the door, the yelling. Running through the streets of Winleigh, smelling the smoke before he saw it, seeing the plumes of flames and knowing in his heart no one within that conflagration was coming out.

David's family had loved and supported one another fiercely, while Dominique's had torn her life asunder. But it did not make her pain any less valid. If anything, it made it more complicated and nuanced. David would miss his father and brother every day until his own death. But their love for one another had never been in question, and their memories were almost all pleasant ones. Dominique would never know such peace with her father.

When her sobs finally eased, turning to whimpers against his chest, David pressed a kiss to the shell of her ear.

"I am so sorry for your loss, Dominique."

She sniffled several times, still not lifting her head.

"Do you know how?" he asked gently.

"No," she said, a whisper against his chest.

"Would you like me to find out?"

She was quiet for several moments, making David wonder if he'd asked the wrong thing. But finally, she turned her head and rested her cheek against his shoulder so he could see her face. "Not yet."

He nodded, a shallow movement of his head so as not to disturb her. His legs were tensing from being in the same position for too long, but he refused to move. Instead he stroked her hair in slow, rhythmic movements.

"Did Amelia contact you?"

A slight shake of her head. "One of my"—she paused— "colleagues."

"I see." Not sure what else to ask but certain she needed him still, he continued his rhythmic caress, moving down to stroke her back.

"Amelia has never contacted me," Dominique said after a while. "I wrote to her after we came to London, telling her our address and asking her to write. We were so close when we were children. She was as upset by what her mother did as I was... or at least, I thought she was. But she never wrote me a single letter. Not even to tell me that our father had died."

It was not just the pain of her father's loss racking through her, David had realized from the start. But now another piece of the puzzle she'd so studiously kept to herself fit into place. Amelia had been a beloved sister—until that fateful day in Winleigh.

David had lost Dominique, the woman he loved and intended to marry.

But Dominique had lost so much more—her home, her sister, her father, and him.

He tightened his arms around her. "You will never suffer like that again. I will not allow it."

He thought she would protest. Even he did not know if that vow was truly within his power to give. But he did not take back the words. He never would.

Instead, she lifted her head and pressed a kiss to his cheek.

In an instant, his body seemed to realize who was pressed against him. It was Dominique's hip nestled against his manhood, hardening by the second. The damp fabric of her gown clung to her breasts, outlining every curve. Her nipples were hardened, straining against the fabric, begging to be suckled.

David turned his face to hers, and her mouth was there, her lips pressing against him. He groaned into her mouth as she slid her tongue between his lips. Shifting uncomfortably, he struggled to get his legs under him. He reached for the armchair to steady him, but Dominique began to uncurl.

"No," he said, swiftly catching her knees and swinging her up, so she was tight against his body. She did not protest, merely reached for his cheek and guided his mouth back to hers.

He crossed to the bed in three long strides, setting her on the edge with delicate precision. Dominique reached for him again, but David stepped backward, his body screaming in protest.

"You are soaked. You'll be shivering in a minute."

Dominique took a shaky breath. "Then perhaps you will warm me up."

The invitation could not have been clearer. David raked his hands through his hair. Through some inner strength he did not know he possessed until that very moment, he turned and strode to the armoire against the wall, tugging open a drawer and extracting a clean, dry shirt.

"Put this on," he said, tossing it to her.

Dominique caught it easily, but a frown marred her perfect face. "I do not understand."

"You are hurting," David said. He reached down and cupped her face, stroking a thumb over her cheek. She leaned into his touch, and he almost forgot his morals. "Let me comfort you tonight, Dominique. Tonight, that is enough."

She stared up at him, dark eyes widening then swelling with wetness that she blinked back. Then she nodded, her teeth clamped on that luscious lower lip once again.

David nodded sharply and withdrew. If he stayed a moment longer, his resolve would falter. He walked to the corner, pouring a bit of water from the ewer and splashing it on his face. Behind him, he heard Dominique undressing, the slap of the wet fabric of her gown and underthings as they hit the floor, then the swing as she slung them over the wooden chair at the dressing table. Finally, the creak of the bed as she sat back down.

He removed his own clothing, leaving his drawers and un-tucked linen shirt, then turned back to her.

It was a mistake.

She'd unpinned what remained of her coiffure, and her dark hair fell in thick locks over her shoulders. Even in his shirt, the outline of her breasts was visible; the open neckline gave a tantalizing peak of her golden skin beneath.

"Shit," David mumbled to himself, turning back to douse the candle beside the armoire. He carefully picked his way around the room, dousing candles as he went.

When he arrived back at the bed, the room was at least mostly shrouded in darkness.

"Are you going to get in?" Dominique's voice floated through the darkness, tinged with amusement.

He should be glad that even in her sadness, she managed some bit of joy. But it was doing little to quell his desire.

"Move over."

"Afraid to touch me?"

"Yes," he said with utter honesty.

Her laugh was audible this time, then through the darkness he felt her arm snake out and her hand close around his wrist.

"I will not bite you," she promised as she tugged him down. "Unless you think you might enjoy it."

David swallowed hard as he forced himself to lie back on the mattress. Dominique sank down beside him. He listened to her move, felt her turn her head on the pillow in his direction. She inhaled sharply as if to speak, but seemed to decide against it.

She did roll up onto her elbow, lean over, and press a soft kiss to his cheek.

"Thank you, David," she murmured, her breath warm against his skin, before she rolled back.

He was sorely regretting his declaration that he would not touch her when she was as vulnerable as this, when he felt her hand curl around his. She threaded her fingers between his, and he pulled them closer so their palms were pressed together.

The desire did not ebb, but inside his chest another sensation took root. It felt so very right, to lie in bed with her and hold her hand. The intimacy of it… Once he had taken it for granted—a promise that had been brutally ripped away.

As Dominique's breathing evened out and she slipped into sleep, David vowed to himself he would not take another moment with her for granted.

Chapter Nineteen

T HE RAIN HAD stopped.

That is my first thought upon waking?

She was on her side, David curled around her, nothing but a few sheets of linen separating the warmth of their bodies, and her first thought was an observation of the weather.

Being a trained spy had its drawbacks, it seemed. She could not stop her mind from racing through the implications. The heavy patter of the rain had covered any sounds of her sneaking into the townhouse; she would have to be more careful when she slipped out. However, she would not have to worry about leaving suspect puddles on the perfectly polished floors, assuming her clothes were sufficiently dry.

Her eyes flicked to the window, and she tried to judge the time from the amount of light slipping through the curtains. There was a grayish tinge to the pale curtains; dawn was not far off. Which meant her clothing had been drying for at least five hours. The muslin dried quickly, so she would not be wet as she snuck out.

Then David shifted, his leg coming forward and hooking around hers.

All thoughts of planning her egress disappeared from her mind.

His arm tightened around her waist, claiming her even in

sleep. Her shirt—his shirt—had ridden up while they slept, revealing her stomach and legs. And everything else.

His fingers spread over her stomach, his fingertips a hairsbreadth away from the tangle of dark curls between her legs. Dominique swallowed hard. How could he possibly be asleep?

But she listened to his breathing, even and low. She might be able to effectively feign sleep, but she doubted David could—at least not well enough to fool someone as well trained as she.

However, even in sleep he was seducing her. His breath tickled her neck, sending tantalizing shivers down her spine that had her wriggling against him. She felt him hardening, his manhood rising in a silent demand where it was nestled against her bum. She was supposed to be the experienced one... yet every move of David's body against hers loosened her control from its tightly held grip.

He shifted in his sleep, moving his hips so his cock slid along her bottom and nestled itself near her entrance. All it would take was an artful maneuver of her hips and he would slide inside her. She knew she was already dripping wet.

Dominique gave up trying to control the moan that ripped from her throat as he unconsciously teased her entrance. She reached for his head, rolling to her other side and taking his lips in one graceful movement.

She arched against him as he stirred from slumber, letting her breasts graze his chest. His cock scraped over her clit as she shifted her hips and cried out against him.

Good heavens, this was better. Or worse. This was heaven.

"Dominique," David mumbled, his voice hoarse from sleep.

"Hush," she murmured against him. There was no need for words now.

She wanted this with every fiber of her being—had wanted it for more than ten years. Once, she had been a naïve young woman on the cusp of adulthood, driven by her feelings and the need to discover everything at David's side. That possibility had been ripped away, but by some miracle she'd been gifted a second chance. She would not allow impossible promises or talk of the future into this moment. Here, safe in David's arms once again, she would just *be*.

"I do not know what I am doing," he whispered against her.

"Then allow me," she said. She nudged his shoulder until he was on his back before swinging her leg over and straddling him.

His eyes snapped open, his irises a sea blue in the predawn light filtering through the curtains. Dominique bit her lower lip to keep from chuckling at the widened surprise in those lovely eyes. She would never forget how they looked in that exact moment.

Bracing one hand on each of his shoulders, she leaned down and kissed him, sliding her tongue past his impossibly soft lips and drawing his tongue into a dance around hers. She felt him begin to relax almost instantly.

She hummed against David, letting the sensation ripple through him. She had settled herself just below his cock, could feel it demanding and pushing up against the curls of her quim. As her tongue circled his, her hips mirrored the motion. David thrust up against her eagerly. This time, she was unable to contain the laugh that bubbled up into her throat.

She drew back just far enough to be able to look into his eyes, close enough that they still shared breath. "All in good time, my love," she purred as she slid down his body.

Dominique began with a kiss at his collarbone, followed by the gentle scrape of her teeth. David sucked in a breath, his hand curling tightly in the bedsheets. She flicked her tongue over the place her teeth had marked. From the corner of her eye, she watched him lift his hand, as if to reach for her, then fall back to the bed, uncertain.

"Touch me," she said, a gentle command.

David needed no more encouragement. He caught her shoulder, stroking up her arm. But he was immediately frustrated—there was still the linen of her shirt between them. Not to mention hers.

"Take it off," he demanded in return, tugging at the shirt.

Dominique pursed her lips as she slowly sat up. Her fingers caught the hem of the shirt and dragged it up over her head in one fluid motion. Dropping it onto the bed behind her, she stretched her arms over her head, watching David through heavy-lidded eyes as her large breasts lifted and moved with her arms.

He reached for her, but Dominique shook her head. "Yours too."

With a half-cocked smile, David sat up and tugged his own shirt over his head, tossing it to the floor. Now he was inches away from her, his mouth within easy claiming distance. But his eyes dropped to her breasts, the quivering tips of her nipples a tight, dark pink, begging for attention.

"You told me to touch you," David murmured with a grin.

She sucked in a ragged breath as he cupped her breasts and took one nipple into his mouth. The whimpers that followed were utterly beyond her control.

Inexperienced he may be, but he was earnest and thorough. His tongue circled her pert nipple until she thought she might die, might have to demand him to suckle. But then he flicked his tongue over the peak and sucked it into his mouth, the slightest graze of his teeth sending her over the edge. He was copying the caress of her tongue on his throat. He may be inexperienced, but he was learning fast.

Most importantly, he was David. No other man could compare, because she'd never wanted another man as deeply as she needed and wanted him.

He kissed a scorching trail to her other breast, repeating the tantalizing twirl of his tongue. She was shivering uncontrollably, each swipe of his tongue sending another delightful wave of sensation through her body.

"I am meant to be seducing you," she said as he took her nipple between his teeth.

"You're making a fabulous job of it," David said, blowing a hot breath across her wet nipple, yet another sensation that sent a shiver through her body.

She grabbed his shoulder and pushed him back, narrowing her eyes as she did. "Stop making me laugh," she ordered him.

"I make no promises," he said, grin wide.

Dominique slid her hand down his chest, resisting the urge to stop and caress his tightly peaked nipples with the same attention he'd given to hers. But she dragged her nails over his abdomen and down the tantalizing V of his hipbones.

She watched with satisfaction as David realized her intention.

She was determined to have him moaning.

DOMINIQUE THOUGHT HE'D taken control?

No.

Oh, no, no, no, no.

When she slid down his body, licking that luscious lower lip of hers, with only one possible destination… control was the furthest thing from his mind.

He belonged to her, body and soul.

He would do whatever she wanted. Let *her* do whatever she wanted to him.

Dominique flicked her gaze up to him as her hand curled around the base of his cock, a slow smile spreading over her face. When she closed her mouth over him, David fell back on the pillows, all ability for coherent thought gone.

She kissed up and down his length with featherlight touches at first, teasing him. He tried to keep himself from thrusting up into her, but he couldn't resist. His body was making demands at a rate his mind had no hope of keeping pace with.

Dominique's low chuckle reverberated over him. "Eager, are we?"

"Who's the one laughing now?" he asked.

"Always me," Dominique said, voice as husky as his.

Then she lowered her head back to his cock, this time taking him fully into her mouth and stroking up with her hand at the same time that she sucked him inside of her. David nearly came off the bed, the pleasure was so intense. She repeated the motion, once, twice.

Christ almighty, he was going to—

"Dominique," he warned desperately.

Her head popped up, dark eyes round with mock innocence.

"Get up here," he demanded, curling his fingers in her hair and gently tugging.

Dominique sucked her lower lip into her mouth, surely knowing it would remind him of where that mouth had been sucking moments before, but she did move until her hips were fitted over his and their mouths joined once again.

David cupped the back of her head, holding her in place so he could devour her mouth with all the desire and need that had been building inside of him for the last ten minutes—the last ten years, really. But when she began to move her hips, maneuvering him toward her hot center, he caught her waist with his hand.

"My turn," he breathed against her lips.

Dominique frowned, confusion furrowing her brow.

He slid the hand that was tangled in her hair down to join the one at her waist. Then with gentle but demanding pressure, he urged her hips upward over his chest. David could sense the moment she realized what he was about—she swallowed audibly, her hips pausing for just a fraction of a second. But he did not stop, urging her forward until her knees were planted on either side of his head and she had to reach up to hold the headboard in order to keep her balance.

"David," she murmured above him. Whether it was an entreaty or a benediction, he did not know. But he slid his hands lower to cup her full bottom and ease her down until he could feel the heat of her pulsing core quivering above his face.

He massaged the soft mounds of her bottom, stroking them with increasing pressure, and then pulled her down the rest of the way.

He delved his tongue into her center, one tentative touch to begin.

She tasted amazing.

Like spices and honey, warm and sweet at the same time—and he could not get enough of her.

He dragged his tongue down her center, from the apex of her dark curls to where her quivering channel welcomed him in. His cock jerked as he drove his tongue into the tunnel of warmth, and her wetness coated his tongue and mouth, soon the entire lower half of his face. He could not get enough of her fast enough. He returned to the top of her slit, inhaling the scent of her, nose buried in the soft curls. He flicked his tongue back and forth, not really knowing what he was doing but knowing that he wanted to explore every part of her.

His tongue flicked over a hardened, rounded nub—

Dominique's moan ripped from her throat, low and nearly feral.

Oh.

He did it again, and she nearly bucked off his face.

"David," she moaned as he licked over the tender bundle of nerves again and again. This time when she said his name, it was a prayer.

He paused in his sensuous assault long enough to murmur: "Who is in control now, darling?"

Dominique did not laugh. She ground her cunny down on his mouth, the rock of her hips begging for his tongue. David found her tender nub again and continued his rhythmic onslaught. The urgency of her hips increased—she was close, he could tell. Christ, so was he. He fought the urge to reach down and stroke his cock, knowing that more than anything he needed to be buried inside of her. But first she would reach her completion.

Her breath came in sharp pants, in time with the lashing of his tongue and the thrust of her hips. He skimmed his hand down her bum, but instead of moving down toward his cock, he slid a finger inside of her.

She exploded over him in a wave of wetness, her keening cry

echoing through his ears as she rode his face through her waves of pleasure. When she finally slowed, he eased her hips down, needing to kiss her. Dominique trembled against him, but allowed him to move her body until they were stretched against one another. She did not flinch away when he claimed her mouth, twirling her tongue with his own. Dominique seemed to enjoy the taste of herself on his tongue.

Then she broke away, her dark eyes capturing his. She did not need to speak to make her demand known. She rolled onto her back, and David moved on top of her, their movements as graceful as any dance.

He held her gaze as he slid inside of her, memorizing the flutter of her eyelids as he fully sheathed himself, every inch of him surrounded by her sweet cunny. Her breath hitched in her throat when he started to move inside of her. David was not sure he was breathing at all.

Dominique slid her hands down over his shoulders to grip his hips. The pleasure was building fast, much faster than he'd expected. He tried to slow himself, but she held firm on his hips. He searched her eyes, words beyond him, but trying to tell her. The gentle curve of her lips and insistent pressure of her hands was his answer.

He exploded inside of her—and by some miracle, a moment later she threw her head back and joined him, her pussy gripping his cock in enthralling spasms of pleasure as her climax took her as well.

When he was fully spent, he rolled back to the bed, Dominique moving with him. She pressed her forehead into his chest. David was sure she could hear the thundering of his heartbeat. It said everything that was needed between them. He stroked her hair, curling it around his fingers and then stroking her back as well.

As the dawn began to peek through the curtains, they both fell into a deep, satisfied sleep.

CHAPTER TWENTY

1807
10 years ago
Wartham Grange, Hampshire

S HE'D MADE THIS walk dozens of times in her seventeen years,
but this felt the longest. Her cloak was tight around her, but
she'd forgotten gloves in her haste. Bella had just left for the
afternoon when the summons arrived. Her mother was visiting
Mrs. Quill—one of the few villagers who had not spurned them
entirely. Dominique had to leave immediately.

This was not a journey she would subject her mother to.

The gates of Wartham Grange stood open, welcoming
guests.

But Dominique was not a guest here. She was an interloper,
and always had been. The foolishness had been hers, in thinking
anything different.

Every step up the long drive was heavy, her feet leaden despite the frost-hardened ground. She was surprised it had taken
this long, really. Five endless days of silence had stretched
between Joseph Bolton's declaration in the town square and the
summons from her father.

She had spent most of them staring at the wall in her room
and stabbing crochet needles together, imagining Lady Wartham

on the sharp ends of the hooks.

Dominique was known for her kindness, but even she had her limits.

The front door of Wartham Grange swung open before she could lift her shivering hand to knock; she was expected. The butler led her through the entry hall to the front parlor, a room she'd seen a hundred times, where community teas were held and newcomers welcomed. A room for guests, not for family.

How appropriate.

"May I take your cloak, Miss Beauchamp?" the butler asked as they paused before the parlor threshold.

Dominique surveyed the room. Her father stood beside the fireplace, straight as a board. Lady Wartham sat on the settee, her face set in hard lines. Amelia was nowhere to be seen.

"That is not necessary. I doubt I will be here long," she said.

The butler cringed. Dominique did not have the mental fortitude to regret her harsh words. She squared her shoulders and faced the room's occupants.

"You summoned me."

Lady Wartham sniffed. "Typical. She cannot even show the proper respect when invited among her betters."

"When I am among my betters, I shall remember the requisite respect."

Lady Wartham shot to her feet.

"Dominique," her father said, stepping toward her. He caught his wife on the shoulder and pushed her back down to the settee.

"Father," she said, her nails biting into her skin. "How could you allow this?"

"It was an accident—"

"An accident?" Dominique nearly choked. "Lady Wartham has resented my existence from the moment my mother and I arrived in Winleigh. This was no accident. She wanted to humiliate me—us."

Her accusation rang in the air. She expected them to refute it—for her father to take her hand and tell her it was indeed an accident, to apologize; for Lady Wartham to force the false words past her tight, puckered lips. She expected them to at least attempt it.

But instead her father stared at her in silence.

The smirk on Lady Wartham's face deepened by the moment.

Gathering the tattered shreds of her pride, Dominique thrust out her chin and looked directly into Lady Wartham's smug face. "You have succeeded in humiliating my mother and me before the village. But Mr. Grisham—"

"Ha!" Lady Wartham's sharp laugh cut through the leaden air. "You foolish, idiotic girl. You think young Mr. Grisham will honor your courtship? What sweet nothings has he whispered in your ear, what childish promises? Have you given him your maidenhead as well?"

Dominique wished she had something to throw at the vile woman.

"Madam, you are out of order—" Her father stepped forward, but Lady Wartham brushed past him.

"Mr. and Mrs. Grisham will not allow your disgrace to dishonor their family. Your courtship is at an end, child. It should never have begun. You are not worthy—of their family or of ours."

"Mother!"

Amelia bounded into the room, her governess on her tail. Her pale skin was flushed, cheeks burning brightly and tears already streaming down her face as she grabbed her elder sister's hand tight.

"Daughter, this is a conversation for adults," their father said. He fixed Amelia with a stern look.

Dominique's heart broke a little more.

Adults. He considered her an adult—all of seventeen years old, with only the protection he would choose to offer. It was an excuse. If she were an adult, he could excuse his choices, his failure to protect her. If she were an adult, she was not his responsibility.

Though he'd provided for her financially, she never really had been.

"This is my family as well," Amelia said stubbornly, literally digging her heels into the carpet.

"We are a family," Lady Wartham said. She grabbed her daughter's hand and wrenched violently. Amelia cried out in pain, not expecting the sudden gesture. She let go of Dominique's hand.

Dominique counted each frantic beat of her heart as she stared across the room at the trio—the father she'd always begged for love, the stepmother who could not understand the meaning of the word, and the dear sister who had always given it so freely.

"*We* are a family."

Regret twisted Dominique's stomach.

But she could not deny the relief that flooded through her veins as her mother stepped into the parlor and wrapped her arm around her waist, pulling her close.

"*This*"—Collette Beauchamp nodded toward the trio—"this is pain and disappointment. I regret that I did not see it sooner, so that I may have spared my daughter."

"You are not welcome in my home," Lady Wartham said, voice shaking with rage. Beside her, arm still clasped in her mother's grasp, Amelia whimpered.

"Nor have I ever had any desire to be," Collette said, her voice calm despite the anger that thrummed through her body. Dominique did not see her mother express the emotion often, but always it was just like this: quiet, devastating rage.

"Take your bastard and get out."

"Wife! That is—"

"Mother, how could you—"

"We all know—"

Fresh tears sprang to Dominique's eyes, but no one saw them. Her mother spun her and caught her opposite hand, leading her out.

"Maman, we must—"

"No. We owe them nothing, Dominique. It was my mistake to think we ever did. I should never have brought you *here*."

The ominous emphasis on that last word made her heart quiver. "What do you mean?"

"I am sorry for Amelia. I truly am. I know how much you care for one another."

Her mother did not wait for the butler, who scrambled behind them. She threw open the door of Wartham Grange herself and started down the drive, holding Dominique tightly at her side.

Dominique did not protest; her mind was a muddled mess. She could hardly make sense of what was happening moment by moment.

"Amelia? Why should you apologize about Amelia?" she mumbled.

"Because we are leaving, Dominique. We are leaving Winleigh."

CHAPTER TWENTY-ONE

1817
Present Day

WHEN SHE WOKE for the second time, there was no doubt that morning was upon them. Miraculously, the dreary springtime rain of the day before had given way to brilliant sunshine that slipped around the edges of the heavy curtains and proclaimed the day.

Dominique allowed herself two whole minutes of luxuriating in David's arms. Already, sneaking out would be near impossible. But it would not be made any more impossible by those two minutes.

While they slept, he'd rolled to his back, and she was now nestled against his chest, his arm curled around her. She could still hear the heavy beat of his heart, the same sound that had echoed through her ears in the aftermath of their lovemaking and lulled her to sleep.

She counted the beats, marveling that there was nothing between them but feeling and pleasure. Not a stitch of clothing. Not a hint of regret, nor the looming specter of their pasts—

But the future, the now… that came crashing down upon her with the force of a tidal wave.

It was still early morning. But come the evening she would be expected to report to her dressing room at Covent Garden, smear rouge on her face, and take the stage. D'Terre would be in the audience, waiting for a private audience with her, which she'd worked hard to make him believe he was entitled to.

He might be entitled to the actress she pretended to be, but he had no claim on her heart.

That, despite all efforts she'd made to the contrary, belonged to David.

Did you really try to stop it? a quiet voice that sounded eerily like Jane's whispered from the recesses of her mind.

No, she had not.

When David reappeared in her life, she ought to have given him a polite smile followed immediately by a firm dismissal. Instead, she'd invited him into her quest. When he'd kissed her, she ought to have requested they keep their relationship professional. Instead, she'd leaned into that kiss, and all the ones that followed.

Because she wanted this. She wanted him, as much as she ever had.

After a night spent in his arms, she had more questions than answers. What did this mean for her future? Not much had really changed… if anything, time had only complicated their circumstances. She was a lady knight, taking on dangerous and secretive quests on the order of Her Majesty the Queen. David was set to inherit an earldom. A marriage between them…

She shoved the thought away. This moment was too sweet; she would not ruin it. Not yet.

But one answer had become stunningly clear, and it was with that firmly in her mind that she eased herself from his arm and crawled across the bed to where her dress and underthings were hanging.

David rolled to his side with a sleepy sigh. "Where are you off to?" he mumbled.

She tugged her shift over her head and began lacing her stays, granting him a glance over her shoulder. Seeing him lying in bed, golden hair falling over his brow, she was sorely tempted to dismiss all good sense and clamber back in with him.

"To sneak out while I still have a chance of it," she said, reaching for her gown.

"Do you need me to provide some sort of distraction?" He waggled his eyebrows suggestively.

Shaking her head, she finished quickly plaiting her hair and fixing the end with a ribbon from the pocket of her gown. A lady knight was always prepared, after all.

She perched on the bed and leaned across, pressing a soft but thorough kiss to his deliciously lush lips. "You have already provided *quite* the distraction."

He smiled against her mouth at the same time that a low groan rumbled from his throat. She thought he would catch her arm, beg her to stay, but when she pulled away, he rolled onto his back and tucked both hands behind his head, watching her with a look of pure male satisfaction.

"When will I see you again?"

Her stomach flipped delicately within her. "I will send word."

"I will do my best to wait."

"You shall have to wait," she said, shaking her head. She contemplated one more kiss, but decided she did not possess that sort of fortitude. "I have something rather important to manage today."

David sat up instantly. "Dangerous?"

She waved her hand. "Not for me," she said. "If I can sneak out of your cousin's house in the busiest part of the day, I can get in anywhere."

"You have not managed it yet," David pointed out, though his grin had returned as she padded to the door.

She blew him a kiss over her shoulder as she eased the door open. "Watch me."

His soft chuckle followed her out into the hall. She carefully made her way out of the townhouse, deftly avoiding servants until she reached the window at the end of the next corridor, then scurrying down the trellis that led into the garden. She'd left the window unlocked for herself last night, before she went into David's room to wait for him.

But when her feet hit the ground and she began to weave her way through the alleyways, her thoughts slipped away from David. She'd stop off at her flat long enough to change into the maid's outfit that had served her so well the last two times she'd snuck into D'Terre's house, as well as one of the reproductions David had made for her.

She needed time to study one of the originals. Perhaps there was something they had missed when making the copies. Whatever this secret message embedded in the drawings was, it was time to decode it.

Because although nothing in her mind was settled regarding David, one thing was clear: she needed to finish this quest and get the hell away from D'Terre now—before her heart broke in two.

Chapter Twenty-Two

WHHHEEEEEEEEEEEEEEEEEEEEEEE!

Dominique jerked, the demanding whistle of the teakettle snapping her to attention.

She shoved aside the drawings spread before her, hurrying to the hearth. Mr. Pritchett in the flat above hers was particularly irritable, and judging by the steam swirling around her, the kettle had been calling for some time. Like clockwork, she was rewarded with three loud stomps above her head.

"I apologize, Mr. Pritchett!" she yelled, knowing there was no chance of obtaining his forgiveness.

She grabbed a cloth and fetched the kettle from the heat, before pouring the water into the dainty pink and white teapot her mother had gifted her when she moved to her own flat three years before. She left the tea to steep, then drifted back toward the desk where she had the drawings laid out.

Crossing her arms over her chest, Dominique considered them for what must have been the hundredth time. There were four in total—she'd taken two each time, David had created a reproduction, then she'd snuck back into D'Terre's townhouse to return the originals.

Convinced they must have missed something in the originals, she'd snuck back into his home this morning—while he was at his club, as was his habit—and swapped two of the reproductions for the original drawings. So, she had two fakes and two authentic drawings. All executed in charcoal. All bearing depictions of different London buildings. That much, at least, she'd been able to deduce.

But what did the four buildings all have in common?

Nothing, so far as she could see. The architect? No. Carlton House was designed by Henry Holland, while the Royal Academy was the provenance of Chambers. Ownership? Carlton House was a Crown possession, while the Temple of the Muses was privately owned. Perhaps it was not the buildings that were meaningful, but the drawings themselves. She counted pillars, trees, clouds, hoping for a pattern to emerge. But none of it amounted to anything.

She rolled her shoulders, hoping to reduce the strain that had built there over the last few hours of fruitless staring. When that failed, she returned to her teapot.

But she froze with her hand an inch above the handle.

Footsteps.

The fifth step from the top of the landing always creaked—she'd wrenched at the board herself upon taking up residence here. She needed a quick tell that someone was approaching her door.

Mr. Pritchett was already in his flat; his son did not visit until Sunday morning. The flat above him was occupied by old Mrs. Fletch, too aged to make the climb up or down without assistance.

She had seconds before the footsteps reached her landing. Dominique used them wisely, swiping the knife she kept behind the books on the mantel and tucking herself into the corner between the hearth and the window. When the stranger stepped through her door, she'd be able to—

Knock! Knock!

A pause.

Knock, knock, knock.

Dominique frowned. The raps were rhythmic, musical almost. Not demanding in the least. In fact, the happy cadence of it reminded her of—

"Miss Beauchamp, are you at home?"

Dominique tucked the knife under her arm as she flicked open the latches and swung open the door.

"I told you I would send word," she said, lips pursed in disapproval.

David merely grinned. "I could not wait," he said.

Shaking her head, she moved aside so he could enter and latch the door behind him.

"How did you know I was here?" she asked, setting down her knife so she could fetch a second teacup.

"Dominique, why were you holding a knife?"

"Because I heard unexpected footsteps outside of my door," she said with complete matter-of-factness. Only when she turned to pour the tea did she realize the horror upon his face. She bit her lower lip to keep from laughing—an action she'd repeated so often since David reentered her life that it was a miracle she hadn't chewed through it completely.

"I am trained to do more than pick locks and steal drawings," she said, motioning over his shoulder to where the sketches were laid out.

David followed her hand, but his gaze went back to hers immediately. "Do you often have cause to use knives to defend yourself?" he asked, his voice hoarse.

Dominique could not stand the worry in his eyes—it was why she'd never told her mother about her work as a lady knight. Of course, the inherent secrecy required was the other reason.

"I have in the past," she said evenly, looking at the tea she was pouring instead of at him. "I am also a decent marksman and can hold my own with a rapier, though it's not my preferred weapon. I also know how to be lethal with my bare hands."

She heard him swallow, but she did not look up. She prepared their tea, stirring cream into hers and a bit of sugar into his.

When she raised the teacup to offer it to him, she met his

eyes. "Does it bother you?"

David's handsome face was set with worry, the lines between his eyes deep enough she could have slipped a coin between them. "I do not want you to be hurt."

Dominique sipped her tea. "I have been injured in the course of my work. But never seriously." There was no use in lying to him. She was proud of what she'd accomplished as a lady knight.

He opened and closed his mouth, clearly struggling with what to say next. She held his gaze. No matter what was between them, the feelings that she'd allowed to grow against her better judgment—if he asked her to walk away from the Lady Knights, it would be over. She would not—could not—surrender that part of herself.

"Have you…" He paused, gripping the teacup so hard she thought it might shatter. "Have you ever killed someone?"

Dominique set her teacup down in front of her. "Only someone who was trying to kill me."

She held his gaze, letting him search her eyes. He would find no hint of regret and no fear. She had taken a life—two, to be precise. Though it had haunted her the first time, she'd made peace with it. As a lady knight, her quests could be dangerous. If she had not protected herself, she would not be alive to stand and have this gut-wrenching conversation.

David cleared his throat, swallowed, and blew out a long breath. He'd made his decision. Dominique braced her hand against the edge of the worktable.

"I am thankful you have the skills to defend yourself."

Dominique inclined her head in acknowledgment.

David shook his head slightly. "The things you put me through, woman," he said under his breath as he took his tea and turned to where the drawings were laid out in a perfect grid.

He paused, cocking his head to the side. "When did you retrieve the originals?"

Frowning, Dominique came to stand beside him. "How did you know?"

It was his turn to shoot her a reproving glance. "I recognize my own work well enough." He nudged her with his hip.

Dominique couldn't help the blush that climbed her cheeks in response—which only deepened when the hand that did not hold his teacup snaked down to curl around her waist and stroke circles on the small of her back.

She swallowed and tried to focus on the set of drawings. "This morning, after I left you. I wanted to have another look at the originals, to see there was something we might have missed."

David's golden eyebrows rose. "Doubting my abilities now, are you?"

It was her turn to nudge him. "Doubting my own," she said. "I know these must be meaningful. There's no other reason to include them with the letters to the other members of Parliament. The most obvious thought would be a code, but I've tried every combination I can think of." As she spoke, she opened the top desk drawer and pulled out the copies she'd made of the four letters that corresponded to each drawing.

"Well versed on secret codes as well," David said wryly.

But Dominique hardly heard him. "Of course," she murmured.

She reached for the edge of the desk, wresting the entire piece away from the wall and rotating it one hundred and eighty degrees, so she was looking at the drawings upside down. They both stared for several long minutes. But still... nothing.

"Carlton House, the Royal Academy, the Temple of the Muses, the Royal Opera House..." she mumbled.

David's head snapped up.

She turned to him immediately, her heart leaping with anticipation—what had he found?

"Why weren't you at the Theatre Royal this evening?"

Dominique rocked back on her heels, both at her disappointment he'd not solved the code, but also at the need for an explanation she wasn't ready to make.

"I begged off sick," she said. "I supposed it would endear me more to Cora, to have a prime performance night. It is always useful to have someone owe you a favor. Besides, I want to solve this." *And I could not stand the possibility of having to kiss D'Terre when I'd spent the night in your bed.*

"I bought a ticket," David said.

Dominique chuckled. "Why?"

"I wanted to be near you, to see you. Even if we could not speak, even if you were working."

She kept her eyes firmly fixed on the drawings, afraid to meet his gaze and what she might find there. The emotions swirling inside her chest were enough; if she saw what she suspected of shining in his eyes...

David cleared his throat and took another long draw of tea, covering any awkwardness. "When I saw Cora on stage, I excused myself and came here."

"I see."

His hand on her back was practically a brand, one that she never wanted to go away. His words fueled the flame they'd lit the night before. When Dominique turned into his arms, there was only one outcome.

They discarded their tea on the table, and Dominique had just enough presence of mind to tug him away before their desire for each other caused them to upend the drinks over the painstakingly obtained and created drawings.

David did not appear to notice. His hands were too busy roaming her body, his mouth fixed on her throat. He sucked and licked at the place where her pulse pounded erratically, urging it to dance with him. Meanwhile, his hands...

Oh, heavens, his hands.

They roamed up and down her back, bracketing her shoulders so her breasts were pressed against him, then sliding down her back again. He cupped her bottom and, with the slightest pressure, lifted her to his waist. Dominique tugged ruthlessly at the skirt of her gown, hiking it above her knees so she could wrap her legs around him.

Yes, there was the hard length of him, pressing at her through her skirts. Bracing one hand on his shoulder, she burrowed the other beneath his tailcoat, determined to dislodge it from his shoulders. When he put her on the bed, she'd lean up and strip him bare…

Except he did not take her to the bed. He took her to the dressing writing desk pressed against the wall. He sat her on the edge, and she immediately ached for his touch. But he was gone only a moment, long enough to shrug off his tailcoat and the waistcoat beneath. He reached for her, but Dominique fisted her hands in the silk of his shirt, demanding that be removed as well.

Only when he was bare-chested before her did satisfaction sizzle through her. She watched her own fingers spread across his broad chest, still not able to match the breadth of him. His muscles were taut beneath her fingers, and his nipples pebbled at her touch.

Glancing up at him, she grinned wickedly at his pained expression. He sank his hands into her hair, but did not stop her when she lowered her mouth and flicked her tongue over one tight bud.

"Dominique," he groaned, low and needy.

She laughed against his chest, reveling in the way his muscles tightened beneath the breathy caress. "What do you want?" she teased, lacing her fingers behind his head and drawing his face down to hers.

"I want you to hear you crying my name, just as I've imagined it all these years," David said before taking her mouth once again.

His assault was thorough, timed with the thrust of his hips and the push of his hands. She wore a simple white muslin dress and an even simpler shift beneath. It was the work of a moment beneath his artist's hands and she was bare beneath him.

He paused a moment above her, simply admiring her. The sight of him watching her was enough to steal his breath.

"David," she whispered.

His eyes cleared, meeting hers. "A little breathier," he instructed her with grin that told her he would make good on that desire of his.

He caught her shoulder and tipped her back, bracing her hand behind her on the desk. She was on full display to him, her breasts peaked and begging for his touch. Between her legs, he slowly began to circle his hips, teasing her hot center with this rigid cock, still confined in his trousers. She reached for him, but he knocked her hand back, positioning it behind her with the other.

Their eyes met again, and Dominique understood. He intended to feast upon her, and she was meant to sit back and enjoy it. And she would... but there was no way she would be able to keep from touching him.

She proved it when his lips went around her nipple and one hand flew to his hair, holding him close. He circled and licked, sucking the sensitive nub into his mouth.

"Harder," she panted.

His teeth grazed her nipple, and she arched off the desk, grinding her hips against him. His deep chuckle of satisfaction reverberated between them. His next pass was firmer still, a sharp suck followed by a delectable nibble that had Dominique reaching for his trousers.

She needed him inside of her. Now.

"What do you want?" he asked her as she tugged with the buttons.

She curled her fingers around his cock, which was hard as steel and so thick she could hardly get around it, as she purred: "David."

He wasted no time, taking his cock from her and nudging at her entrance. "Tell me again."

"David," she moaned, thrusting her hips forward. But his other hand was at her waist, holding her in place. "David, please," she cried. "Please, David, I need you now."

His groan of satisfaction matched hers as he shoved inside of her and sheathed himself to the hilt in one thrust.

She nearly came right then from the fullness of him. But he began to move, slowly pulling back and then driving back inside of her. The discovery of one another's bodies was replaced by an urgent fire to be together as closely and as quickly as possible.

Dominique sat up as much as she could, grabbing his shoulder for leverage so she could kiss and suck on his shoulder. The pressure was building, her climax coming. She bit down on his skin, ripping a cry from his mouth that was nearly feral.

"Christ, Dominique," David groaned, his pace increasing.

She slid her hand to where their bodies were joined, desperate to come with him. But he was a beat ahead of her; his fingers swirled around the bundle of nerves at the apex of her legs before she could reach it. He stroked and circled in time with his thrusts, increasing the pressure and the speed until her groans matched the intensity of his.

"David, I—"

But the words were lost. She cried his name again and again as each wave of her climax poured over her. A half-second later, she felt the wave that rocked through David's entire body as he emptied himself within her, coming as hard as she had moments before.

He'd asked her what she wanted—from him, from them? The answer was startlingly clear and complex in her mind as she collapsed into his arms: *David, David, David.*

⟫⟩⟩⟨⟨⟨

"Is your cousin expecting you?" Dominique asked quietly. She drew swirls across his chest with her index finger as their breathing slowly returned to normal, now curled together in the bed.

"I left word that I would be out late," David said.

He debated whether to tell her the rest, but decided that with as far as they'd come, there was no room for secrets between them. Not if they were to have the future he was dreaming of nightly.

"He knows that there is a lady in my life," he continued slowly. Dominique stiffened. David drew her closer, pressing a kiss to her hair, praying she would not retreat. "That is all he knows, my love. I promise you."

Slowly, ever so slowly, she relaxed again. Only when her fingers had resumed their ministrations on his chest, this time tapping out a beat that might have been a song for the pianoforte, did he speak again.

"Geoffrey will not be concerned if I do not return this evening," he said.

He could hear Dominique worrying her bottom lip—that lush bottom lip that was the fixation of so many of his fantasies.

"Will you stay?"

Joy surged through his chest. *Yes, my love. Tonight and every night.*

But instead, he tugged her tighter and kissed her forehead. "Of course," he murmured.

Only then did the rhythm of her fingers on his chest stop and she truly relaxed into him.

CHAPTER TWENTY-THREE

Even in sleep she was irresistible.

He'd lost all feeling in his arm, but he'd gladly sacrifice the limb for every second he spent with Dominique stretched against him, peaceful in sleep. He watched her face, the steady rise and fall of her chest, thinking how few peaceful moments her life had afforded her.

From the time she'd been a small child, she'd lived with the knowledge that her status was different. She'd been marked—a feeling that could only have intensified when she and her mother settled in Winleigh.

David remembered clearly the first time he laid eyes upon her. He'd been a cheeky lad of ten, playing cricket on the town green with his elder brother and a smattering of other local boys. She'd emerged from the bakery on her mother's arm, dressed in periwinkle, dark hair swallowing the gray autumn light.

All of seven years old and she had stolen his breath. He was much too young for feelings of attraction, but something in his soul knew she was different. She'd turned her sunny smile upon him and he was lost. They'd been fast friends after that. Until the evening in her father's orangery at Wartham Grange, where friendship had turned to something headier.

It had taken ten more years, but by some miracle he once again held her in his arms. This time, he would not let her go.

But how would he convince Dominique of the fact?

She had feelings for him—intense ones that matched his own, he suspected. But whereas he could easily admit to himself that he was deeply in love with Dominique Beauchamp, he doubted the admission would come as easily for her. Unsurprising—she had so much at stake. She was a lady knight, a profession she'd built on her own intelligence and determination. She would protect her mother at all costs... and perhaps that was the more challenging proposition to overcome. If she believed that marrying him and becoming his countess would put her mother into any type of danger of pain or humiliation, she would not do it.

With the hand that was not pinned, David reached over and stroked the hair away from her face so he could see it more clearly. He admired the high cheekbones, their delicate exoticism that hinted at her Gallic heritage. The crisp white sheet beneath her cheek highlighted the warm olive of her skin, several shades darker than was fashionable among the debutantes he'd been forced to chat with night after night.

Would their children have his ruddy complexion and golden hair, or would they take after her, thoughtful and dark? They'd name them for their family—her mother, his brother or father—the ones who'd loved them and given so much.

He could see their entire future unfurling before his eyes with every breath she took. Now he had only to convince her to take his hand as they reached for it.

Unable to resist, he reached for where her hand rested upon the sheet, intent upon linking their fingers together. It was all he could manage for the moment, but he would let it be enough for now.

But before he could grasp her hand, a creak sounded outside the quiet flat.

In one swift motion, Dominique rolled away, swiping her hand underneath her pillow as she moved. It happened so quickly that David had to blink several times to convince himself he was not having a dream—or a nightmare.

No, it was real.

Dominique stood before him, completely nude, with a knife gripped in her hand and a challenge upon her face. She looked like a goddamned warrior goddess. If he wasn't so surprised, he'd be aroused.

No, he was aroused.

"You sleep with a knife below your pillow?" he managed to choke out, pulling himself upright.

But Dominique was already halfway across the flat, pulling on a wrapper as she went. "Hush," she commanded in a whisper. "There is someone in the hall."

David rolled to his feet, searching around for his trousers while Dominique edged closed to the door, eyes intent as she cocked her head to listen.

It was not as if she was the only occupant of the building. But David kept that thought to himself as he pulled his shirt over his head and stalked across the flat after Dominique. He pressed his hand to his mouth to try to muffle the cough in his scratchy throat, but judging by the daggers in Dominique's eyes when she looked back at him, he did not do as well as he thought.

A sharp, succinct succession of three knocks rang out on the door.

Dominique sagged visibly, a sigh slipping from her throat. She paused long enough to stash the knife in the drawer of her desk before unlatching and opening the door.

"Good morning, Maman," she said.

"Were you still abed, *ma fille?*" Collette Beauchamp said, disbelief and a hint of admonishment in her voice as she leaned forward and kissed each of her daughter's cheeks.

"Maman, I—"

"You have a guest." Her mother stilled, cheek mere inches from her daughters. Her brows gathered as she peered at him, then recognition filled her dark eyes. "Young Mr. Grisham."

Ridiculous as the situation was, being that he was only half-clothed, David bowed.

Dominique cringed, trying to catch her mother's arm. "Maman, allow me to explain—"

"I do not think there is much to explain. I think I understand things perfectly." The reproach in her voice had disappeared, replaced by something else. It had deepened by an octave, and her brow furrowed as she stepped around her daughter to get a better look at him.

The years had been kind to Collette Beauchamp, even if the world had not. She moved with the same grace and poise as her daughter, sported the same thick, dark hair and olive skin. There were a few strands of gray at her temples, but it only added an air of elegance and mystery to her smoky, dark eyes.

"It is a pleasure to see you again, Madam Beauchamp," David said. He ignored the embarrassment on Dominique's face and took her mother's hand, kissing it with as much courtly respect as he would for any grand dame of the *ton*.

"Not so young anymore, Mr. Grisham. You've grown into a very handsome gentleman," Collette said, looking him over without a hint of compunction.

"Thank you, madam."

"What has brought you to London, after all this time?"

David glanced to Dominique, who nodded almost imperceptibly. "I am a guest of my cousin, the Earl of Danby. I have recently been named his heir."

The words hurt more than David expected—because he knew what was coming next. Collette's eyes flashed with understanding.

"I am so sorry for your loss," she said quietly. "How?"

David cleared his throat. "A fire at the foundry."

Collette dipped her head respectfully. "Your father was a good man. He was always kind and respectful to me, even after… Well, after everything that occurred in Winleigh. I did not know your brother well, but I can only assume he shared you and your father's upstanding nature."

David could only nod his thanks, the emotion clogging his throat preventing anything more. Behind them, Dominique moved toward the hearth, collecting the kettle.

Collette glanced over her shoulder to mark her daughter's movements but then turned her attention back to David. "How is your mother?"

Thankfully, a topic David could speak of without struggle. "She is well, despite the losses of the last year. She has left Winleigh and is ensconced at my cousin's estate in Derbyshire. I will be joining her there, after my sojourn in London, to fully assume my duties as heir."

This time the look that Collette cut to Dominique was full of meaning. But Dominique did not look at her mother, instead busying herself with readying a tea tray.

"Will you join us for tea, Maman?"

"Of course."

"If you will excuse me, Madam Beauchamp, Miss Beauchamp. I believe it is best that I return to my lodgings. My cousin and I have an appointment to review the accounts this morning." It was a complete lie. Judging by the looks on both of the women's faces, they knew it. But neither challenged him.

Collette nodded and turned to help her daughter, giving him as much privacy as was possible in the small flat to finish dressing. Dominique spoke quietly with her mother in French, but David only caught the occasional word.

Shrugging on his tailcoat, he started toward the door.

"I am honored to have renewed our acquaintance, Madam Beauchamp," he said, offering yet another bow.

The lady's brows rose in amusement. "A most interesting happenstance, I agree," she said.

Dominique made a sound in her throat akin to a snort, though marginally more ladylike, before circling around the worktable and joining him at the door.

"I did not know she was coming," she said quietly, apology written all over her lovely face.

"Should I kiss you goodbye, to seal your embarrassment?" he teased, longing to do exactly that.

Her fingers curled at her side—she wanted to pinch him or something of the like—but she smiled. "You shall do no such thing. I will send word soon—try to wait for it this time."

David winked broadly. "I make no promises, my love."

Dominique rolled her eyes and swung open the door, though she stopped short of actually shoving him out of it.

David chuckled all the way down the stairs.

⟫⟩✦⟨⟪

"Cream, Maman?" Dominique asked as she crossed back to where her mother was already pouring the tea.

"Not this morning," Collette answered, before lifting the teacup to her lips and taking a long drink, all while fixing her daughter with a knowing stare.

"Have you something to say?" Dominique said, fixing her own cup and avoiding her mother's gaze.

"Many things."

"Shall we sit?" Dominique gestured weakly to the settee and armchair arranged cozily before the hearth.

"How long has Mr. Grisham been in London?"

"So, we shall begin the inquisition immediately, then." Dominique sighed and dropped into the armchair. "Two months or so, I believe. Next are you going to ask how long I've been sharing his bed?"

Her mother made a sound so distinctly French as she perched on the edge of the settee, Dominique wished she could bottle it. "You are the keeper of your own heart, Dominique. As you have always been."

Dominique wanted to retort that her heart and her bed were entirely separate entities. But when it came to David, she knew that they were not. From the mixture of emotions playing across

Collette's face, her mother knew it too.

"Are you taking the proper precautions?"

Dominique choked on her tea. "Maman—"

"Dominique, the last thing in the world I want for you is to find yourself in my situation."

"Your situation." Dominique set down her tea, afraid that she would drop it. "David is not Father."

"No, he is not," her mother agreed readily. "But I still worry for you."

"I am taking the necessary steps to ensure I do not fall pregnant," she said. Her mother had ensured she knew all the methods—those traditional, and those whispered about by Parisian ballerinas—as soon as she came of age. Collette was determined her daughter would not suffer as she had.

"*Bonne*." Her mother nibbled daintily on one of the biscuits Dominique had set out with the tea. "I am happy for you that Mr. Grisham has reentered your life."

Dominique was grateful she'd set down her tea. Otherwise, she had no doubt it would have covered her lap. "How... how can you say so?"

Her mother laughed softly. "Are you not happy?"

"Yes, of course. But Maman, it was you who convinced me all those years ago that our courtship could end in nothing but heartache."

Collette shrugged. "Circumstances change. He is to be an earl now."

Dominique shook her head, not able to comprehend. "Which makes a bastard daughter of a country baron an even more unsuitable match—"

"Dominique, please—"

"No, Maman, I—"

Her hand dropped to her lap abruptly, her next words forgotten. She had to tell her mother.

"Maman, I must tell you something," she said. Dominique moved to sit beside her mother on the settee, taking her hand.

She could not bring herself to look into her eyes, the dark mirror of her own.

"Anything, *mon amour*," Collette said.

How could it be that in this moment, her mother was the one soothing her? Dominique stroked her thumb across the back of Collette's hand. On the third pass, she forced the words out. "Amelia has also come to Town."

Her mother breathed in sharply, shifting in her seat. But Dominique had to get the rest out before she dissolved into tears.

"Lady Wartham is with her. But Father... Father is dead."

Her mother stilled.

Dominique waited, expecting a heave of the chest or a quaver of the hand she held. But Collette remained stiff and erect. When she finally dragged her eyes up to meet her daughter's, there were no tears.

"Perhaps that is for the best," Collette said.

Dominique's mouth fell open, and a tear spilled out of her eye.

"Oh, Dominique, *ma fille*." Her mother caught her chin and stroked the tear away, then gathered her into her arms. "You deserve to grieve your father as much as you need. Things between you were always so difficult. But do not grieve for me."

To Dominique's surprise, no other tears followed—as if they had all been spent that night in David's arms. But she did lay her head on her mother's shoulder, letting her perfume fill her nose and the soft wisps of her hair to tickle her face.

"I loved your father once," Collette said quietly. "But those feelings died long ago. The love I have now is for you, my daughter. And for myself. As it should be."

Another wave of surprise rolled through Dominique; she understood precisely what her mother meant. For her entire childhood, she had waited for her father to love her the way that a parent was meant to. When he'd failed her so spectacularly, she and her mother had come to London and built their own lives. They'd both learned to love themselves. There was a freedom in that.

"What shall you do about Amelia?" Collette asked.

Dominique sat up and reached for her tea, taking a fortifying sip. "I shall do nothing. She has known my address in London for years and chosen not to seek me out. I do not think anything has changed now."

Her mother nodded, though the pursing of her lips suggested she wished to say more.

They sipped for a few moments in silence, both contemplating. Dominique stood and refilled her teacup, and her mother finished the biscuit. When the pot was empty and the food eaten, Collette stood and brushed a few errant crumbs from her reserved plum day gown.

"The weather is fine; the season feels as if it is finally changing. Come and have a turn through the park with me. I need your counsel on Annabelle Foster's younger sister, now that she is coming of age," she said.

Dominique could not help but smile at the invitation. Her mother was careful never to ask about Dominique's profession, but she still often shared her own.

"Allow me a moment to ready myself," Dominique said, stepping over to the wardrobe in the corner as she began to untie her wrapper.

Her mother cleaned up the tea set and then drifted around the room, wiping away a bit of dust, rearranging the floral arrangement on the windowsill. Dominique chuckled to herself as she laced her stays and selected a shimmery golden-beige gown. A mother never stopped mothering, it seemed.

"These drawings are most peculiar."

Dominique paused with the tie beneath her bust; she'd left the drawings out on her desk. But the letters were safely tucked away in the drawer.

"Are they?" she called back, keeping her voice carefully casual.

"They are all wrong."

"Pardon?" Dominique turned, hands falling away from the forgotten gown.

"Carlton House has three columns on each side; not four," Collette said, pointing to the bottom-left drawing. "And the angle of the steeple of St. Clements is all wrong."

"How can you be certain?" Dominique stared at the depiction of the little church.

"It is two blocks from my flat. I have walked by it every day for the last ten years. I am certain," her mother said, annoyance tinging her voice. She pointed to the others. "I am not familiar with that building. But at the Regent's Canal, the trees were recently cut down to make way for Mr. Nash's expansion."

"It could be an old drawing," Dominique reasoned, but excitement was building in her stomach.

"It could not. It shows the Camden Town connection, which was only opened last year."

"Maman…" Dominique bit down hard on her lip to keep her exclamation in. "Maman, you must excuse me. I am suddenly taken quite queer," she said, eyes fixed on the drawings. She had to get the letters out. The code was there.

"Taken queerly?" Her mother folded her arms in front of her and peered at her daughter. But Dominique was already sweeping her toward the door.

"I shall call on you tomorrow or the next day, Maman, I promise."

"Yes, well, if you do not at least send word that you are well, do not force me to embarrass you further by seeking you out at the residence of Mr. Grisham's cousin."

"Yes, yes," Dominique murmured. But she did not truly hear the false threat in her mother's voice or see the understanding in the older woman's eyes as Collette allowed herself to be shooed out the door.

She slid the latches into place by reflex and then returned to the desk.

Finally, she would untangle the code.

CHAPTER TWENTY-FOUR

FOUR HOURS LATER, she sat on a bench in Green Park, her leg bouncing excitedly. It was almost over. Once her mother was gone, it had taken her less than an hour to break the code. Another hour and she'd lifted the hidden messages from the letters.

D'Terre was blackmailing each of the different Parliament members. Lord Hawley had taken a bribe two years before. Mr. Harding was having an affair with Lord Chapman's wife—a clever double-blackmailing ruse. Lord Rogers, the last of the victims, was engaged in something more nefarious—the buying and selling of illegal imports from overseas. That would be dealt with directly. She'd already sent word to the duchess so she could open an investigation.

Precisely as the duchess had suspected, D'Terre was trading in secrets to steal votes on influential legislation within both the House of Lords and the House of Commons. All Dominique needed now was the proof.

"Who is the overeager one this time?"

Dominique did not jump—she'd heard him approaching from several yards away—but she did let David think that he'd successfully snuck up on her. She tossed a smile over her shoulder and stood, aiming for the tree line. Her mother had been correct about the weather. The summer had finally come, and with it a park full of Londoners eager to enjoy the sunshine.

Green Park was still noticeably less populated than its more fashionable counterpart, Hyde Park, but it was better for them to remain in the cover of the trees.

David fell into step beside her, his movements easy and relaxed. He seemed to have learned her habits, waiting until they were in the shade of the trees and far from any other park patrons before speaking again.

"I did not expect to hear from you so soon," he said, taking her hand and tucking it neatly into his arm.

Dominique let him, enjoying the familiarity of it. They were hiding in the trees. Why not be close to one another?

"Do not overly flatter yourself," she teased. "The pleasure of your company is but one of the reasons I have summoned you here."

As she spoke, David ran his fingertips along the underside of her arm and very intentionally grazed her breast. Despite the seriousness of the news she bore, Dominique felt her nipples pebbling against the thin muslin of her gown.

"And what is the other?" he said, his smile growing at her sharp intake of breath.

Dominique swatted his hand away and turned to look up at him, letting the triumph glow in her eyes. "I've solved it."

David's blue eyes widened instantly. "The code? What—"

"It was my mother, really. I can't show you precisely how I worked it out, as I haven't brought all the drawings and letters with me," she said, taking his arm again and continuing through the trees.

"What do we do now?" David asked, rubbing at his jaw with his free hand.

"I must sneak back into D'Terre's townhouse and obtain the remainder of the originals. I will leave the reproductions you created in their place. Even if he finds them and realizes they are fake, there will be little he can do. He will not know I've been the one to take them, and before he can act, he will be arrested." As she spoke, she watched David closely. She saw the relief course through him, his entire body relaxing. His hand tightened over hers; his feelings for her were as strong as ever. But then his step hitched slightly—worry taking hold in his mind.

"By tonight, it will all be over," he said slowly.

"Tomorrow," she corrected him. "I must apprise my colleagues of my intentions, so they may intervene if anything goes amiss."

She watched his throat bob. "Do you expect anything to go amiss?" he asked.

"Of course not. But it is protocol, if possible, to give notice before going into a situation such as this." *A potentially dangerous one,* her mind finished, though she did not relay that part to David.

"How much longer will you remain at the Theatre Royal?" David asked.

"Another week or so, I would imagine. Until D'Terre is arrested and then a few days more, to make it more difficult for the casual observer to connect our absences." She was already looking forward to having her evenings to herself again. Or perhaps... not entirely to herself.

Dominique paused again, but this time when she turned to David, she reached up and stroked her thumb across his face. He caught her hand, pressing a kiss to the inside of her wrist.

"I shall finally have you all to myself," he said, breath hot against her skin.

"Yes," she said, chuckling softly.

The answers to what else was between them and what they would do about it... she could let those go for now. With her quest resolved, she could be with David without the specter of danger or duty hanging above their heads. She could seduce him properly; they could spend luxurious days in bed feasting on one another.

With one quick glance around them to reassure herself they were well and truly alone—now completely concealed by the close-growing trees in the corner of the park—Dominique caught his lips with hers.

Oh, but she could do this forever. She slid her tongue into his mouth, finding him waiting and ready for her. She could taste the tea he'd drunk before coming, the taste of him as heady on her tongue as any liquor had ever been.

David caught her waist, drawing her close so her breasts strained against the thin material of her gown and rubbed against the stiff lapels of his tailcoat. She imagined undressing him slowly, kissing every inch of his golden body. There was so much to explore and do, and she wanted all of it with David.

He curled the tail of her intricate French-inspired plait around his fingers and tugged her head back, kissing her chin and her throat before arriving back at her lips.

"I love you," he breathed against her mouth between kisses.

Not a grand, proud declaration, but a prayer. A promise.

Which made it even more painful as she ripped herself away.

"David," she whispered. "David, no."

His mouth fell open, shock registering on his handsome features. "Dominique, you cannot say no. Not after all of this time, not after all of this. You *know* that I love you—"

"Stop!" Her hand shot up, forcing him back. She could not let him embrace her again.

If she did, her resolve would falter.

Because David was right—she knew that he loved her.

And she loved him.

And it did not change a damn thing.

She was the bastard daughter of a country lord. More importantly, she was a lady knight. While David would eventually become the Earl of Danby.

Why had he said it? Why could he not let them enjoy these moments and days together, free of the responsibility of the future?

David stared directly at her, no twinkle in his eye or affable grin to be seen. The intensity of his gaze bored into her very soul.

"Do not ask me to take it back," he said sharply.

Dominique shook her head. "I would not ask that of you."

"But you will not return the words." From the pain lining his face, Dominique knew he had already discerned the answer.

"What we feel for one another does not change the circumstances."

David sighed heavily. "For you, I suppose not."

His arms fell to his sides, forlorn, empty—she should be in them.

But it was David who stalked back toward the path, pausing before he stepped out of the privacy of the grove of trees.

"I have always loved you. I always shall—regardless of the walls you choose to hide behind. I would give you the world, Dominique, if only you would let yourself accept it."

"I—" she began.

But he was already gone.

CHAPTER TWENTY-FIVE

CHERRY CORDIAL WAS delicious.

Whisky was not delicious.

Sherry was passable.

Where was the rest of the cherry cordial?

David dropped to his knees and crawled across the floor of the study, checking under chairs as he passed. Where had that bottle gotten to?

Not under the armchair or the settee.

Could it have rolled all the way to the desk…?

"Not bloody likely," he mumbled.

But just as he was rolling back onto his bottom, he caught a glint of green out of the corner of his eye. "Ssssson of a bitch!"

He tumbled over face-first, just managing to get his arm beneath him at the last second. The cherry cordial *had* rolled all the way under Geoffrey's desk!

He lurched forward, shouldering past the settee. He'd have to lie on his stomach to reach it, but—

"What in the name of the Almighty are you doing?"

David's head hit the underside of the desk with a resounding *smack!*

He hunched forward, letting the thick Persian rug and his copious hair cushion his forehead. Vaguely, he heard Geoffrey's footsteps padding across the room. David cracked his eyelids open just enough to see the polished black tops of his cousin's boots from beneath the desk.

"Are you ill?"

David groaned. "I want more cherry cordial."

Geoffrey paused, then his hand appeared alongside his boot. But instead of offering it to David, he tugged on the green bottle that lingered just a few inches beyond David's reach.

"Blazes, David! This bottle is nearly empty!"

"I liked it better than the whisky."

David listened as Geoffrey turned and laughed sharply. "You've put back an admirable portion of that as well. At least you didn't find the brandy; it was rather expensive."

"But I did find the sherry."

Geoffrey muttered another oath, then his face appeared. "You've got the tastes of a seventy-year-old lady."

"I have the tastes of a gentleman!" David protested.

But the real protest came from his stomach when Geoffrey grabbed his arm and tugged him up. And his head—his head was spinning frightfully.

"Why are you moving like that?" David grumbled as his cousin stuffed him into the armchair.

"I am not moving. That is all your own doing. Yours, and half of my sideboard." Geoffrey looked thoughtfully between the bottles strewn about the various surfaces of his study, finally selecting the whisky.

David's stomach turned over at the thought. Thankfully, Geoffrey handed him what remained of the cherry cordial instead. He popped the cork free and tipped the remnants down his throat.

Geoffrey watched with a silent, incredulous laugh before uncorking and taking a more dignified draw of the whisky.

David ignored him, studying the label on the cherry cordial. "Have you any more of this delicioussssss stuff?" he slurred.

"I absolutely do not. It was a gift to Lily many years ago. Even she could not stand the sweetness of it."

David tipped the bottle completely upside down over his head, hopeful for a few remaining drops. That failed. When he looked back at his cousin, Geoffrey was watching with open-mouthed shock.

"What has come over you?" he asked. "In my fifty-six years, I've never seen you behave like this. Never a drop of wine with dinner or brandy over a cigar. What happened?"

"*She* happened."

"Ah. The mysterious woman."

"I cannot tell you about her," David said. A second later, a very ungentlemanly burp erupted from his chest. "I cannot," he mumbled again.

"I won't ask you to," Geoffrey said after another pull of whisky.

"She broke my heart. Twice." David began to eye the remains of the sherry across the room, still on the sideboard.

"A true pity," Geoffrey said. He drained the whisky and stood up.

"Aren't you going to offer me some sage bit of wisdom?" David turned his eyes up to Geoffrey. "Or, at least, bring me the sherry before you go?"

"I have no wisdom to offer where women are concerned. I loved only one, and now that she's left me, I'm content to wait until the day I will rejoin her." Geoffrey pounded his fist twice against his own chest, burping in a much more masculine manner than David had managed. Then he crossed to the sideboard, returning with the sherry in hand. He dropped it into David's lap. "Besides, there will be no talking to you until at least noon tomorrow. I expect you will not even recall this conversation."

"I most certainly—"

"Goodnight, David. I'll send along one of the footmen to ensure you don't choke on your own vomit."

"That is most ungentlemanly—"

But the door of the study had already snapped closed.

David picked up the sherry, wrenching the cork free and

taking a swig.

He smacked his lips noisily, looking hard at the bottle. "It is just you and I tonight, then."

When the bottle did not answer, he took another drink.

DING DONG DING *dong ding dong—*

David shot up, trying to count the chimes—

"Oh bollocks!"

He just made it to the chamber pot Geoffrey's footman had set beside him the night before. Once he finished emptying his stomach, he fell back against the chair.

He was still in the study. Though instead of sitting in the armchair, he was leaning back against it. He tried to lift his head, but that was impossible too. Christ, why was it so damn bright? Had someone come to draw the curtains already?

They were probably never closed the night before, his better sense chimed in from the recesses of his mind. He'd been holding his drunken, solo court in Geoffrey's study since midafternoon yesterday.

David vaguely recalled the footman trying to get him to eat something. Then the same footman had delivered the chamber pot sometime after dark. Had Geoffrey been there as well? Or was that before?

He tried to pry an eye open, but the scalding light was too much. He'd just rest a few minutes more, and then he would get himself in order…

Ding dong ding dong ding dong—

This time when he shot up, he managed to grab the side of the chair and steady himself. His stomach rolled, but by some miracle, what remained inside of him managed to stay there. The second miracle was that David managed to count the chimes.

Twelve. It was noon.

There will be no talking to you until at least noon tomorrow.

That was what Geoffrey had said. Of course, he was right.

David peeped his eyes open—still a painful endeavor, but at least not impossible. As he did, he recalled the rest of his cousin's words.

Geoffrey had insisted he had no meaningful advice to offer, but he was wrong. He'd loved only one woman. Just as David always had and always would. While Geoffrey's love was now beyond his reach, David's was not.

Dominique was very much alive. Despite the pain of her words, despite the rejection, he'd seen the truth in her eyes and felt it in her touch. She loved him as much as he loved her. He would make her see that it would be all right between them. He would make it right.

He had approximately seven hours to clean himself up and figure out what to say to convince her.

SEVEN HOURS LATER, nearly to the minute, he stood outside of Dominique's flat. The stairs were so damn squeaky; if she was going to remain here much longer, he'd hire a carpenter to come and fix them so they did not drive him to insanity.

He knocked at the door but was unsurprised when she did not answer. The evening's production was set to begin any minute. Which meant that Dominique was likely already at D'Terre's townhouse, waiting for her opportunity to sneak in and truly conclude her quest.

For a minute, he contemplated trying to pick the lock so he might wait inside. But if an accomplished lockpick had installed those locks, he doubted the likes of him would be able to get inside without breaking the door itself down. Then he remembered.

It was the work of a minute to move back down the stairs, find the right board in the landing, and retrieve the key. The door swung open to her flat waiting empty.

David put the kettle on and sat down to wait. When Dominique returned, her quest would be settled. Then they could turn their attention to settling the love that was between them.

DOMINIQUE WAITED TEN minutes after D'Terre's carriage departed for the theater before dodging across the alley. She did not have much time; when he arrived at the theater and discovered she was not in attendance, it was possible he would return home. Not because he suspected her, but because his chance to bed her that night was ruined.

She suppressed the shiver that came unbidden. She would not have to bed the awful beast. Sneak in, steal the letters and swap out the reproductions for the original drawings, and she would be on her way. Smoothing her maid's uniform, she dodged one of the few remaining puddles from the wet spring.

It was pressing her luck to attempt a third entrance and egress in the maid's uniform; she'd contemplated dressing as a chimney sweep instead. But she needed the wide pockets of her apron to conceal the evidence on her way in and out. It would have to do.

She ran her hand along her bust and checked her pocket one last time, ensuring her blade and lockpick roll were still in place. Then she lifted her skirts and slipped in through the rear door.

CHAPTER TWENTY-SIX

1807
10 years ago
Winleigh, Hampshire

THERE WAS A snag in the embroidery.

Dominique rubbed her thumb over the little leaf, one tiny part of the intricate embroidery along the edge of her grandmother's amethyst shawl. Very carefully, she tried to coax the thread back into place, in line with all its siblings.

But it would not go. The snagged loop remained just a little bit longer than its fellows, determined to go its own way. Even as she folded the beloved garment, she mourned. The bit of thread would eventually catch on something and pull out a little more. Over months or years, that delicate little leaf would unravel until there was a barren spot in the shawl. If she was lucky, the damage would end there. If not, the rest of the detailed decoration might follow, until nothing remained.

That first stolen moment with David in the orangery had seemed so perfect, the start of a life she'd only allowed herself to dream about.

But now Dominique recognized it for what it had truly been—the first snag in the fabric of her life.

She folded the shawl so that the damaged bit was protected

and added it to the trunk. A moment later, footsteps sounded on the landing.

"Are you finished, Miss Beauchamp?" Bella asked, huffing slightly. She'd been up and down the stairs at least a dozen times in the last hour, busily readying for their departure.

Once Dominique and her mother left, Bella would stay behind to give the cottage a final tidying before the new owners arrived to take possession of the property.

Dominique could still hear the two men's voices as they walked through her home, dissecting and assessing the value of every nook and cranny. How well maintained the floors were; yes, the rugs could stay for the right price; the roof was clay tile, an unheard-of luxury in a cottage of this size.

We will make our own home, now, her mother had assured her. *Away from this place that has caused us nothing but pain.*

Yes, pain there was in spades. It rattled through her dreams and greeted her in the morning upon waking.

But beneath the pain of her father's rejection and her own humiliation, Dominique's heart broke for a reason all its own.

David.

"Dominique?" Bella said gently, the floor creaking under her as she stepped forward. It always creaked in that spot, even under Bella's slight weight.

"Yes, I am finished." Dominique snapped the lid of the trunk down and pushed the two clasps into place, and the metallic click clanged through her soul.

"Very good, miss. I will fetch the driver to carry down your trunk. I believe your mother is ready as well," Bella said. She bustled back down the stairs, leaving Dominique alone once again.

Her eyes flitted around the small bedroom that had been hers for nearly a decade. Most of the furniture would remain here, sold along with the cottage. A new beginning, her mother kept saying. A complete, final divorce from the life she had known, Dominique's mind countered.

The armoire was slightly ajar, its shelves once filled with colorful frocks now dark and empty. The vanity, where she'd sat for hours learning to plait her own hair, looked so small with all of her combs and personal belongings packed away.

There was one item left.

She opened the drawer of the vanity as her mother set foot upon the landing.

"The driver will be along for your trunk in a moment and then we will be off," Collette said, rubbing her hands together against the crisp air. The door of the cottage had been open all morning as the carriage was loaded with their belongings, and the early November chill had permeated nearly every square foot.

Her mother paused at the doorframe. "What is that?"

Dominique stared at the parchment in her hand, carefully folded and sealed with a bit of wax from the very same candle she'd used to light her room as she'd written it late last night.

"A letter."

A sharp intake of breath. "For your father."

"For David."

"My sweet…" Collette reached for her, but Dominique jerked away.

"I… I cannot help but feel that I am betraying him," she said, her voice so soft she almost did not hear the words herself. But her mother did.

"You have done nothing wrong," Collette said, her tone soothing. But she did not reach for Dominique again.

"Perhaps if I had told David earlier, in my own way, then we could have told his family together. We could have formed a plan…"

"David cares for you deeply, I have no doubt of that."

Dominique's heart clenched, the pain so intense she had to grab the corner post of the bed to keep herself from crumpling.

"But," her mother continued, "sometimes that is not enough."

Had her mother and father once loved one another?

Dominique wondered. She'd never been able to bring herself to ask, afraid of the pain it would cause her mother.

But she could read the subtext of her mother's words clearly enough. She and David may care deeply for one another, but it would not be enough to overcome the humiliation. The only chance at happiness they had together was if they left Winleigh, and Dominique would not ask it of him. His family was close-knit, warm, and loving—everything Dominique had missed out on. She would not be the cause of yet another person's unhappiness. Most importantly, not that of the man she loved.

She breathed the cool air in slowly, letting it fill her chest and flow out of her lips. The chill was harsh, even a bit painful. But she welcomed it in contrast to the burning pain of her breaking heart.

Finally, she reached for her mother. "Come, let us get on."

It had been too damn long. He'd waited for the word she promised to send, but after more than a week without seeing or hearing from Dominique, David could stand it no more.

She'd told him of what occurred at Wartham Grange tearfully as they walked through Farmer Jones's apple orchard in the twilight.

His mother and father had not asked him about their courtship, though he could surmise from the mournful looks on their faces and the stilted glances they exchanged that they assumed he'd broken it off. He had not appeared with Dominique in public, nor mentioned her to his family after that disastrous day when the truth of Dominique's birth had roared through Winleigh like wildfire.

He'd yet to form a plan, wanting to give Dominique the time to grieve the upheaval of her life. But when she was ready, they would talk together and decide how to proceed.

He loved her.

That was all that truly mattered.

Whether his family could accept that and her into their family, or whether he had to take her back to France in order for her to find peace—it did not matter to him. So long as he had Dominique at his side, he could conquer any challenge.

David would remind her of it every day until the sorrow faded from her beautiful, beloved face.

He knew something was amiss as soon as he rounded the corner where the Quill cottage stood. Dominique and her mother's cottage was another quarter mile down the lane. On a brisk evening like tonight, the chimney should have been huffing smoke, cheery light glowing from the perimeters of the tightly closed window shutters.

But the cottage ahead of him was still. Dark.

He shifted into a jog, sure that if he only got a bit closer he would see the telltale signs of occupation. It must be a trick of the light.

Then a sprint, because he could not believe what his eyes were seeing.

Empty.

Empty. Empty. Empty.

The cruel word ricocheted through him with each mighty beat of his heart.

He wrenched open the door, already knowing what he would find within—nothing.

The cottage was empty. Even in the darkness, he looked around the room, able to discern the barren residence stripped of the small touches and belongings that had made it a home.

Dominique was gone.

David stumbled forward, grasping the edge of the dining table. His eyes adjusted to the dim light, searching. She would not have left without a word. She would have left him *something…*

His eyes landed on the parchment, waiting on the low table slung between the armchairs and the settee in the corner.

Could it only have been weeks ago that he sat on that very chaise, asking to court Dominique?

The ghost of her smiling face mocked him as he broke open the wax seal and read what she'd left for him. It was achingly brief.

Dearest David,

After all that has occurred, it is impossible for my mother and I to stay in Winleigh. The happiness we have enjoyed here was always fragile, but even I did not realize just how much.

I will always be grateful for your friendship in this cruel world.

I hope that you find your own happiness. There is no one who deserves it more.

Though it is not fair, I ask you one last favor.

Let me go. Do not look for me. I fear that if you do, it will only bring more pain upon us both. More than anything, I cannot bear to cause you more pain than I already have.

Adieu,
Dominique

If there had been a fire, he would have thrown the letter into it.

In the years that would come, he would be grateful that instead, he folded the parchment and shoved it into his pocket.

He would not honor her request. He would find her.

If it took him a month, a year, or a decade, he would always find her.

CHAPTER TWENTY-SEVEN

1817
Present Day

TWO POTS OF tea later and the only footsteps he'd heard on the stairs were the slow, cranky steps of Dominique's upstairs neighbor Mr. Pritchett. He could have sworn the man muttered a derogatory oath as he passed her door, but David decided to ignore it. The man was older than sin.

He pulled his father's pocket watch from inside his tailcoat and checked it for the fourth time in an hour. Never mind that there was also a pretty—and accurate—crystal clock atop the mantel.

It was after nine o'clock.

She ought to be back by now.

Unless something had gone badly.

Perhaps she'd gone directly to meet with her other lady knights, he reasoned. After the row they'd had, there was no reason for her to expect him to be waiting for her. Was it possible she'd called at his cousin's house or left word there?

Maybe, he decided.

But if he left her flat, he might miss her entirely.

She might be in trouble.

No matter how many reasonable scenarios David ran

through his mind, he could not dismiss that one.

He had to do something or he would jump out of his skin. He could not drink another pot of wretched tea. Pushing to his feet, he scoured the room. Was there a way to contact her colleagues secreted somewhere here? He tentatively opened her desk, but dismissed that avenue. Dominique was too intelligent to leave such pertinent details where someone ransacking her flat could find them, even if the person doing the ransacking did so out of love and concern.

He'd have to go to D'Terre's townhouse. There was nothing else for it. He'd stop by Geoffrey's residence en route to ensure she hadn't left word there, but that was the only concession he would make. If she'd been caught, her life could be in danger.

He was no lady knight, nor gentleman knight, nor any type of hero. But he loved Dominique more than life itself. That would have to be enough.

After snapping the desk drawer closed, he swiped the knife from beneath her pillow—though he had never used one for anything more than cutting meat—and tucked it into his tailcoat. At the very least, he could hand it off to Dominique if he found her.

When he found her.

But before he was halfway across the flat, the door swung open.

David managed to get the knife out of his tailcoat, but before he could get a solid grip upon the hilt, it was knocked forcibly out of his hand and he was shoved hard up against the wall.

"She's not here—"

"Mr. Grisham!"

The pressure across his chest eased immediately. The woman who'd pinned him to the wall fell back, a wide smile spreading across her face.

"Mr. David Grisham," he huffed, straightening his lapels.

Based upon the speed at which she had moved and her brutal efficiency, this could only be a fellow lady knight.

While he did not really appreciate being pinned against a wall, he did feel relief course through his veins. This woman would surely know Dominique's whereabouts.

He'd imagined Dominique's colleagues to be a bit like her—mysterious, sensual, elusive. But the woman before him was the opposite. She had full, generous curves and bright, coppery red hair that would mark her anywhere. Her pale skin was liberally sprinkled with freckles, and the smile she gave him was completely free of avarice.

Or, he supposed, was meant to appear so.

"Miss Ethelreda McGovern," she said with a tilt of her head. "I am pleased to finally make your acquaintance."

David fought the urge to fiddle awkwardly with his cravat. "You have me at a disadvantage, Miss McGovern. I find I know nothing of you."

"By design." She winked. "Please, call me Red."

"If you insist," he said.

Red had backed up, hands at her hips, surveying the flat with quick, sharp eyes. "Has Dominique stepped out to get a bite? I am half-starved."

Icy fear trickled down David's spine.

"No," he said. "She has not returned."

Red's hand stilled halfway to the breadbox against the wall. "She has not returned from D'Terre's house?"

The even tone of her voice scared him even more. "No."

"Hound's teeth." Red swirled for the door. "Stay here," she ordered him over her shoulder.

"Like hell. If Dominique is in danger, I am accompanying you to retrieve her."

"We do not know that she is in danger," Red said. "There are any multitude of reasons she may have been detained. If we rush in after her, we may be putting her in more danger."

"I will not sit by while the woman I love risks her life for—"

Red spun on him, advancing two steps until she was so close that if they'd been in public, she'd have been thoroughly compromised.

"Dominique is a highly trained and skilled agent of Her Majesty the Queen. Love her you may, but this choice has been and always will be hers," Red said fiercely.

David clenched his teeth. He knew if he tried to brush past the woman, she'd have him on the floor in a second. She probably had weapons hidden all over her person. He forced the calm into his voice, though he felt none of it in his heart.

"I am not questioning any of that. But I cannot stand by while she is harmed."

Red glared at him, her gaze boring into his as if she was trying to read his very soul. Several moments passed, each of them an eternity when Dominique might be in danger. But then Red stepped back and stabbed the air with her chin.

"You may come with me if you follow my instruction to the letter." David opened his mouth to respond, but she cut him off. "If I tell you to stay behind, you must do so without question. I am breaking every rule and protocol by bringing you along."

"Fine."

Red still looked unconvinced, but she said, "We leave now."

They turned for the door, Red a half-step ahead of David. "Do you have the k—Who are you?"

She'd swung the door open to reveal a petite dark-blonde woman with her hand raised to knock. She jumped backward across the landing, pulling her cloak tight around her. But not fast enough to cover the costume she wore—the same one Dominique wore for the final scene of the play.

David pushed past Red. Somewhere from the depths of his memory, he pulled a name. "Cora?"

The woman frowned at him, but nodded. "You're the gentleman who has been visiting Miss Beauchamp's dressing room."

Red shot him a reproving look, but David ignored it. "I am— Mr. David Grisham, heir to the Earl of Danby." He was not sure why he said it. But the woman let out the breath she'd been holding, so the title must have comforted her.

"Is Miss Beauchamp here?" Cora asked, rising to her tiptoes to look over their shoulders.

"She is not," Red said, pushing David aside again in the small doorway. "Have you seen her?"

"No," Cora said. Her hands were tangled nervously in her cloak. "I came as quickly as I could, as soon as the curtain fell."

David breathed in sharply, but Red grabbed his arm and held him in place. She turned back to Cora and said in a calm, soothing voice, "Tell us what happened."

"Miss Beauchamp sent word that she was unwell again. I am her understudy. When I stepped onto the stage, there was a commotion in one of the boxes—chairs overturned, someone yelling. It was quite unusual…" The pulse in Cora's throat was fluttering terribly. David could see her stumbling to keep her words steady.

He wanted to grab her by the arms and shake the rest of the story from her, but Red only said, "Which box?"

"Mr. D'Terre's."

"Did he come backstage?" Red asked.

Cora's chin trembled as she shook her head. "I was terrified to go back to the dressing room. But he was not there. He was expecting Dominique on the stage, I know it. I ran here to warn her, but… she is not here."

"No, she is not," Red said, still unruffled. She reached into the reticule attached to her wrist, the one David had scarcely even noticed, and extracted several golden guineas. "For your silence. Now go back to the theater. You are in no danger."

It took every bit of control in David's possession to stand there silently while Cora looked between them, then slowly made her way back down the stairs. She sent several nervous glances over her shoulder, but did not inquire more.

Only when the outer door had closed behind Cora did Red speak again.

"He knows."

※※※

Mops and brooms were better company than rats and cockroaches.

They did not bite. Though they were considerably smaller.

As far as one to share a cupboard with, she'd choose the former every time.

Which was lucky, because that was precisely what she was doing at that moment.

She waited for D'Terre's footsteps to fade away, listening carefully to see which direction he took.

Invisible ink.

How could she have failed to check for it?

In addition to the code embedded in the drawings, there was invisible ink written on the back side. Which meant when she switched the originals out to examine them closer, she'd unknowingly alerted D'Terre that someone was onto his dealings.

When he'd seen Cora in her place on the stage that evening, Dominique was found out—discovered with the incriminating documents quite literally in her hands.

She could pass herself off as a fill-in to the other servants if need be, but there was no chance of fooling D'Terre when he looked her straight in the face. Then he'd rambled about his invisible ink and shoved her into a cabinet.

She'd fought him hard enough to make a good show and earn a few bruises. She could have dispatched him easily enough. But then she would have had to run from the house without the proof she needed, which was not an option. Locked in a cupboard was a circumstance she could easily handle.

The difficult part was judging the timing of it all. The longer she waited, the more likely D'Terre was to execute whatever nefarious plan he had for her. If she did not report to Red within a few hours, she too would become a complicating factor. David…

He was surely waiting for word from her following their row. At least she could relieve her mind of worrying about him for this interval.

I suppose being locked in a cabinet does have certain benefits.

However, she needed to wait long enough for D'Terre to vacate his study and lower his guard. His head would still be pounding with triumph at having caught her, and judging by his footsteps, he'd returned to his study. She could only hope that with her safely tucked in the cabinet, he would not feel the need to relocate the letters and corresponding drawings. If she had to search the study all over again, it would waste valuable time.

She silently hummed two-thirds of Beethoven's Ninth Symphony to herself. Which meant forty minutes had passed and she had not heard D'Terre's footsteps, nor anyone else. The only servants left in the house were the maid and butler, who kept rooms in the attic. But if D'Terre was awake, they likely were as well.

If she came across them… she'd be as gentle as she could. Dominique had no quarrel with either of them, and there was no reason to think they were complicit in D'Terre's nefarious dealings. But time was slipping by, and she could not waste any more of it.

Slowly, careful not to disturb her friends the mops and create a hullabaloo, she drew her gown upward. Her roll of picks was unrolled at present, molded around the inside of her upper thigh. Damn near undetectable. With a bit of maneuvering, she was able to untie the loop from her thigh and tug the entire roll up around her leg and into her palm.

Calm composure spread over her with the familiar leather roll in her hand.

She selected two petite picks and began to work. Even in the dark, she knew just where each pick was located within the roll. Picking a lock in the dark was easy work—it merely allowed her to focus more easily on the feel and sound as she manipulated the tumblers. One soft click, and the door sprang free.

Dominique caught it with her left hand, while her right replaced the picks and stored the roll away in her pocket—but not before she pulled out the two she'd need for D'Terre's desk. She slipped those down her bodice.

Pushing the door open slowly, she peered into the hallway beyond. It was deserted, as she'd expected. He'd stuffed her into a cupboard near the back of the house, which meant she'd have to navigate back to his study past the stairwell to the kitchen. The kitchen was the most perilous. If she met the butler or maid having a spot of evening tea, it would complicate things.

Still crouching in the cupboard, Dominique plotted her route.

Down the hallway and into the formal dining room. Through the butler's pantry that connected to the sitting room. From there she'd have to dash across the foyer, the largest expanse of open space. Then it was a quick slide past the small morning room, down the hall of paintings, and into the study.

Pulling her penknife free from her bodice, she slipped out of the cupboard.

⟫⟫⟪⟪

"I THINK IT is unoccupied," Red said after several long moments of pressing her ear to the rear door of D'Terre's townhouse.

"What if it is not?" David was not quite wringing his hands, but he'd certainly decided he was not made for spy craft.

"Then I shall see it taken care of." Red dipped her chin to the parasol tucked under her arm.

As if that was supposed to have any meaning to David. He had no notion why she was carrying a parasol to begin with.

"Stay back and be quiet." With that, she produced two slender metal instruments similar to the ones he'd seen Dominique use and set to work on the lock. Based upon the murmured curses, he gleaned she was not as adept as Dominique.

But she did manage it, and two minutes later, they were

stepping cautiously into D'Terre's deserted kitchen.

"Luck is with us," David murmured.

"For the moment. Be quiet," Red whispered.

David decided he did not much like Ethelreda McGovern. But if it meant getting Dominique to safety, he'd have bartered with the devil himself.

She crossed the stone-flagged floor with impressive speed and silence that David tried to emulate. The eye-roll she did not quite hide told him he'd done a less-than-satisfactory job. But nonetheless, she motioned for him to follow as she snuck into the hallway.

The candles on the walls were already burning low, ready to be snuffed out for the night, but even so, there was nowhere for them to hide in the long corridor. Red ducked through the first doorway, and David followed. A dining room. She skirted around the table and behind a wall of curtains.

During their hasty hackney ride from Dominique's flat, Red had interrogated him for all he knew of D'Terre. Which, despite his involvement in the quest, was shockingly little. His attention had been on Dominique. For not the first time that night, David cursed himself for not paying closer attention.

He paused, a glimmer of reflected moonlight drawing his gaze. Red was already moving, out of the protection of the curtains and toward the next door. But David remained fixed, squinting through the window in the low light.

Red reappeared, grabbing his arm. "Do not make me regret—"

"Look."

Her eyes followed the tilt of his head, but she remained unfazed.

If Dominique had not been in danger, David might have enjoyed lording something over Red. Instead, he explained: "Dominique mentioned D'Terre's study has a wall of windows. Look there."

He saw the recognition in Red's eyes. Across the courtyard diagonally from them was a break in the brickwork. Two stacked rows of narrow, repeating windows lined the wall.

"You ought to have mentioned that before." Red glowered at him. "At least we have a direction." That was the extent of recognition or admonition she was willing to give. She was already speeding for the next door. David could do nothing but follow at her heels and pray for the best.

⟫⟫⟫⟪⟪⟪

DOMINIQUE WAS TWO steps from the morning room when her foot slipped. She flailed, reaching for anything to steady herself, then checking the urge and falling back instead, forcing her body to roll to cushion the sound of the impact. She could not afford to bring furniture crashing down along with her.

For two long breaths, she lay on her stomach, arms curled under her, waiting.

Some idiot had overwatered the potted plant that stood sentinel between the foyer and morning room, leaving a puddle of water that her satin slippers had no hope against.

A quick inventory of her limbs—uninjured—and she pushed to her feet.

She'd made it to the morning room. All that remained was to verify that D'Terre was not in the study, sneak down the hall of paintings, and get what she needed. And get out, of course.

She poked her head into the gallery, looking for any sign of life behind the double doors at the end of the hall—

A scuff.

Like a boot heel dragged carelessly over tile.

She melted into the wall, trying to conceal herself in shadows. Perhaps it was a coincidence, the butler coming down to do his evening rounds. He likely did not even know she was in the house. With even more care than before, she edged back around the morning room to peer into the foyer.

Nothing.

But she had not imagined it. Her instincts screamed that someone—

Dominique stepped from behind the potted plant and waved her hands emphatically.

Red froze, halfway across the foyer, in plain sight.

Why is Red here? What is—David? David!

Dominique shoved those useless wonderings away and pointed to the puddle, motioning around it with her arms. Red understood immediately, taking a wide berth and joining her in the morning room quickly. David was not as quick—he was trying to keep his steps silent—but by some miracle, he reached the morning room undiscovered as well.

"What are you doing here?" Dominique whispered.

"I—"

"We—"

"Red!" Dominique cut her gaze directly to her fellow lady knight. David's ill judgment, she could understand. Red's was unforgivable.

"You did not come back," Red said, meeting her eye with unflinching panache.

"I was not due to report for another hour."

"You were found out. The other actress from Covent Garden came—"

"Cora?"

"We are here now. Use us."

They'd already made more noise than either of them was comfortable with, given the way Red were glancing around constantly to assess for threats.

Dominique let her eyes travel to David, ready for the surge of emotion. It was there, sure enough, but her composure won out. Until they were away from this house, they were all in danger.

"The study is down that gallery," she whispered, nodding toward it. "There's a candle lit, but I don't think D'Terre is inside."

"We saw through the windows from the dining room. There

are several lamps burning, but we did not see any movement," Red confirmed.

It was the best Dominique could hope for—if the study was empty, she could steal the documents and they'd be away. If D'Terre waited inside… at least she had Red at her back. And David… though he was like to be more liability than anything.

But the light shining in his eyes as they turned to the gallery… Dominique suppressed a sigh. He loved her and would do anything to protect her. Including facing off with D'Terre, even as untrained in fisticuffs as he was. She would ensure it did not come to that.

"What shall our signal be?" Red murmured, scanning the possible entry points to the gallery.

"An owl seems appropriate," Dominique said, glancing over her shoulder to where the moonlight spilled in through the window.

"Not a lot of owls in Mayfair," Red said, but she nodded agreement. "I'll signal if I see or hear anyone."

Dominique nodded her assent and stepped into the hall, but something caught her hand. Someone.

She looked up into David's eyes, expressive and full even in the darkness. There was no time for words, so she squeezed his hand tightly and then slipped her fingers free. It was nowhere near enough for what lay between them.

Down the gallery she went, each step a danger. But there was no hooting or other commotion. She tried the doors of the study, but knew they would be locked. A Barron lock. Simple. She pulled one pick from her bodice and had it open in seconds.

Her chest was tight as she stepped into the room, her body taut and ready to spring into action on the exhale.

But the study was empty.

Please be there. Please, please, please, she prayed silently as she crossed to the desk, picked the lock, and wrested the bottom drawer open.

✤

DAVID COUNTED EVERY second Dominique was inside the study. He could tell from Red's composure that the lack of sounds or scuffle was good, but worried his bottom lip nonetheless. Only when Dominique appeared again, hand possessively draped over her maid's apron, did he breathe unhitched.

"I have them all. Let's go before we all end up shoved in a cupboard," she said, already leading the way back through the morning room.

"He locked you in a cupboard!"

"Hush!" both women cried in unison. They all froze, waiting. No one had heard them.

"Where the hell is D'Terre that he isn't hearing this?" Red whispered.

"I do not want to stay and find out." Dominique sprinted across the foyer, avoiding the puddle of water she'd shown them earlier.

"I might. He deserves a solid trashing for locking her in a cupboard," Red muttered before following Dominique.

David was inclined to agree. But he did not say a word as he followed the two women silently out of the house. Dominique was safe—nothing else mattered.

CHAPTER TWENTY-EIGHT

DOMINIQUE'S HEART DID not return to normal until they were out the back alley, five blocks away, and skirting the perimeter of Hyde Park. By some miracle, the worst of their injuries were the bruises from where she'd struggled against D'Terre as he shoved her into the closet—which had been entirely for show, of course.

David and Red were both unscathed, though the latter was still huffing.

"We ought to have bashed him over the head and have done with it," Red grumbled.

"My quest was to secure the evidence," Dominique reminded her. That very evidence was in her apron. She would need to get it to the duchess promptly; there was no doubt in her mind that once D'Terre discovered the letters and drawings were missing, he would raise a ruckus trying to find her.

"You've managed that, at least, though with less finesse than you're known for," Red said, pausing on the corner. She tucked an errant red curl behind her ear, though it did little for the wild locks springing forth from her coiffure.

Dominique rolled her eyes at the rejoinder. "Thank you for your assistance, Red."

She just managed to keep her eyes from sliding to David.

Red had no such compunction. She stared between the two

of them with obvious interest. When neither of them spoke, she sighed.

"Well then, I suppose I will be off. Now that you've dragged me into this mess, I shall have to write up a report of my own." She sighed again for emphasis.

Dominique bit down on the retort that sprang to her lips. Red had been long without a quest. Though she thought she was being punished, Dominique suspected the duchess had something brewing for her fellow lady knight. Her intuition told her Red would not be long for London.

"You have my thanks, Red." Dominique squeezed her friend's arm. She'd have been fine on her own, but just the knowing she was not alone was worth more than she could articulate.

Red inclined her head sharply before spinning on her heel and making for the park, though not before Dominique detected the faint blush climbing her neck. She smiled softly after her friend, a rush of affection surging through her chest now that the danger was past.

"Your colleague is quite interesting," David said.

Dominique swallowed, knowing that now they were alone, there would be no avoiding the words and feelings hanging between them.

"She is a dear friend," Dominique said as she turned to face him. She glanced around; she had no reason to think they'd been followed, but prudence won out. "It is best if we keep walking."

And it also made it easier to have a conversation that could only hurt them both.

"I will escort you home," David said as he fell into step beside her.

"I cannot go home. If Cora knows where I live, so do the others at the theater. Once D'Terre discovers I've gotten away with his letters, he'll be on the hunt for me," Dominique explained.

She would go to the flat where she'd first met the duchess,

one of several sanctuaries scattered throughout London. She'd had occasion to use many over the past few years, but the flat near Regent's Park was her favorite. It reminded her of that first night where everything had changed. When she'd stepped into her full power as a woman and become a lady knight.

David cleared his throat. She read it as awkwardness, as his trying to fill the space between them. But then he reached for her hand, curling his fingers around hers.

"Come with me, back to Geoffrey's residence," he implored her, stopping on the street despite her earlier warning.

Half of her tried to jerk back her hand while the other gripped his instinctively. One foot stepped forward while the other dug in, adamant to stay with David. The dancer's grace that helped her move silently through D'Terre's house deserted her. Her body and heart were inescapably torn.

"You'll be safe there. No one knows of our connection," David said. "I would like to introduce you to Geoffrey."

The pleading in his face… It was only matched by the pain in her chest.

"I cannot."

David's face fell, but he did not release her hand. He tried again: "Cannot or will not?"

Although half of her was screaming a rebuke, she managed to pull her hand back and tuck it beneath her apron. She opened her mouth to explain, but he was already shaking his head, taking a half-step back.

"David… please."

He would not look at her. Why wouldn't he look at her?

Because I am breaking his heart.

She could not stand here arguing with him any longer—it was asking for trouble. They'd be discovered by D'Terre, and then they would both be in an even more precarious situation.

Part of her wished for it. The physical danger she could run from; the peril her heart was in would not be avoided forever.

"I must deliver my report. I will send word once D'Terre is

apprehended." Dominique forced the words out into the air between them.

David turned away, refusing to meet her eyes... or unable to. "Fine."

"David, please..." But even Dominique did not know what she was asking for.

"We'd both best be on our way," David said.

But unlike their disastrous row in the park two days before, he did not walk away from her. He stood on the roadside, unable to look at her but also unwilling to leave her.

Were those tears shining in his eyes or a trick of the light? Heavens, how was she to manage this?

Dominique's fingers began to tremble beneath her apron. But as they did, they brushed up against the thick packet of papers tucked into the pocket.

She had to get the evidence to the duchess and document all that had happened in a report. Everything must always be in order—another tenet of her life as a lady knight. No carelessly untended ends, everything secure and managed.

Evidence. Duchess. Report.

Evidence. Duchess. Report.

Dominique repeated the words to herself over and over as she turned away and continued on alone down the street, pausing at the corner.

Evidence. Duchess. Report.

David.

CHAPTER TWENTY-NINE

THREE DAYS PASSED before she heard the lock turning in the key that meant she could no longer hide from the problems of her own life.

Dominique's lockpick kit was spread before her, gleaming in the early-afternoon sunlight. She'd finished polishing the last pick when the door swung open and the Duchess of Guilford swept into the little flat.

"Gotten a bit bored, have we?" the duchess asked, eyes immediately combing over the room and assessing its state: gleaming. Dominique had cleaned every inch of it in the last three days out of a desperate need to drown out the sound of her own thoughts.

"If you have any other sanctuaries you'd like me to tidy before my next quest, I am happy to accommodate you," Dominique said, rolling the silver implements away and tying off the leather roll neatly. "Unless Red has already beaten me to it."

"Ethelreda left for the country this morning," the duchess said, perching behind the chair on the other side of the table where Dominique sat, but making no move to sit herself.

Dominique quirked a brow. "A quest?"

The duchess nodded. "I must ask that you not attempt to contact her, even through our usual channels."

"Of course," Dominique said, tucking the neat leather roll

away in the pocket of her skirt. "Will she contact us if she needs aid?"

The older woman tilted her head to the side, considering. "I doubt it. Ethelreda has struggled of late. I predict that no matter what comes of this new quest, she will be determined to sort it out on her own."

Dominique was inclined to agree. But she wished Red did not feel so desperate to prove herself. The Lady Knights were just that—knights, plural. A fellowship of friendship and support.

The duchess hummed quietly from across the table.

Dominique did not hold back her frown. "Yes?"

"I was going to offer a penny for your thoughts, but I do not think I have quite enough coins in my reticule at the moment."

Dominique ducked her head. She ought not to forget that the duchess was the one who had trained her; if she was good at hiding her emotions, the duchess was more than apt at reading them.

"I have made bit of a mess of things," Dominique said, leaning back and meeting the duchess's dark eyes with her own.

A smile played across Her Grace's thick, bow-shaped lips. "I came here to commend you. D'Terre has been apprehended and the proof you collected distributed to the appropriate parties. The Home Office has opened an investigation into Lord Rogers. All that remains is for you to complete your run at the Theatre Royal and this quest will be neatly wrapped up."

Sighing, Dominique shook her head. "You have most conveniently left out the bit about my bringing in my childhood friend as a consultant, then nearly getting him, myself, and Red all caught thieving."

The duchess ought to have been angry, or irritated as she had been that day when Dominique first told her she'd taken on David's help. But as she stared across the table, she looked rather amused.

"Childhood friend or childhood lover?"

Dominique dropped her face into her hands.

"I am only jesting," the duchess said.

"You are not given to jesting," Dominique said through her fingers.

"That is true. But perhaps I have changed. Look around you." Her Grace motioned at the flat. "Even this room has changed since that first day I asked you to join the Lady Knights. It would be unreasonable to expect anything different from the brilliant women who populate it."

Dominique lifted her head, looking around the room. The coverlet on the bed was new—Red had burned a hole in the old one. The tea set on the sideboard Dominique had brought herself, after her mother gifted her a new one of her own. The changes were subtle, but there nonetheless.

"It feels as if the young woman who came to you in this room, nervous and alone, was a different person altogether," she finally said.

"Nervous you may have been, Dominique, but you've never been alone."

Dominique's eyes snapped back to the duchess. "How do you mean?"

"Your mother, for one," Her Grace said pointedly. "But even then, when I put my proposal to you—even then your young Mr. Grisham loved you."

Her chest began to burn. "How can you know that?"

"Because he has none of the finesse of a lady knight. And I am very good at finding things out. He never stopped searching for you, Dominique."

"But it does not change the situation, nor my birth, nor any of it," Dominique said. How could she be having this same argument she'd had with David, now with the Duchess of Guilford? She ought to understand better than anyone the importance of good birth and social standing.

But the duchess did not argue with her. She merely shrugged and changed the direction of the conversation entirely.

"If I may ask, what was it about my proposal that night that convinced you?"

Dominique frowned. She had the answer ready at a moment. "That first day we met, you attended a party hosted by Mr. and Mrs. Foster."

"Yes, I recall. Their daughter is married to the Earl of Brisbane now, is she not?"

Dominique smiled. Quite a coup, that had been. "Indeed."

Miranda raised her eyebrows, a silent indication for Dominique to continue.

"It worried me to see you there—a duchess. My mother and I made such a point of avoiding all *ton* functions. After you passed me your card at the refreshment station, I set to finding out who you were and why you were there."

Understanding flashed in Miranda's eyes. Her face softened, and a smile turned up the corners of her mouth, now slightly lined with age.

"Mrs. Foster was the daughter of your childhood governess. Not only did you maintain a correspondence with her, but when she asked you to attend, you granted the favor."

Miranda nodded. "I was quite fond of her mother. She passed only a few years ago." Grief flitted across her eyes.

Dominique shifted in her seat so she could face her mentor directly. "Not many duchesses would do such a thing for a former employee."

"I am a person first, and a duchess second," Miranda said.

"And that is why I chose to join the Lady Knights."

The duchess straightened her pelisse and smiled again. "You are more than a servant of Her Majesty, Dominique. You are a person first, and a lady knight second."

THE DUCHESS'S WORDS rang in her ears long after she'd given the flat one final tidy and started the long walk across town to her own home. She left off her cloak, consigning it to her small portmanteau instead, so she could feel the early summer sunshine on her arms. It was a lovely day, despite the rain clouds swirling through her mind.

Perhaps they weren't all rain clouds. But if her mind had been full before Miranda's visit, it was positively bursting now. Which must have accounted for how she walked directly past her sister.

"Dominique!"

"Amelia?" She nearly dropped her bag. There was no chance of her keeping the surprise off her face, even with years of training on how to school her features.

When Amelia threw her arms around her shoulders and pulled her elder sister tight, Dominique did drop the portmanteau—almost in comical unison with her mouth falling open.

"You've the most odious neighbor! Mr. Critchett? Pratchett? My, was he surly—"

"Mr. Pritchett—"

"Ah, yes, Mr. Pritchett. He said you were interminably noisy, which had me wondering right off if I'd bungled the address. But when I described your appearance, he was—"

"Amelia!" Dominique disentangled herself and stepped back, surprise and anger colliding in her painfully. "Why are you waiting on my doorstep?"

"I could not very well wait upstairs. Mr. Pritchett did not invite me for tea, which would have been the polite thing to do," Amelia said loud enough to carry above their heads to Mr. Pritchett's open window.

Hands on her hips, dander high and cheeks flushed, she was a vision of life and light. Dominique's heart ached to see the lovely young women her sister had become. Dressed in a rose pink that accented her fair complexion and glowing chestnut hair, she was as beautiful as her youth had promised—and torturously favored their father.

"But Amelia, why are you here at all?"

Amelia frowned, glancing over her shoulder. Dominique

followed her gaze across the street to where a well-appointed carriage waited, a footman and driver posted outside and watching them with too much interest to be casual.

"Perhaps this is a conversation better had inside," Amelia said, tilting her head meaningfully toward the building.

Dominique wanted to refuse. She opened her mouth to refuse. Amelia had ignored her for ten years. What could she possibly have to say to her now? But instead she said:

"You may come up. Your escorts may not."

Amelia brightened instantly, waving to the two servants waiting with the carriage. Dominique cursed inwardly but led her sister inside and up to the first floor nonetheless. How many painfully emotional conversations would she be forced to endure in one day? Once she'd finished with Amelia, she would lock the door and hide under her blankets for at least the next twenty-four hours.

Her sister hummed softly behind her, a wordless tune that nonetheless felt familiar as she unlocked the column of latches securing her door. Only when the door swung open and they stepped into the flat did it occur to Dominique to be self-conscious.

Nothing about her younger sister was subtle. She wore an expensively tailored gown embroidered with intricate gold flowers at the neckline, hem, and sleeves. Her dark hair, several shades lighter and warmer than Dominique's, was held in place with an ornate diamond and mother-of-pearl clip in the shape of her a butterfly. She wore jewelry in every place one could—rings, bracelets, earrings. Even an armband. It all suited her. Amelia had always been a shining light, destined to be a diamond of the first water.

But seeing her standing in the middle of her modest flat, looking around eagerly at every corner and cranny, Dominique could not help but feel a flush of inadequacy.

"Your home is lovely," Amelia said, offering a smile.

Dominique watched her closely, trying to detect any hint of

avarice—and finding none.

"Thank you," she responded, moving toward the cupboard. "Tea?"

She did not wait for a response, moving for the kettle just to have something to do with her hands.

"Perhaps later," Amelia said, picking at the diamond and pearl bracelet twinkling around her wrist.

Dominique stilled. Forcing in a breath, she set the kettle back in its station and turned to her sister. No niceties, then. She could handle this—this was her home. This was the life she'd built for herself after Amelia's horrible mother had ruined everything.

You have nothing to be ashamed of, a voice whispered in the back of her mind. Not her own—David's. *You are perfect.*

Words he'd spoken in another life echoed in her head still.

They were true.

Dominique squared her shoulders. "No tea," she said. "Then let us sit." She motioned to the settee and armchair.

Amelia lowered herself to the settee, leaving Dominique to take the chair across from her. She folded her hands carefully in her lap and fixed her sister with a steady look.

"Why have you come to London, Amelia?"

Amelia continued to pick at her bracelet, but she did not look away. "I am to make my debut this Season," she said.

"You've left it rather late. It is already June." Dominique watched Amelia's lips tighten at the sharp clip to her voice. But to her credit, the younger women was not cowed.

"Indeed. That is why I have come to speak with you. Our arrival in London was delayed because… Oh, Dominique, I am so sorry to tell you this." The bracelet dropped away from her fingers, and she leaned forward as if she would take Dominique's hands. But when Dominique continued to hold herself apart, Amelia rocked back and squeezed her hands together in her own lap. "Father is dead."

Dominique stared in silence.

Of course Amelia did not realize that she already knew.

"It happened months ago. I would have told you sooner, would have come to London immediately, but Mother—"

"I would rather not discuss Lady Wartham."

Amelia's teeth came down on her lower lip sharply, and Dominique nearly hurled up the contents of her stomach. The action was so familiar, one she'd done herself a thousand times. Was it an affectation her sister had gained from her during their briefly shared childhood? Or some familial trait neither of them could help?

"I can respect that desire," Amelia said carefully. "I would have come immediately, but I had no notion of where to find you until the mourning period ended and we came to London."

Dominique stared at her sister, mulling over what to say next. There were tears in Amelia's eyes, but she was trying fiercely to hold them back. Tears for their father? After so many fraught conversations, Dominique had none left.

Or were they tears for something—or someone—else?

"A friend told me of Father's death more than a week ago," Dominique finally said. "I am sorry for your loss."

Amelia frowned, clearly wanting to ask who had shared the information, but instead she nodded. How different it was to see her as a polished young woman making calculated decisions, rather than a brash child, Dominique mused. What other secrets had she missed in their past ten years apart?

"It is your loss as well," Amelia said tentatively.

"Father was lost to me long ago."

"I suppose so." Amelia sighed heavily, finger twirling around her bracelet once again. "I am so sorry for what happened, for my mo—for all of it. I should have intervened. I should have done *something.*"

The vehemence in her voice surprised Dominique. "You were a child. There was nothing you could have done." But there was—and Dominique tried very hard not to let her voice tremble as she added quietly, "You could have written to me."

"Oh, Dominique!" Suddenly Amelia was on her knees, holding Dominique's hand to her chest in a flutter of pink and sparkles. "Did you not hear me? I did not know where you were!"

Dominique tried to pull her hand back, but Amelia held it tight. "I wrote you as soon as my mother and I were settled in London. I sent you dozens of letters—but you spared me not even a word to tell me you were well!"

The tears Amelia had held back spilled forth, covering her cheeks in a thick deluge. "No, no, I did not," she sobbed. "My mother, she took them all. She hid them!"

Without making any sort of conscious decision, Dominique found herself sliding out of the chair to join her sister on the floor—as if her body were melting and had lost all ability to support her.

"I found your letters here in London, hidden away in father's study. My mother…" Anger lined her lovely face. "She took them. I think she even hid them from Father, thinking that if he knew where to find you, he would eventually seek you out."

Dominique's lower lip trembled. "I thought you had forsaken me."

"I could never have forsaken you. Dominique, I love you." With that, Amelia collapsed against her, and the two of them sobbed in each other's arms. For the years lost, the children who'd been hurt, and the women they had become.

The sun had trekked far across the sky, dipping toward the horizon with the promise of early evening, when they both breathed steadily enough to speak. Dominique rocked back on her heels, but her hair tangled around the bauble dangling from Amelia's ear.

"You've developed quite expensive tastes." Dominique laughed through the wetness still rimming her eyes.

"That is the other reason I sought you out," Amelia said once they'd disentangled themselves, reaching into her reticule and pulling out a carefully folded sheaf of papers. "Here."

She held it out to Dominique, who took it with a frown. Even as she scanned the words and disbelief bloomed in her chest,

Amelia smiled softly.

"You are an heiress," her sister said.

"This cannot be right. All of this income and property... it should go to you."

"I have my own list, I assure you. It is quite lengthy."

"How...?"

"Father was much wealthier than he ever let on, it seems. He never even told Mother the extent of his holdings... probably because he thought she'd exploit them somehow." Amelia snorted.

"I am... This cannot be," Dominique stammered. How could her father have hidden this? Surely the Duchess of Guilford must have known—she'd found out Dominique's parentage easily enough.

But even if the duchess had known the extent of her father's wealth, there would have been no reason to share that with her, Dominique realized. It would only have served to wound her. And the Duchess of Guilford protected her Lady Knights fiercely.

Amelia leaned across the froth of skirts surrounding them and kissed her cheek. When she settled back, she still held Dominique's hand, and a small smile graced her face.

"Father failed you in so many ways, my dear sister," she said. "But he did give you this—your freedom."

Dominique shook her head. "It is a small fortune, to be sure—"

"No, Dominique. It is a large fortune, and it is yours." Amelia squeezed her hands. "Go to America or to France. Build yourself a castle and reign from the tallest tower. Or find a gentleman worthy of your love and have a houseful of children."

Dominique thought she was beyond tears, but one spilled down her cheek. "I am still a bastard."

"You are my sister," Amelia said fiercely, swiping the tear away. "I am proud to tell it to every *ton* socialite I meet."

"You will ruin your reputation. I cannot let you do such a thing."

"We are heiresses—mistresses of our own destinies. Wealthy as Midas… perhaps wealthier." She chuckled, tilting her head to the side. "What matters to me now is you. No one shall ever keep us apart again. Do you promise?"

Dominique was suddenly transported back—ten years, a dozen, more. They were once again the children they'd been at Wartham Grange. Young and unhurt by the world, but their love for one another strong and pure.

By some miracle, she had regained her sister.

But it was not the only love she'd lost and found again.

Rising to her knees, Dominique squeezed her back and made her vow.

"I promise I will not waste another moment."

CHAPTER THIRTY

D AVID TOLD HIMSELF he would wait until evening to approach her, but after three endless days and nights, he gave in. It would be evening by the time he reached her flat, he reasoned with himself. But at the pace his eager feet traveled, the sun was still lingering about the buildings when he turned onto her street.

He knew she'd been liberated from whatever sanctuary she'd taken up residence in for the last several days, but he had no way of knowing whether she was at home. If she was not, he would take a turn around the park and then try again. In this precise moment, using the key he'd taken the other night felt like a violation. There was so much unresolved between them.

He was five yards from her building when a voice calling from across the street halted him.

"Mr. Grisham!"

He scanned the edge of the park, recognizing the voice but not quite able to fit it with a face—Ah, yes.

He found her just a few yards past a well-appointed carriage attended by two bored footmen. Collette Beauchamp was dressed in a forest-green walking dress that blended into the trees. Combined with her dark hair, unmarred by any cap, she could have been a wise goddess of the forest.

"Madam Beauchamp," David said, bowing politely.

Collette smiled and bent her knees in a small curtsey, but her eyes were fixed over David's shoulder.

"Do I take this to mean that Miss Beauchamp is not at home?"

"She is." Collette nodded to the building. "She has company."

Dominique's flat was on the second floor. There was only one window visible from this side, and the curtains were shut. But as he stared at it, he just made out the movement of a body and a lantern being lit.

"Her sister," Collette answered before he could even voice the question.

"Miss Wartham?" Of all the possibilities, that was the one he'd least expected. The pain between them... He lurched forward, ready to intervene and protect in whatever way he could.

But Collette's hand landed on his arm. "Let them be."

David tried to shake her off. "Begging your pardon, ma'am, but things are not well between them. She has endured enough—"

"I know that well, sir." She infused her voice with steel.

But still it was not enough for David. He could protect Dominique from so little, breathtaking and capable lady knight that she was. But he would not leave her to endure this meeting alone.

"I have been watching Miss Wartham," Collette admitted. "Things are not well between her and her mother. Which can only mean that between them"—she nodded up at the window—"perhaps things will finally be mended."

David glanced between her and the window, unconvinced.

Collette offered him her arm. "Come, take a turn with me through the park. Then you may go and rescue her."

He did not like it, but he did as she asked. "You have been watching Miss Wartham and her mother?" he asked.

Collette shrugged nonchalantly. "I thought it prudent to be prepared, especially where Lady Wartham is concerned. No good has ever come from that woman."

David suppressed the chuckle in his chest. Did Collette realize how alike she and her daughter were?

"Next you will perhaps tell me that you've been watching me as well," he said.

Collette winked. "If I had, you would never know it. I have learned a few tricks from my daughter."

David blinked. "You know—"

"I know nothing," she burst in. "And you would do well to tell me nothing."

Ah. She suspected something of Dominique's profession, then. But she'd chosen to respect her daughter's secrecy, respect her daughter—which had her rising in David's esteem all the more.

They reached the opposite side of the park. David wanted to turn on his heel and walk directly back to Dominique, but Collette steered him toward the far corner instead.

"I was very sad to hear about your father and brother's passing. I have spent much time the last week thinking about your mother."

David had been thinking of her too. More precisely, of the quiet way she bore her pain. She'd loved his father so deeply that she could not bear to remain in Winleigh without him and had retreated to Derbyshire. David wondered how far he would have to go to escape the memory of Dominique. Nowhere on Earth seemed far enough.

"Would your mother be opposed, do you think, if I were to write to her?"

David drew back at the tentative quaver in her words, hiding beneath the bravado. He'd heard just such a manner of speaking from Dominique. It made his answer all the easier.

"I think she would be glad to receive it," he said. "Nay, warmed and pleased. She is quite lonely," he admitted.

Collette smiled, but it did not reach her eyes. "It is a feeling I am intimately familiar with." They rounded the far corner and started back in the direction of the flat. "One I wish fervently my daughter does not have to suffer any longer."

"It is not for my lack of trying, madam." David sighed.

Collette held his arm tight as they walked the final yards back to where they'd begun. "Keep trying, David. Please... She has been hurt so deeply. But she has such great capacity for loving. Do not give up on her."

David squeezed her hand tightly as he lifted it off his arm. The carriage with the bored footmen was gone, leaving them alone on the corner.

"I never intended to," he promised.

"I AM HIRING a carpenter to fix that stair," David said as she opened the door.

"I would have to wrench it back out as soon as you did," she countered, surprised but thankful that David had spared them at least a moment of awkwardness. "It is my most reliable way of detecting intruders."

"Is that what I am, an intruder?"

That was where the reprieve ended, it seemed.

Dominique stepped aside to let him pass, but he caught her hand. "I'll fasten the latches."

His fingertips on her wrist scalded her skin, sending burning tendrils of desire and heat up her arm. But she only nodded and stepped back, watching silently as his nimble fingers moved up over each lock, securing them one by one into place.

As he turned to face her, she shifted her weight toward the hearth where the teakettle waited. But David forestalled her favorite crutch.

"Your sister was here. Are you well?"

Dominique frowned. "How did you know?"

He shrugged, not evasive but not forthcoming. How odd.

"I saw the carriage outside," he offered.

"And you knew it was hers?"

"Did you quarrel?"

She moved toward the hearth, but he stepped in front of her, very effectively blocking her path. "What is the matter with you, David?"

"Nothing," he said. But he rubbed at his chin at some imaginary stubble that they both knew was not there. "I am concerned."

"I can care for myself," she said slowly.

"I damn well know that you can, Dominique. You are an agent of the Crown—a blasted lady knight! But I can still ask after your well-being!"

"Why are you shouting at me?" She'd never seen him like this—his cheeks flushed with frustration and his blue eyes practically glowed with emotion.

"I cannot protect you from the dangers of your profession. But I will shield you from the pain society tries to inflict upon you." He was breathing so heavily, he might have run all the way to her flat.

She swallowed down the lump in her throat. "My sister and I are reconciled. It was Lady Wartham who kept us apart all of these years."

"Bloody hell… I ought to have known."

"Why are you intent on punishing yourself for things you have no control over?" Dominique caught the irony of the words the moment they left her mouth. She no longer tried to move past him, but sank into the chair behind her. David caught her hand on the way down.

"I am angry at myself and at the world," he said quietly, staring down at her hand where it was cradled within his own. "I should not have shouted."

"I much prefer your smiles," she said, pushing her fingers back into his until they were laced together. "And when you are making me laugh."

"There has not been much laughter between us of late."

"Perhaps it is time to change that."

Her tentative offering hung in the air between them. Dominique could practically feel the weight of the thoughts turning through David's head. But she said nothing, letting him take the next step in this dance of their future.

Finally, David spoke. "Geoffrey's estate is one hundred and seventy-two miles from Winleigh."

She cocked her head backward so he could see the confusion on her face.

"I worked it out on the maps in Geoffrey's study while I was closeted inside for the last three days," David continued. "We never have to go back. You never have to see a single one of those people. I will ensure you are never in a room with Lady Wartham ever again."

Dominique bit her bottom lip.

"No one knows you there. It will be a fresh start and a convenient base for your work with the Lady Knights."

Despite the churning of her stomach, she laughed nervously. "How do you figure that?"

"Geoffrey has many years ahead of him; you will not be expected to assume the role of countess anytime in the near future. But you will have entrée to any room you desire, while maintaining the anonymity of someone outside the peerage," David said quickly.

She was not sure she quite agreed with him on the particulars, but she could see the wisdom behind his words. The duchess did her work very aptly, and she was the next thing to royalty. There was no reason Dominique could not also continue.

If she agreed with David.

"You are contemplating it," he whispered, awe clear in his voice… as if he'd expected this presentation to be met with more argument. She supposed she'd set him up for nothing less.

"I want to say yes, David. So badly," she said. Not a yes. But very close.

"Perhaps this will help convince you." David reached into the inner pocket of his tailcoat and pulled out a sheaf of paper, the wax seal already broken. Whatever it was, he'd already read it. Indeed, it was his name scrawled across the front.

"What is this?" she asked, a bit afraid. She'd already had one bit of parchment change her life immeasurably today; was this another?

David unfolded the paper. "It's a special license," he said softly. "From the Archbishop of Canterbury."

"How did you obtain this?" she asked, checking it by reflex for signs of forgery. Special marriage licenses were notoriously difficult to come by and could only be obtained by petitioning the archbishop directly.

"I did not," David said, chuckling. "It arrived at Geoffrey's residence this morning."

Dominique shook her head. "I do not understand."

"It arrived care of the Duchess of Guilford."

Her hand flew to her mouth.

"I take it she is a colleague of yours?" David was smiling now. Dominique could only nod. "This means the banns will not have to be read. We can go to Derbyshire and marry privately."

It was a show of approval from the duchess herself.

A kindness, to be sure, but not one Dominique had needed. She realized as she held the license in one hand, and David's hand in the other, that she already had all the assurance she would ever need.

Leaning over, she carefully set the special license on the table. Then she turned all of her love and attention back to David. "Ask me."

The question flared in his blue eyes. *Are you certain?*

Dominique smiled, feeling tears threatening once again. It seemed a day for all the feelings to be felt. This one, she would finally yield to. *Yes, I love you.*

"Dominique Beauchamp, my lifetime love, my friend in all things, I am continually in awe of you. I have loved you forever. I will love you forever. Will you consent to be my wife?"

"Yes," she breathed. "Yes, yes, a thousand times, yes."

She collapsed into his arms, breathing in the scent of him. Her David. *Hers*. After so much time, hers for always.

David kissed her hair, then the shell of her ear and down her neck. He left a line of kisses along her chin and paused only when he reached her lips. She stared into the blue eyes that she'd never been able to forget and finally gave him the real answer—the words that had lived secretly within her heart for more than a decade:

"I love you."

EPILOGUE

"WHY DID I bother bringing a trunk?" David asked, staring at the nearly empty contraption. A silk scarf, a threadbare cloak, one dress, and a set of petticoats. That was the totality of personal effects in her dressing room at the Theatre Royal.

"You have seen my dressing room enough times," Dominique admonished him, checking through the drawers of the dressing table one last time.

She peered at the undersides of the drawers at well, in the case that perhaps the duchess or one of her retainers had affixed something secret. But there was nothing. She was truly done.

"That first time, when I saw you on stage and came back here, I was struck by the lack of *you* in this room," David admitted as he leaned down to latch the trunk.

"It was only ever a temporary arrangement." With the last of her things packed, all that remained was to pin her hair into place and they could be on their way.

She ran her fingers through her thick hair, detangling the strands slowly as she went. She did not even have a comb here. David watched her from the other side of the dressing room, his blue eyes intent. As he drifted closer, visible over her shoulder in the mirror, she could see the desire in his eyes.

"Have I mentioned that you have magnificent hair?" he

murmured, catching one lock and twining it around his finger.

"You have not." She smiled, tugging the lock back.

David responded by burying both of his hands in the dark mass of her hair, tugging her head back until she was looking up at him. He leaned over her, brushing his lips over her forehead, then the tip of her nose, lingering above her mouth but not quite kissing her.

"It is glorious. Every time I see it, I imagine removing pin after pin, until it is loose over your shoulders, the ends tickling your breasts," he said against her lips.

Dominique's purr was absolutely feline.

"The door is not locked," she whispered as one hand slid free of her hair and curved around her breast. She'd only intended them to be in the room for a few minutes.

"How forgetful of you." He teased with his words, while his hands began to tease her nipples through her dress.

"You are terrible—Hold a moment!" She sprang from her chair, sending it careening backward into David. He groaned and clutched his groin.

"Bollocks," he cried.

"Precisely." She giggled, stepping around him to the door. Whoever had knocked had at least spared them the embarrassment of being caught *in flagrante delicto*, even if David was a bit the worse for the surprise.

"Oh, Cora—hello, dear." Dominique smiled genuinely at the other woman. "I will clear out in just a moment, I promise."

Cora waved her hand dismissively, though her stance was anxious—arms crossed, teeth worrying her bottom lip. "There is no rush. I shall have plenty of time to arrange my things tomorrow."

"I saw your rehearsal this afternoon. You were wonderful. Much better than I ever was," Dominique said. It was true—Cora must have been watching all these nights that Dominique had performed, for she'd taken all of her best affects and improved upon them herself. "You will do magnificently finishing out the run."

Cora blushed prettily, a small smile finally pulling at her coral-pink lips. "Thank you, Miss Beauchamp. I have something for you."

Dominique frowned, hoping it was not some sort of cruel trick. She'd thought she and Cora past such things, when Red and David told her of how the other woman had come to her aid regarding D'Terre.

But Cora uncurled her arms and held out an open palm.

"It is the brooch from your costume at the beginning of act two," she explained unnecessarily. Dominique recognized it immediately. She felt her brow wrinkle—Cora must have noticed it as well, for she rushed to explain. "I asked the prop master if I might have it for you, as a memento of sorts. I suspect you will not be taking the stage again anytime soon."

Cora's smile was knowing, and surprisingly kind.

Dominique reached for the brooch, clasping her hand around Cora's as she did and squeezing tightly. "Thank you, Cora. I appreciate your kindness. You shall stun them every time you dance across that stage," she said.

"Thank you." Cora's gaze flicked over Dominique's shoulder, and her smile deepened. "I shall leave you to finish packing. It seems the dressing room is still rather crowded."

Dominique opened her mouth to make some excuse, but Cora merely winked and disappeared down the corridor, a melodic hum trailing behind her.

Watching her go, Dominique waited for the stab of sadness she always felt when a quest ended. But the only emotion in her heart now was love. It made for an immeasurably better end.

"Where were we?" David asked, catching her around the hips when she leaned down to open the trunk and add the brooch to the small collection of items inside.

"We were about to leave for dinner," she insisted. But he began to grind her hips back against his, teasing her with his rigid length.

She managed to get the brooch into the chest without losing control of herself. But if she did not get space between them soon, she'd be lost to her baser instincts.

At least the door was locked this time, she thought as she spun around, landing her palms on David's chest.

"Your mother only arrived in town this morning. We ought to go welcome her," she said, giving him a gentle shove.

He caught her wrists and pulled her with him. "Which means she's hardly had any time to reminisce with your mother," he said, leaning forward to nip at her ear.

Heavens, maybe he was right. Mrs. Grisham and Collette were meeting in person for the first time in a decade, their children newly engaged. They would have mountains of things to speak about.

David trailed his tongue down from her ear to her collarbone. Her legs began to wobble. He knew how sensitive her collarbones were, the rogue.

She decided to take a different tack. If decisions were a thing she was still capable of making—*Heavens, his teeth now too*—she was acting on instinct alone now.

"My sister has done me a great service, sending her mother back to Winleigh. It would be unforgivably rude for us to be late to her first dinner party."

David pulled back long enough to say, "Amelia sent Lady Wartham away because she is a venomous snake that neither of you ought to deal with." Venom laced his voice. "She will enjoy playing host to our mothers. Besides, she might be more excited about our engagement than either of us."

It was an overstatement, but Dominique smiled through her moans. He was correct about Amelia's excitement. Her sister had squealed loud enough to be heard across the Channel when they'd told her their news.

"We must finalize plans for the wedding," Dominique murmured. The wedding that would take place in less than two weeks at his cousin Geoffrey's country seat in Derbyshire. The shiver of anticipation this time was not from desire, but pure, undiluted joy.

"Let them wait," he said. "I have waited a lifetime for you."

"So you intend to torture everyone else?" But she was already tugging the tail of his shirt free from his trousers.

"No, my love, I intend to torture you." He nipped at her collarbone in demonstration.

She shivered with anticipation. "Do your worst, *mon amour.*"

About the Author

A lifetime reader of romance, Cara put pen to paper (or rather, fingers to keyboard) in 2019 and published her first book. She hasn't slowed down from there. Cara is an avid traveler. As she explores new places, she imagines her characters walking hand-in-hand down a cobblestone path or sharing a passionate kiss in a secluded alcove. Cara is living out her own happily ever after in Seattle, Washington, where she resides with her husband, daughter, and two cats, RoseArt and Etch-o-Sketch.

Instagram: caramaxwellromance
Facebook: caramaxwellromance

www.ingramcontent.com/pod-product-compliance
Lightning Source LLC
Chambersburg PA
CBHW061230210726
48293CB00003B/722